Killer in

Best wishes to Susan
from Marilyn.

FROM THE #1 BESTSELLING *WALL STREET JOURNAL* AUTHOR OF
AFTER MIDNIGHT IN THE GARDEN OF GOOD AND EVIL AND
AWARD-WINNING AUTHOR AND LAW ENFORCEMENT
OFFICER MARK GADO

Killer in the
Holy City

A novel by
Marilyn J. Bardsley and Mark Gado

DARKHORSE MULTIMEDIA, INC.

First Edition
ISBN: 978-0-9983516-2-9 (Print)
ISBN: 978-0-9983516-3-6 (Kindle)

Chapter 1

Charleston, South Carolina
Saturday, June 30, 2012

RUNNING.

Always running.

She ran all the way from the bus stop to Miss Rachel's house. It was the third time this month Justine was late for work, and she was certain she was going to be fired. Miss Rachel would not put up with her being late again. Justine had to find a way to fix this problem.

She didn't get off her second job at the bakery until six in the morning, and by the time she got home, had her daughter fed, dressed, and to the daycare, it was over an hour and a half later. She couldn't make that lazy son of hers understand he had to pitch in and help. His summer job didn't start until ten, and there was no reason in the world that he couldn't have his sister ready so she could get her to the daycare and then arrive at Miss Rachel's by eight.

She was out of breath when she arrived at the grand house on Meeting Street in Charleston's historic district. It was almost 8:20 a.m. There would be hell to pay, but it wasn't because Miss Rachel had anything special to do that morning—or any morning for that matter. The rich never make appointments before noon. It was one of the many things Justine had learned after working for Miss Rachel the past three years. It was just a rule that Justine should arrive on time.

She scooped the newspaper off the sidewalk, punched in the code for the wrought iron gate, and ran the twenty feet to the side of the house. It was on beautiful mornings like this that Justine enjoyed sitting for a few stolen minutes in the old lady's manicured garden. But not today.

When she knocked on the side porch door just off the garden, it wasn't completely shut. Pushing it open, she walked quickly to the kitchen. The coffee pot was not on, and there were no breakfast dishes in the sink. Justine's hopes soared. Maybe Miss Rachel overslept and wouldn't know she was late.

Justine looked in the library and family room and saw the lights were on, odd for this early in the morning. Then she crept up the large, curved stairway to the second floor, straining to hear any sound that might indicate Miss Rachel was up and about. She peeked into the upstairs living room and the dining room, but there was no sign of her. Some of the lamps were on here as well. Had they been left on from last night?

Finally, she summoned the courage to tiptoe down the hallway outside the master bedroom. The door to Miss Rachel's room was closed. She listened for any sign that her employer was moving around or taking a bath, but she couldn't hear a thing from inside. After a moment, it dawned on her that maybe the old woman might be sick or could have fallen and was waiting for her maid to rescue her.

Justine didn't know what to do. If Miss Rachel had slept late, she had no right to wake her. If she were up late, Miss Rachel would be angry she was awakened. When Miss Rachel yelled at her, Justine felt like crying. Nobody she ever worked for made her feel so bad. But she tolerated it because she desperately needed the money, and work was so hard to find these days.

She stood outside in the hall for several minutes, hearing only the sounds of her own breathing and the ticking of the antique grandfather clock at the bottom of the steps. Better to leave well enough alone and go back downstairs. When Miss Rachel finally woke up, Justine could pretend she had been there on time.

She started toward the stairs, but stopped, thought for a moment, and turned back. It was her Christian duty to be sure that her employer was okay, even if Miss Rachel yelled at her. She went back to the bedroom door and first made sure there was no sound inside.

"Miss Rachel?" she called softly and waited. "Miss Rachel?" A little louder this time. When there was still no reply, she knocked. "Miss Rachel, you all right?" She knocked again, only harder.

Now she was worried. Slowly, Justine pushed the door open part way and called out again. The room was hot and smelled bad. Really bad. She opened the door further and called for Miss Rachel again. The heavy drapes were drawn, making it hard to see inside. She flipped the switch for the overhead light.

Justine stood mute for a moment, her brain struggling to understand what she saw. When she tried to yell for help, her throat tightened, and she couldn't get the words out. A tidal wave of panic enveloped her. She bolted down the stairs, almost colliding with the grandfather clock, fumbled with the front door lock, and flew out of the house into the quiet street and the glorious, sunny morning.

Screaming.

Chapter 2

HER DREAMS WERE OF MURDER.

That may sound odd to some people, but to her, it seemed natural. After all, she had thought about murder for as far back as she could remember. It wasn't so much the act of violence that intrigued her, but the motives behind it. Her fascination with the psychology of those who kill was established in her mind long before her first day of high school. When other kids her age were reading *The Catcher in the Rye* and *Moby Dick*, she read Capote's *In Cold Blood* and Bugliosi's *Helter Skelter* in her spare time.

This obsession with murder began at an early age. She didn't know exactly when or how, but her father, an officer of the Cleveland Police Department, was central to her career choice and the driving force behind her desire to enter the twisted, often enigmatic world of forensic psychology.

When Danielle Callahan was ten years old, her father took her and her younger brother, Johnny, to watch the planes taking off from Burke Lakefront Airport on Lake Erie. Along the way, they stopped at a Polish deli where they feasted on ham and muenster sandwiches and chocolate milkshakes. "The best sandwiches in Cleveland, Danie," he told her.

He always called her that, and it became the name she preferred. Even today, she could still recall how that sandwich tasted. As they devoured their lunch, other customers yelled, "Hey, Bob!" and "How's things going?" or "Glad to see you, Officer!" Everyone knew him, and everyone liked him. Danie could see that right away. Her father was a man who commanded respect, enjoyed many friends, and never had a bad word to say about anyone, even criminals.

Danie tried hard to be outgoing like him, but she was, by nature, an introvert, and there was no changing that. Making new friends was never important to her. Rather, she regretted she never had enough time to devote to the few close friends she treasured.

Despite working in the toughest areas of downtown Cleveland, her father had that Irish happy-go-lucky demeanor Danie wished she had inherited. Always ready with a joke or a funny line, he possessed a natural affinity for people wherever he went. However, behind the easy-going façade was the soul of a high achiever, a man driven to success.

Raised dirt poor by immigrant parents, her father's goal in life was to prove to himself and everyone that he, his parents, and by extension, his children, were as good or better than any Irish who came before them. He didn't have a college education, but what he lacked in schooling, he made up for by being a compulsive, incessant reader, a habit he was determined to pass on to her.

She was expected to excel, to work as hard as she could in every endeavor, for there would be no excuses for failure. Every step of advancement was measured by what Danie read or achieved in one week. Her father never let up, not even once. She and her brother, Johnny, were told over and over again they were destined for greatness in life, but they had to earn it. By the time she was eleven, Danie was in a special school for gifted children.

During that summer, she set a goal for herself to read *The Illiad*, *The Odyssey*, *The Aeneid*, and all three books of Dante's *Divine Comedy*. By the end of July, she was finished and needed another project. So, for the remainder of the summer, she sat in a chair in their living room day after day, night after night, with the full blessing of her proud father, listening to Puccini, Verdi, and Wagner with the librettos in her hand, memorizing each word, including the correct pronunciation, repeating the phrases endlessly until she could recite them in her sleep.

Such was her determination and her inner craving to please her father. For a while, she and Johnny competed for their father's attention, but Johnny was more like their mother, and while he never said so, seemed to dislike the need to outdo his sister for his father's approval.

The bond between Danie and her father flourished as she took up tennis, his favorite way of releasing the pressure of his work. For him, slamming the tennis ball was his revenge on the day's frustrations, but for Danie, it was perfecting her competitive skills. More importantly, it was a sport that didn't depend on the talent of anyone but herself to win.

This morning, as she finished packing for the trip to Charleston, Danie looked wistfully at the tennis rackets in the closet and decided to take them along. Surely, she and Cal would be able to find time for at least a game or two.

Danie's thoughts were interrupted by the rambunctious collie puppy at her feet. "Magic! Are you hungry?"

He wagged his tail in anticipation.

"C'mon! Let's go downstairs!" They went to the kitchen where Danie poured some fresh water in his water bowl and filled his food dish. Magic plunged head first into the crunchy meal as Cal walked in.

"Morning, baby," he said, putting his arms around her shoulders and kissing her. It was a tradition that he began right after their wedding and continued to this very day.

"Morning, darling. Sleep well?"

"Like a rock." Irish was written all over Cal Callahan's face. His shock of straight, dark hair and fair skin told the story, but not all of it. Cal was a typical Savannah boy, a Scots-Irish blend. His mother made sure that her Scottish maiden name, Monroe, came between Calvin and Callahan.

When they first met, Danie was immediately attracted to his athleticism, his manly look, and quiet, confident demeanor. He was just himself, with a take-it-or-leave-it attitude that wasn't haughty or pretentious. From almost the moment they were introduced, Danie felt deep inside her that he would be the man she would one day marry. After more than twenty years of marriage, her intuition had been spot on.

Danie was unexpectedly tired this morning. When she looked in the mirror, she imagined dark circles under her eyes, perhaps because she rarely slept more than six hours a night, most times less than that. She had to look twice to make sure it was just a shadow. Cal liked to say that she had the metabolism of a hamster running on its treadmill for hours.

Danie, with her adrenaline highs, seemed to always be pushing herself intellectually and physically. More often than not she was completely immersed in solving a thorny problem that always demanded an immediate solution. Cal, on the other hand, was laid-back, thoughtful, and never quick to make judgments.

For the first time in their marriage, they would be working together as a team. They hoped to eventually make a career out of it. After more than a decade of being a medical examiner in the Atlanta area, Cal had his fill of typical big city homicides. They were squalid, depressing, and uninteresting.

A couple of years ago, when Danie worked as a profiler in the Atlanta FBI offices, Cal's father got sick. They decided to move back to his hometown of Savannah where Cal earned his living as an expert witness and consulting for law enforcement. As a profiler with a stellar reputation, Danie was in demand by police departments around the country.

The money was good, but the travel was exhausting, and she hated being away from Cal, her daughter, Chloe, and Magic. When Cal's father passed away last year, he learned that his father had left him some money in trust. It enabled Cal and Danie to cut back on their careers and pursue their dream of working as forensic consultants to police agencies across the country.

After breakfast, they got Magic into the Range Rover, loaded up the luggage, and hit the road for Charleston, a drive of about two and a half hours, depending on traffic. With a little luck, they should arrive around 10 a.m. They were scheduled to meet with Charleston Police Chief Billy Murphy, a college friend of Cal's who he hadn't seen in a year. But this time, the visit would be more business than pleasure.

Billy had called Cal a week before to ask for their assistance with a recent murder case in the nearby town of Mt. Pleasant. The victim was a wealthy woman in her sixties named Peggy Walsh who was found strangled and possibly raped in her own home. Her body was deliberately posed in a manner to provoke shock which, according to Billy, suggested that "a fucking sex maniac may be on the loose."

As they drove up Route 17 in South Carolina, Danie immersed herself in the police reports Billy had sent over. The color images provided a vivid display of the gruesome crime scene in Mt. Pleasant. She had already begun to formulate an opinion on the case and made a few notes which would be the foundation for a psychological profile of the killer. Cal's ringing phone broke her concentration.

"Hey, Billy," Cal said.

"Where are you guys right now?"

His friend's voice sounded urgent. "We're about fifteen minutes from your office." Cal switched the phone to Bluetooth so Danie could hear the conversation through the car speakers.

"Well, we got another murder, Cal. Looks like a hurricane went through the house. I can tell you, it's not pretty. Why don't you drive right to the scene? I'll wait for you here."

"No problem," Cal said. "Where exactly are you?"

"We're on Meeting Street, just off South Battery. You'll see our cars out front."

"Okay, we'll be there shortly."

Cal stepped on the accelerator as Danie packed away the reports. "Sounds bad," she said.

Cal glanced over at her. "Yeah, you know Billy. He don't rattle very easy."

That was for sure. Billy was one tough cop and had the commendations and experience to prove it. In all the years she'd known him, she could honestly say he didn't know the meaning of fear. But she heard something different in Billy's voice now, not fear exactly, maybe anxiety or trepidation.

Up ahead, she saw the approaching signs for downtown Charleston. One sign indicated the last exit before the bridge that crossed the Ashley River. An odd feeling swept over her. She couldn't say why. It wasn't exactly a premonition, but for one brief moment, she imagined they should turn around and go home.

Chapter 3

Rachel Ackerman's residence
10:20 a.m.

AS A CRIMINAL PSYCHOLOGIST FOR MORE than a decade and a former FBI profiler, Danie had seen hundreds of crime scenes, but nothing prepared her for what she saw in Rachel Ackerman's bedroom this morning. Obscene was an understatement. If ever a killer staged a scene to trigger a gut reaction, this was it.

Anyone who entered the room was forced to see the woman's bloodstained pubic area, exposed in a hideous caricature of a gynecological exam position. She lay face-up on the floor at the foot of the bed. Her thick, flabby legs were spread wide, and her feet propped up high on chairs, tied to wooden rungs with hosiery. Pillows under her head left the dead woman staring lifelessly at the large mound of wrinkled flesh her aging body had become. Blood had clotted on her face, in her gray hair, and on the nightgown that hung in shreds on the sides of her naked body.

As she looked around, Danie found the room itself even more unsettling than the presence of a corpse. In the midst of Charleston's summer heat and humidity, someone had closed the air conditioning vents, making the air heavy with the smell of death. Thick, velvet drapes covered the windows, and the nightstand lamp lay broken on the floor, leaving only weak light from a chandelier with several burned-out bulbs. Beside the bed, busy flies feasted on a shattered dish of melted chocolate ice cream. In the corner of the room, an old electric fan rotated slowly on its ceramic base, providing only a hint of stale, warm breeze.

"Jesus," Danie said. After the disastrous events of the past several weeks, she still felt a little shaky.

"Steady, love." Cal placed his hand on her arm. Twenty years of marriage and he knew how little or much to say.

"I'm okay. It's just so damn hot in here. I feel lightheaded."

"Let me get us some water."

"Maybe later. This is something you don't see every day, and I want to get my head around it." She leaned against one of the bed posters and changed the subject. "Was she actually strangled?"

Cal examined the woman's neck under the pillowcase. "Yeah, but most likely with his hands. We'll have to wait for the autopsy to know for sure."

"Then why on earth tie a pillowcase around her neck?" She knelt down to get a better look.

"Not sure. A decorative touch?"

"I don't think so, Cal." Then as an afterthought, "Do you suppose he tied her up like this while she was still alive?" The possibility was so repugnant that she hoped it wasn't so.

Cal motioned her over to one side of the bed and pointed to the blood on the sheets. "I think he killed her in bed. Notice how the top sheet and blanket are both at the foot of the bed? He probably pulled her down to the bottom and let her drop onto the floor. It would be the easiest thing to do with a body that must weigh over two hundred pounds."

As a former Atlanta medical examiner, Cal knew what to expect at a murder scene. There were varying degrees of ugliness in the world of homicide, and this one was high on the scale. He learned early in his career to deal with the facts. There was no room for speculation in a death investigation; it was all about knowledge and experience. Disregard the natural feelings of disgust and revulsion. They're only distractions. To the average cop on the street, medical examiners may seem apathetic because they rarely display any emotion at the goriest of crime scenes. Cal remembered well the comment a detective once made during a murder case early in his career.

The victim was a ten-year-old boy who had been tortured and beaten to death by his mother's boyfriend. The boy's eyes hung from his head like marbles on a string, and every one of his fingers had been broken like twigs. His body had been smashed into an unrecognizable bag of bones. When a detective first saw the victim, he vomited. Cal arrived and immediately examined the child without a word about the brutality in front of him.

"You ain't fucking human," the detective said.

How far that was from the truth. What could be accomplished if the medical examiner broke down at every murder or expressed disgust at what he had to do? How reliable would his conclusions be if he couldn't stand to be in the same room with a mutilated corpse? Cal was doing what he knew he should: maintaining his composure and professionalism to gather the most accurate information possible. Those were his objectives at every homicide he ever attended, including Rachel Ackerman's.

Danie heard Chief Murphy before he came through the door. Billy Murphy, a mountain of a man with a head of curly blond hair and a sunburned face, had spent his entire career in the city's police department, the last seven as Charleston's police chief.

"Hi, Danie. Isn't this a hell of a scene?" he said quietly, putting his hand on Cal's shoulder. "Thanks to you both for coming. I sure didn't know this was gonna happen when I talked to you last week."

"Hey, that's okay. At least it got us ol' Georgia Bulldogs together again," Cal said giving Billy a slap on the back. "It's good to see you, man. Despite the circumstances." Billy and Cal were college room-mates at Georgia over twenty-five years ago, and they'd been friends ever since. Billy had been best man at Danie and Cal's wedding and was one of the few people who he let call him "Calvin."

"Looks to me like you'll need all the help you can get, and we'll do whatever we can." As gruesome as this murder was, it got Danie's mind off her own problems.

"I know you will." Billy gave her a hug. "I'm glad you're here. What the hell kind of crazy wacko you think did this?"

"Don't know yet, but it looks complicated." Her voice trailed off as she watched one of the detectives pull Billy from the room.

Danie wiped the beads of sweat from her forehead and con-centrated on the spectacle before her. Her first thought had been that someone had hated this poor woman, but then if this was a sexually motivated crime, it probably had little to do with the killer's personal interaction with her. Sexual posing was rare in homicide cases, and the most common reason for it was acting out a violent fantasy. Retaliation as a motive was a distant second.

While Cal examined Rachel Ackerman's body, Danie tried to make sense of the chaos in the bedroom. She had never experienced a crime scene like it. The first things she examined were the two beautiful oak chests and the matching nightstands that flanked each side of the bed. Every single drawer in the highboy and the mirrored dresser had been left open, their contents strewn all over the room.

One nightstand drawer was on the floor, and its contents appeared to have been dumped on the carpet. Nothing looked particularly valuable: snapshots, a key chain, handkerchiefs, playing cards, and hard candies in cellophane wrappers. On the floor in front of the nightstand, were two stacks, one of letters and the other of envelopes. Did the killer read all of it, even her credit card statements? What was he looking for? And why stack the letters and envelopes neatly when everything else was scattered around on the floor?

On the other nightstand was a digital photo album of Rachel Ackerman at different times in her life, along with a younger woman who looked like her daughter, a middle-aged man, and a young man who was probably her grandson.

Danie watched several rotations. Rachel Ackerman had been an attractive child and young woman, but as she aged, she transformed into an overweight, dour-faced old lady. Danie took a deep breath. No matter how unpleasant this elderly woman might have become, she didn't deserve to die for it. Danie had been thinking a lot about that lately, but she didn't want to dwell on it anymore. She turned away from the photos and concentrated on what the killer had done to the room. Surely, there had to be a reason for it.

Remembering the huge diamond ring on Rachel Ackerman's finger, Danie expected she would have had some other expensive pieces. The killer had turned over an old jewelry box on top of the dresser, scattering bulky necklaces and matching clip earrings that contemporary fashion had long forgotten. She wondered briefly where the good stuff was, and then her gaze wandered to the closet. She walked over and sure enough, inside the closet an unopened wall safe appeared.

The area outside the closet looked like a tornado had touched down. Every dress, blouse, and skirt had been ripped off its hanger and thrown in piles. Shoes and slippers too numerous to count were purposely stacked outside the closet door next to a tangled mound of belts. A pile of purses lay together on the carpet, each one opened and dumped just outside the closet walls. Combs, toothpicks, keys, nail files, and lipstick had been thrown together in another pile.

As she stepped carefully over the mess, Danie had been so distracted by the disarray outside the closet she almost missed a remarkable thing inside the closet. In the far right-hand corner were stacks of coins. She counted eighteen perfectly spaced stacks of pennies that appeared to have the same number of coins in each stack. Not wanting to contaminate evidence, she knelt on the plush carpet and tried to count the pennies in one of the stacks visually, just in case the number in each stack might have some significance. This was easier said than done, especially when there were about thirty pennies in the stack. The first time she counted twenty-nine. The second time she counted thirty. What was the significance of these eighteen stacks of thirty pennies each?

"What are you doing?" Cal said.

Danie hadn't heard him come up behind her. Startled, she knocked over three stacks of the pennies. She stood up and brushed the carpet lint off her slacks. "The killer stacked all these pennies, and I was wondering how hard it would be to do on this thick carpet without them toppling over. He must have spent some serious time here and with his victim."

This crime scene was incomprehensible to her. Why would the killer scatter his victim's possessions all over her room but carefully read her mail and then meticulously stack pennies in her closet? It would take some analysis, but she was determined she would ultimately understand what was going on in his mind.

Billy came back in the bedroom. "The techs are going to have to get in here. If you're finished looking around, I'd like you to go over to Mt. Pleasant. Detectives are waiting for you, and they'll brief you on what they've got on their homicide."

"No problem, Billy. By the way," Cal said, "did the coroner give an estimate about the time of death?"

"You know, it's a bitch getting that right, but she believes it was sometime in the early morning hours."

"I'd agree with that," Cal said.

Billy's phone rang.

"Hey, Walter," he said. As Billy ran his free hand through his hair, he frowned. "Oh, you're kidding! Don't tell him anything yet. Let's get together at my office in about an hour." Billy put the phone back in his pocket. "That was my new deputy chief. He just got a call from the news director of WCBD-TV. Someone sent Ricky Ramirez, the most obnoxious news anchor in the city, crime-scene photos of Rachel Ackerman. Ramirez wants to interview me on the evening news."

"What?" Cal said. "How did someone get the crime scene photos that fast?"

"I don't know. We haven't processed our photos yet." Then Billy's eyes opened wide. "Jesus. The killer. The killer must have taken them."

Chapter 4

Mt. Pleasant, South Carolina
11:30 a.m.

"GOD! THAT WAS AWFUL." DANIE OPENED the car windows and cranked up the air conditioning full blast, trying to rid their clothes of the stench of Ackerman's corpse. Magic, their rambunctious collie pup, immediately sensing that something had upset her, crawled into her lap and gently nuzzled her shoulder.

She forced herself to ignore her recent turmoil and focus on the extraordinary complexity of the Ackerman scene. It was as though an avenging force was bent on destroying the woman, but then there was also the puzzling combination of reading her letters and stacking pennies in her closet.

"Not a good morning," Cal said, hoping that Danie would be able to shake off the oppressive atmosphere they had just left. Had he known in advance how disturbing the scene would be, he would have done something to prepare her for it. Yes, she was one tough cookie, but she had been through hell in the past month. He glanced over at them, satisfied that Magic had provided a soothing effect.

He wondered if the killer had intentionally closed the air-conditioning vents in that room or if Ackerman, like many older folks, had found the room too cold that night and closed the vents herself. It was days like this that reinforced his reasons for retiring from his career as a medical examiner. Decades of death had left a scar on his mind and soul. From his perspective, it was more productive and less stressful to use his expertise to help professionals like Billy.

As Cal navigated the traffic over the Ravenel Bridge to Mt. Pleasant, they debated the motive for the savagery of the scene they had just left. Cal believed that the killer hated Ackerman so much that he did everything in his power to degrade her and then tried to broadcast it to the entire city. Danie disagreed. She argued that his theory did not consider the sexual aspects of the scene, which she believed were central to the case.

Billy told them how a murder two weeks earlier had thoroughly disrupted the genteel character of Mt. Pleasant's Old Village. Cal knew the small well-to-do Old Village from his high school days at the Porter Military Academy in Charleston where his father had enrolled him after yanking him out of Savannah's schools. Murder here was unthinkable. Many residents didn't lock their doors unless they went away, but now, Billy said, they were buying guard dogs, ammunition, and organizing neighborhood patrols.

Driving into the tiny village center, he saw that the news of this morning's murder in Charleston had fueled a sense of panic. Instead of the Saturday shoppers that usually buzzed around the stores, a growing crowd had gathered to listen to a police official who attempted to calm their fears.

Just outside the village center, they turned off Pitt Street to a lane overlooking Charleston Harbor. Until then, they hadn't given any thought to the victim's home but expected it to be like the others in the village—upscale, attractive, and unpretentious. However, when they pulled into the expansive circular driveway of a stunning brick manor house, they were surprised.

"The last time I visited a house like this, I had to buy an admission ticket," Cal said.

"Breathtaking," Danie said as she viewed the intricate façade of the Georgian mansion.

"Two wealthy women killed in their homes a couple of weeks apart. I'll bet that doesn't happen often." Cal knew that the likelihood of murdering a woman living in this neighborhood was statistically near zero. Maybe it was a tad higher for Rachel Ackerman because she lived in Charleston's historic district, close to commercial areas. Still, a tall wrought iron gate with a keypad and a top-of-the-line security system protected Ackerman's mansion. It wasn't the kind of home that invited intrusion. In contrast, the huge house in front of him had no fence, but the affluent neighborhood was one where the residents would notice suspicious activity.

He wondered what secrets this crime scene concealed. There was no threat of street crime, so how would a killer know if one or two nights a month the owner forgot to arm the security system or that neighbors weren't out in their yards on a summer evening? Cal realized that murders in a neighborhood like this required a lot of detailed planning.

As the Callahans walked toward the massive front door, two men got out of a dark sedan parked in the driveway.

"Hey, you don't have to lock your car," the older man yelled, "the police are already here." Cal immediately knew that he was not a South Carolina native but couldn't place the accent. It wasn't New England or New York, but it was distinctive.

Mt. Pleasant Detective Mike Cecchi was a powerfully built man with a strong handshake and a broad, friendly face. His partner was a handsome Asian man with an easy smile. "Glad to meet you. I'm Detective Ira Shapiro," he said.

"Ira looks forward to meeting somebody new," Mike said. "Everyone wonders why a Chinese guy has a Jewish name."

"I figured there was a good story behind it," Cal said.

"Yep. My brother, Howie, and I were orphans in Hong Kong. The Shapiros rescued us and brought us here. It was the luckiest day of our lives."

Danie introduced herself. "I love to hear stories like that. How old were you when they adopted you?"

"Howie was four, and I was almost three. We were living on this old junk in Kowloon Bay when our parents died in an accident. It was a lot different than the Shapiro's home."

"That's an understatement," Mike said. "His dad owns several sporting goods stores in this area. Howie runs them now. The boys went from a leaky boat and no future to a mansion in the suburbs and free tennis racquets."

"That's right," Ira said. "America, the beautiful."

Mike paused for a moment and looked back at the house. "Mrs. Walsh's son is waiting for us."

"By the way, Chief Murphy speaks very highly of you two," Ira said as they walked to the front entrance. "Mike and I are happy to get your views on this case."

Judging from Mike's expressionless face, Danie wasn't sure that he shared his partner's enthusiasm.

"From what we heard this morning, there are some similarities between the two murders," Mike said as he rang the doorbell. "Margaret Walsh's older son, Ethan, is here today. By the way, he has some problems with his right hand so don't offer to shake it."

A few seconds later, a voice came over the intercom. "Detective Cecchi?"

"Yes, Ethan. I'm here with Detective Shapiro, Dr. Danielle Callahan, and Dr. Calvin Callahan."

The front door opened slowly into an empty hallway. From the library, a slender man in a wheelchair appeared.

"Thank you for letting us visit, Ethan." She knew how crushing it was to suddenly lose a close family member to violence and then have strangers asking a lot of personal questions. Even if the strangers were there to help.

"When Detective Cecchi said you and your husband were coming, I read all about you on the Net," Ethan said. "I'm very glad that you're here."

"You holding up okay, Ethan?" Mike said.

"As well as anyone could expect. I never imagined in my worst nightmares I'd lose my father and my mother in less than a year. Today I wanted to sort through my mother's things to give to charity, but now that I'm here, I don't think I'm up to it."

"You need more time, Ethan," Danie said. "Your mom's clothes will still be here months from now."

"You're probably right, Dr. Callahan. I'm just so used to making a list of what I have to do and crossing things off one by one. I didn't realize how tough it would be even to go into her bedroom." He choked on his words.

Cal noticed how Ethan focused on Danie, which was not unusual in his experience. Without a doubt, her silky blonde hair and gentle blue eyes were attractive to most men, but it wasn't only that. She had an intangible quality that could immediately draw people to her. He called it Danie's private polygraph, constructed from empathy, intuition, and experience, and refined to determine if people were telling the truth.

"Ethan," Mike said, "we'll be talking about things related to your mother's death. It might be painful to hear it."

Ethan switched his attention back to the detective. "I couldn't stand to listen. My mother and I were very close. I'll go into the library, shut the door, and do some work. Let me know if I can help."

"Are Noah and his wife around?" Mike said.

"They weren't when I came. Our relationship became very tense after the lawyer explained the will, so I try to stay out of their way." Ethan turned his wheelchair, rubber squeaking on wood, and disappeared down the hallway.

Once the library door closed, Mike explained that Noah was Ethan's younger brother who was married to a German woman named Julia. "She's a real bitch."

"It's pronounced 'Yoo-lee-uh,'" Ira said. "Better practice or she'll correct you like you're an idiot. Remind me to give you a copy of her rap sheet in Germany," he added with a grin, "but don't judge her harshly because of the prostitution charges."

Mike led the Callahans and his partner down the main hallway towards the back of the house. They paused at the entrance to the family room, where there was an empty mahogany stand. He showed them a photo of a beautiful polished bronze statue of a soaring American eagle.

"The bastard took this statue and bashed her skull with it." Mike paused for a moment, his face colored with anger. "She fell forward onto the rug in the hallway."

"Mike takes this case personally," Ira said.

"I do take it personally. I don't like some shithead coming into my territory and killing my neighbors. That's why I left South Philly."

Danie felt sick to her stomach as she envisioned the attack. She looked for Cal's reaction, but there was none. The emotional distance he had cultivated as a medical examiner kept him focused on what Billy asked him to do.

"I hope you don't mind if Danie and I have some questions as we go. I'd like to be sure we fully understand the sequence of events."

"Fine," Mike said, his tone slightly clipped.

"How about we start with the killer entering the house, Mike?"

"Sure. We think Mrs. Walsh may have let him in for some reason, probably through the front door, considering she was bludgeoned from behind just after she passed by the eagle statue on this stand. Ethan said his mother didn't lock the back door and turn on the alarm until she was going to bed. The front door was secured most of the time. The coroner believes she died sometime mid to late afternoon."

"How do we know for sure this assault takes place in the hall?" Cal said.

"Well, the rug and the statue were part of the furnishings here," Ira said, "and her blood was on both items and the floor and walls. The blood spatter shows that the initial impact was right about here."

Mike explained that when two Mt. Pleasant officers arrived that evening after nine o'clock to investigate a burglar alarm call, the house was completely dark. They determined that the killer set off the alarm by throwing the eagle statue through the sliding glass door.

Cal tried to imagine why the killer would do such a thing. "What? He set the alarm and then made it go off by sending the statue through the glass in the sliding door?"

"We think this was a murder made to look like a burglary," Ira said. "If the killer got into the house when the alarm went off after nine o'clock, there's no way he would've had enough time to do what he did before our guys got here."

"But why set off the alarm at all? If you just committed a murder, that's insane, right?"

Mike shrugged. "Well Cal, I'm not convinced insanity is off the table, as you may see as we go along. Another thing, while we're here in this part of the house. A chair was placed just inside the broken sliding door. One of the officers fell over it when he came in."

"Do you think that the killer put it there?" Danie said.

"We don't know for sure, but we couldn't think of any reason for the chair being in that odd place."

Mike led them into the kitchen and showed them a photo of an empty wallet on the counter. Credit cards and cash were plainly visible next to it. "The only thing missing was her driver's license."

"Driver's license?" Danie looked up from the photo. "You're certain that it wasn't somewhere else in the house? Maybe in a different purse?"

"We looked everywhere for it," Ira said, "even in the pockets of all her clothes. She used her car more than once a day, and she wasn't the kind of person who would drive without a license. The reason we discounted burglary is that her sons couldn't find anything else missing. There was valuable jewelry in the bedroom, expensive antiques and paintings throughout the house, and cash in several of her purses.

"Can we go back to the missing driver's license? I know this is going to sound strange, but did you contact the local newspapers and TV stations to see if they had her license?"

Mike looked perplexed at Danie's question. "No, there wasn't any reason to. Wouldn't a newspaper or TV station contact us if that happened?"

Cal understood why she focused on the missing license. "Remember that guy in Kansas who sent crime scene photos and his victim's driver's license to the newspaper?"

"Dennis Rader was his name," she said. "He called himself BTK."

"Ah yes, Mr. Bind Torture Kill," Ira said. "The local dogcatcher gone rogue. I hadn't thought of that, but we'll contact the media outlets."

"Sending her driver's license to a newspaper doesn't make any sense," Mike said. "The newspapers know she's dead. They all have copies of her obituary."

"BTK sent the driver's license to make the police realize that he murdered her," Danie said. "He was annoyed that he hadn't gotten credit for her death."

Mike shook his head. The look on his face made it clear he didn't buy into the BTK theory until Cal told them about the Ackerman photos that the killer had sent to the TV news anchor.

"Great," Mike said. "That's just great. Okay. Let's finish in here." He pointed to the cabinet under the sink. "In the trash container were orange peels, coffee grounds, and receipts from a grocery store. The killer went through it and pulled out the receipts, unfolded the ones that were crumpled up, and laid them out on the counter. Weird, huh?"

"Do you have a photo of that scene with you?" Danie said.

"Sure." Mike browsed through a stack of photos in a folder, pulled out three, and handed them to Danie.

As she scrutinized the pictures, Danie appeared increasingly uneasy. She told them how the killer at the Charleston scene went through everything in the bedroom, including the victim's letters and credit card statements.

They moved from the kitchen to the master bedroom suite. The four-poster bed was unmade, and brightly-colored slacks and blouses adorned the back of every chair. A half-full bottle of Russian vodka stood next to an empty glass on the nightstand. In the corner of the dressing room was a large pile of dirty clothes. Above it, hanging on a hook was a garish red thong and a matching plus-size see-through lace brassiere.

"These belonged to Margaret Walsh?" Cal thought that if she wore this underwear, he was ready to entertain some new theories about her death.

Ira rolled his eyes. "No, Doc. The lingerie was put here quite recently."

Mike handed Danie a couple of photos. "This is where the bastard brought her. Next to her body was a small purse with sunglasses, a comb, and some change."

"Take a good look at the drawers here in these photos." Ira pointed to the three built-in drawers in the dressing room.

Danie studied a close-up. "The bottom drawer looks like it's open a couple of inches. The one right above it appears like it's open maybe a half-inch less and the top drawer looks open a half-inch less than the one below it."

"Yeah, very strange, isn't it? The measurements are almost exactly what you just said. Did you ever hear of a killer bringing a ruler to the scene?"

Danie told them about the eighteen stacks of pennies in Ackerman's closet. "Anything like that here?"

"No, nothing like that," Mike said as he showed them the palatial bathroom with a large whirlpool tub. "When we got here that night, we found the tub partially filled with water and a pair of pink fluffy slippers next to it."

Back in the dressing room, Mike handed them photos of the body. Margaret Walsh lay naked, face up on the floor, her lifeless eyes staring into space like a plastic doll, dressed in a pink housecoat with a dark colored cord tightly tied around the neck in a large bow. The killer arranged her legs so that anyone entering the room would see her pubic area first.

Cal looked at each photo twice. "Did Mrs. Walsh have any drug dependencies or a boyfriend before or after her husband passed away?"

"The simple answer is no and no," Ira said. "We checked those issues very carefully."

"She was a very respectable woman," Mike said. "Also, she gave a lot of money and time to cerebral palsy charities."

"These photographs here in the bedroom." Cal pointed to the dresser and nightstand. "Are these recent photos of Mrs. Walsh and her family?" The framed snapshots showed an attractive woman with a distinguished-looking husband.

"These are the most recent," Mike said. "Her husband died of a stroke last year at the age of sixty-six. Mrs. Walsh was sixty-four."

"She certainly didn't look her age," Danie said.

"That's for sure." Cal was surprised at how young she looked in her photos and wondered if her looks had anything to do with her murder. "Was she wearing the robe over her naked body when he bludgeoned her in the front hall?"

"No, she wasn't," Ira said. "She wore a short-sleeved blouse and slacks. Both of these bloodstained items were at the top of the hamper, so he wasn't trying to hide the fact that he changed her clothes."

"What kind of clothing was she was wearing, Ira?" Danie said. "I mean, was it the sort of thing you'd put on if you're going to work in the garden or going to a restaurant?"

"Let me think for a second, Danie. She wore white socks and an old pair of tennis shoes, or at least that was what was on top of her blouse and slacks in the hamper."

"So, she probably wasn't planning to go anywhere with him, and if she was expecting him, she didn't think he was important enough to wear something special. Do you agree?"

"We're on the same page," Mike said.

"While she's still unconscious," Cal continued to construct his narrative of the event, "he turns her over on her back and sexually assaults her with some object that causes her to bleed vaginally. The pink housecoat she was wearing, was it from her closet?"

"Yes, it's hers," Ira said. "But the blue cord he strangled her with is from a dress in her closet. The pink housecoat had buttons."

"Okay," Cal said. "He takes off what she's wearing and dresses her in a housecoat. Then the fluffy pink slippers in front of the tub are staged. She wasn't really ready to take a bath, right?"

"That's right," Mike said.

"Wonder why the hell he bothered to make it look like she was going to?"

"That's one of the many things we don't understand," Mike said.

"This staging has a purpose," Danie said. "It's too specific not to have. It may be an essential part of the killer's fantasy. Altering the scene in such minute detail could mean that he had been constructing an elaborate ritualistic fantasy in his mind for quite some time. He must create every bit of it to be satisfied."

"Let me be sure I got this right," Cal said. "After he kills her and positions her body, he sits around for several hours. Then when he leaves, he sets the alarm, goes outside, and throws the statue through the glass door?" Cal couldn't see any reason for the killer to risk hanging around for so long. "Any guess as to why?"

"Maybe to avoid being seen during daylight?" Ira said.

Cal wasn't sure. "That part makes sense, but why deliberately set off the alarm? That's a risky thing to do. What if your guys had been very close by?"

"Maybe he wanted police to find her body the same day," Danie said, "because that particular day had some significance to him." It made perfect sense to her considering the elaborate scene he created for himself. She glanced at Cal and the two detectives and could see by their expressions that her suggestion didn't get any traction.

Cal folded his arms in front of his chest. "For what it's worth, my initial view is this is a carefully planned event. He'd been in the house at least once before when he selected the statue to knock her out. The timing was critical so that he may have had an appointment with her.

He walked to the front door in broad daylight on a Thursday afternoon, and no one remembered seeing him or whatever he drove. He made sure his clothes and vehicle wouldn't attract attention."

"I think we're pretty much in agreement," Mike said. "We've checked the alibis of the men she knew from her charity work, her church, her friends, and the guys that did her home repairs. Ethan was very helpful. There were only a few people that we couldn't locate."

"What about the family?" Danie said. "Have you cleared them yet?"

Ira smiled. "Not entirely..." Before he could finish his sentence, he heard noises coming from the driveway outside. He went to the window and looked out at the courtyard. A gray Mercedes convertible had pulled up to the house. The woman driver got out of the car and marched up to the front door while the male passenger followed behind her. "Noah! Noah!" the woman yelled. "Why the hell are these cars here?"

"The lovely Julia has arrived!" Ira said.

Soon, the staccato sound of high heels clicking on the wooden floor echoed through the house. Within moments, Julia stormed into the bedroom.

She was a captivating figure, easily six feet without the high heels. A short black skirt exposed thighs and calves that could have belonged to a bodybuilder, and her turquoise top was cut so low that her oversized breasts seemed ready to bounce out of captivity. As she approached, her eyes narrowed down to slits floating in a sea of bright blue-green eye shadow.

"Get out of my bedroom! Now! You can't come in here without a warrant!"

"Now Julia, don't get upset," Mike said. "Ethan gave us permission to take another look at the place where your mother-in-law died."

"I'm going to call my lawyer. Ethan has no right to let you in our house. How do I know you haven't planted bugs in here? Get out, all of you!"

The mousy-looking man stood in the doorway. "Please, dear. Ethan and I told the detectives that they could come back if they needed to."

Julia stood silently, eyeing everyone in the room with suspicion.

Mike introduced the Callahans and explained why they were at the house. "We're finished now. Sorry to disturb you, but thanks very much for letting us take another look at the house."

Her face contorted in anger. "Go to hell."

After they said their goodbyes in front of the house and the detectives drove away, the Callahans took Magic for a walk, giving them a chance to take in the full ambiance of the neighborhood before they headed over to Billy's office.

"Cal, you can't let me forget anything. The receipts in the waste-basket, the chair in front of the door, and dragging her from the hall into the bedroom."

He glanced over at her. "Your old FBI profiler instincts are back in battle mode. Good. I haven't seen you this intense since our days in Atlanta."

"I'll have to do some research." She struggled to keep the stiff breeze off the harbor from blowing her hair in her eyes. As she watched the nameless people in the street going about their lives, hurrying to their appointments, gabbing on their ubiquitous cell phones, and altogether oblivious to the horrors of murder, Danie had one ominous thought. Without realizing it, she said it aloud.

"I just hope it's not what I think it is."

Chapter 5

WHY WOULD RACHEL ACKERMAN'S KILLER SEND crime scene photos to the press? Did he think the TV station would make them public? As he drove to Billy's office, Cal tried to comprehend what this guy hoped to gain. He could only imagine that her murderer hated her with such intensity he needed to humiliate her again in death. Danie was glued to her tablet, which she rested on Magic's back as he lay across her lap.

He came away from Mt. Pleasant viewing Margaret Walsh as a woman who cared a great deal about her appearance. He wondered if her youthful good looks had inadvertently attracted a stalker. With her active social life, she probably had a large number of male friends and acquaintances, many of whom knew she was widowed and lived alone. She might have opened the door to one of those men under some innocent pretext.

Maneuvering through the Saturday afternoon traffic on the Crosstown Expressway, Cal thought more about whether the same man killed both women. It was hard to ignore the similarities between the two murders, but there were differences as well. For one, Walsh's killer had not sent crime scene photos to the TV station. Walsh was strangled with a cord and Ackerman most likely with the killer's hands. Manual strangulation was a very personal act, which in Cal's mind fit better with his theory that Ackerman's death was motivated by hatred, and therefore, she knew her killer. There were a few strange things Walsh's killer did in her house, but nothing like the chaos in Ackerman's bedroom.

For the time being, he wasn't convinced Rachel Ackerman's killer was the same man who murdered Margaret Walsh, and he hoped he was right for Billy's sake. A clever psychopath focused on getting attention for himself could do serious damage to his friend's reputation and his whole department.

In Atlanta, Cal had witnessed a city in an uproar and careers ruined when a killer wasn't caught fast enough for an insatiable media and glory-hungry politicians. He didn't want to see the same thing happen in Charleston.

Throughout the drive, Danie hadn't said a word. As they approached Billy's office, Cal noticed how somber she looked. Something was bothering her about what she had experienced today.

The new deputy chief, Walter Johnson, opened the door to Billy's office where he and the chief were meeting. An imposing figure, well over six feet tall with broad shoulders, a military haircut, and a flawless milk chocolate complexion, he introduced himself in a voice that commanded respect and erased any doubt that he was a man who liked being in charge.

"I know you and the chief were undergrads at Georgia," Walter said. "Emory for medicine?"

"Harvard. My dad went there."

"His dad was the best damn cardiac surgeon in the Southeast," Billy said.

"Why'd you become a medical examiner and not a heart surgeon like your old man?"

Cal smiled. He didn't tell Walter that the idea of having a person's life in his hands every day wasn't the kind of career he wanted. "Someone has to solve the mysteries of the dead."

"But you don't do that anymore, now, right?"

"Mostly for private patients," Cal said. "Folks who want to know what secrets their parents kept from them. Like, 'Did my mother really have Alzheimer's?' 'Was that son of a bitch actually my father?' I also give some testimony in criminal cases."

"How about you, Doc?" He turned to Danie. "Harvard, too?"

Danie laughed. "No, the cost was out of the question for a cop's daughter. Got a scholarship in my hometown to Case Western in Cleveland for undergrad and grad school."

Walter wasn't quite through with his interrogation. "You two work together on cases?"

"Not often. We have our own specialties," Cal said. "She's a criminal psychologist. Consults with police departments and also has her own patients. I just wish she didn't have to travel so damn much."

"Have some sandwiches and iced tea," Billy said as they sat at the conference table.

"Thanks." Cal put a couple of sandwiches on a plate.

"I'll eat later," Danie said, reaching for a bottle of tea. The events of the day had her stomach rebelling against any kind of food.

"What did you think of the Mt. Pleasant case?" Billy said. "Sex crime, burglary, or something else?"

"Sex crime on the face of it." Danie sipped some tea. "It definitely wasn't a burglary. That said, he did things that don't make a whole lot of sense. Like changing her clothes to look as if she was going to take a bath. Now, those things could be explained as parts of his fantasy and nothing more. Obsessive fantasies can build over time and finally explode into who knows what. More than likely, he has a history of sexual assault of increasing intensity. Although he may not have been arrested for any of them."

"Interesting theory, Danie." Billy turned to Cal. "What do you think?"

Cal hesitated before he answered. "I agree with Danie that it wasn't a burglary."

"Do you think the murders are related?" Walter had noticed his limited agreement.

"I think so," Danie said before Cal had a chance to respond. "These murders are the kind a serial killer with highly-developed violent fantasies would commit. In just a couple of weeks, he's escalated both the sexual staging and the disruption of the crime scene. The increased intensity suggests that he is losing control of himself."

Almost immediately, she regretted not being more careful about the words she'd chosen. She, of all people, understood why no police chief ever wanted to hear "serial killer" in his jurisdiction. From her experience, a case like that can turn a city upside down because police departments were never funded or staffed enough to deal with the staggering demands of an investigation that may take years to resolve.

"Whoa, Danie!" Billy said. "I feel like I've missed a couple of steps. What makes you think this guy's acting like a serial killer? Even if it's the same guy in both murders—and I haven't bought into that conclusion at all—there's only two victims. Your buddies at the Bureau tell us there has to be three for it to be a serial killer, right?"

Danie doubled-down on her initial statement. "Sometimes you might get a warning of what you may be facing in the future. Maybe you can get out ahead of this in case another woman is killed."

Cal didn't want to openly disagree with Danie, but he felt obligated to tell them he believed it was too soon to conclude that it was the same killer. He chose his words carefully.

"I'm not as confident as Danie is about a single killer, but in case, here's a suggestion. It's probably worth giving a heads-up to a few key people, like the mayor, the county prosecutor, and definitely the Mt. Pleasant's chief. You don't want them blindsided if you determine it's the same guy." He preferred to address the practical steps to take regardless of whether there was one killer or two.

"I'd also recommend doing what we did in Atlanta and put together a small group with a couple of your detectives and some from Mt. Pleasant. Even if there are no more deaths, you still have two very unusual murders and a killer who wants to be his own publicity agent. Danie and I can help you structure it this weekend while we're here in Charleston. We both have experience in that area."

Billy was silent for a minute and then looked at his deputy chief to gauge his reaction.

Walter nodded. "Makes sense to me."

Billy leaned back in his chair and looked at each of the three expectant faces across from him. "Done. I'll call Mayor Campbell and then Chief Allman over in Mt. Pleasant. Walter, what say we get a few key people together from our department and Mt. Pleasant and shoot for a meeting around five-thirty?"

"Okay, Chief," Walter said. "Danie and Cal, could you be ready by five-thirty to discuss the similarities and differences between the two murders?"

"Sure thing," Danie said. "Could you have some of these crime scene photos enlarged so I can use them at the meeting? If you can, I'd like to have copies of them for both the mayor and Mt. Pleasant's chief. It'll just take me a few minutes to select the ones I need."

"No problem."

It was clear to Cal that Danie was energized. The killings fit perfectly into the expertise she had developed throughout her career. Her FBI profiling work, therapy with sex offenders, and her doctoral thesis on the role of fantasies in sex crimes, all made her confident she understood this killer. He was thankful Danie was excited about the case. She seemed back to her former self again—confident, upbeat, and ready to work.

However, when they left Billy's office, he was uneasy about the meeting they had just left and the next one that was a few hours away. He couldn't help thinking that while some pieces fit the puzzle—there were lots more that didn't.

Chapter 6

How could something so horrible happen in a beautiful place like this?

Danie's thoughts wandered as she watched the birds lining up at the copper-roofed feeder in the magnificent garden while just ahead on the veranda, Cal tied Magic's leash to a railing. They'd returned to the Ackerman mansion to get the very latest information on the investigation for Walter's five-thirty meeting.

She was happy their friend of many years, CPD Detective Joe Asher, was the lead detective on the case. Despite his twice-broken nose, once in a college football game and the other during a shop-lifting arrest, he had a face that looked years younger than forty-six.

"Good to see you again." He shook Cal's hand and hugged Danie.

"Still fishing with the boys?" Danie referred to the outreach program Joe began that took troubled kids on fishing trips several times a year.

"Of course, Danie. You know my creed: everyone deserves a second chance," he said. "We have access to three boats now and more than thirty volunteers. Speaking of which, I'd like you to meet

Master Police Officer Delores Goodall. She's head of our Crime Scene Unit."

A tall, middle-aged woman shook hands. "I'm one of the thirty volunteers," she said with a distinctive New England accent. "Glad to meet you."

"And here's another one of them," Joe said as a young man walked onto the veranda. "This is Rod Karlovec, my partner. Everyone calls him RK."

He paused for a moment while his protégé shook hands with Danie and Cal. "He might seem a little young but RK is a good investigator. He doesn't miss a thing."

A playful smile spread across RK's face. "My uncle, Lieutenant Eric Karlovec, is the CO of our traffic unit. He's also given me a couple of pointers."

"Come on, we don't have much time." Delores led them through the French doors into an elegant breakfast room and kitchen. A large family room with a stone fireplace lay just beyond.

Joe motioned to the large, round breakfast table. "Have a seat. Let me start. Delores, RK, stop me if I miss something. Rachel Ackerman was seventy-six and divorced. She has a son and daughter who live in the area and two grandchildren. The coroner's office was able to notify the son and get some basic information.

"Justine, the maid, found her this morning around eight-thirty. Normally, she knocks on that door over there by the kitchen, and Ackerman lets her in. This morning, the door was slightly ajar, and she came right in. There was no sign of forced entry. The house has a good security system, but it hadn't been turned on."

"Did the maid say whether Mrs. Ackerman was expecting visitors last night?" Cal said.

Joe shook his head. "She said that when Ackerman had visitors, which didn't happen very often, she'd ask her to cut some flowers from the garden and arrange them in vases. The maid figured since she wasn't asked to cut any flowers and no special food was ordered, Ackerman wasn't expecting anyone that evening."

"Have you interviewed the son or daughter yet?" Danie said.

"Yeah, me and RK interviewed her son, Greg. He said his mother was an unhappy woman who became very bitter after she divorced his father seven years ago, who now lives in Colorado with a wife half his age. Greg told us he and his son got along better with Mrs. Ackerman than his sister and her boy. Ackerman always put a guilt trip on them because they didn't give her enough attention, and she disapproved of his sister's lifestyle."

"Greg's son, who's twenty-two, doesn't live with his parents," RK said. "He wasn't at the place he rents, and we couldn't reach him on his phone."

"What about her daughter?" Cal said.

"Her name is Camilla," Joe said. "She's forty-five and has a fifteen-year-old boy. Neither one was home."

"Did you have a chance to talk to any of the neighbors?" Danie said. "Were they friendly with her?"

"The neighbors weren't much help," RK said. "The ones who were home didn't hear or see anything unusual. None of them really knew her—and from what I gathered, never wanted to get to know her. The only thing they said was she had a reputation for shouting at the people who worked for her."

"Before I forget," Delores picked up her camera, "we found an empty plastic Stouffer's lasagna tray just inside the kitchen trash container. The autopsy will tell us whether she ate the lasagna last night. But that's not all."

She showed them a photo of the black granite counter next to the sink. "See the empty wine bottle? The maid said it wasn't there yesterday when she left. She'd worked for the woman for three years and never saw any evidence that she drank alcohol except when she had guests."

Danie looked at the bottle's distinctive label. "This is a very expensive red wine."

"I know," Joe said. "I called a wine store. The 1997 Silver Oak California cabernet cost over a hundred bucks a bottle."

Cal nodded in agreement. "Not generally what you'd drink with frozen dinners."

Joe laughed. "I wouldn't, but a rich woman like Mrs. Ackerman might."

"Interestingly, there weren't any fingerprints on the bottle," Delores said. "Or on the crystal glass we found in the dishwasher."

"Crystal? What kind of crystal?" Danie said.

Delores looked puzzled. "Oh, I don't know. Does it make a difference? It's not here anymore. We took it as evidence."

Danie stood up quickly and looked in the kitchen cabinets. There were some everyday glasses but nothing crystal. "I know the bar near the dining room is on the second floor, Joe, but is there one here on this floor?"

"There's a small one in the library, I'll show you."

The large library was right out of a movie set for a British manor house. Bookcases extended up to the high ceiling on three walls, stuffed with mostly leather-bound volumes. A catwalk about eight feet from the floor let one climb a small stairway to reach the upper shelves. Danie imagined them to be the kind of books wealthy people buy for appearances but never read.

The fourth wall had a small bar cabinet between two windows. Inside, an empty crystal decanter sat on a mirrored tray. Danie found five crystal wine glasses on one of the shelves. Joe thought they looked similar to the one in the dishwasher, so she brought one back to the kitchen.

"Was it anything like this, Delores?"

"Yes, just like the one you're holding."

"This is Baccarat crystal," Danie said. "My aunt has four glasses very much like these. Her son paid close to two hundred dollars for each one. It's hard to believe Mrs. Ackerman would put such expensive crystal in the dishwasher, especially since she has a maid to wash it by hand."

Cal had a plausible explanation. "Maybe she had a visitor that evening who thought putting the glass in the dishwasher was doing her a favor."

Danie shook her head. "What friend wipes off fingerprints from a wine bottle and glass?"

It was a good question, but there wasn't much time to dwell on it. They had to get back to headquarters for a meeting with the city mayor, some detectives, and the police chief of Mt. Pleasant.

"We don't know if the glass was wiped clean or not," Delores said. "Whoever put it in the dishwasher turned it on—with only the one glass, a coffee cup, and a couple plates and forks inside." After the crime scene briefing, the Callahans returned to police headquarters where they were fortunate enough to find a suitably shady spot in the back of the building to park the car so Magic wouldn't be too hot.

It was a small group consisting of Joe and RK from CPD, and from Mt. Pleasant PD, Chief Bert Allman, Detectives Mike Cecchi, and Ira Shapiro. The last to arrive was Charleston Mayor LC Campbell, a dapper man who looked to be in his seventies, well dressed in a light beige suit accented by a handsome lavender tie.

"What does the LC stand for?" Danie whispered to Joe as they sat around the conference table.

"Lutrell Cassius," Joe said. "He's a good guy."

Walter began the meeting by thanking the mayor and the head of Mt. Pleasant's PD for attending. He introduced each person in the room and saved the Callahans for last.

"We have here with us two experts to give us some insight into what we may be facing. Dr. Danielle Callahan, a former FBI profiler and criminal psychologist with an excellent reputation in the field. She's earned kudos from many PDs across the country. Her husband, Dr. Calvin Callahan, has had a distinguished career as a medical examiner in the Atlanta area. We have a unique challenge with these recent murders, and we're grateful they have agreed to share their skill and experience."

After his upbeat introduction of the Callahans, Walter's demeanor became noticeably more solemn.

"We called this meeting so we can examine the possibility that we may have a serial killer on our hands. Naturally, we hope this isn't the case, but we believe the Walsh murder and the Ackerman murder may have been committed by the same person. Dr. Danielle Callahan will explain why."

Using a few crime scene photos from both murders to point out the similarities in the method of strangulation, she emphasized the elaborate staging of the crime scenes and the social status of the victims. Danie was accustomed to speaking at meetings, although she didn't have much time to prepare for this one. She had mentally organized what she wanted to say and managed to write a few notes to guide her through but made sure not to leave anything out.

She was surprised to see that it took only twenty minutes to review both murders and get her points across. When she was finished, Walter Johnson handed out copies of the photos.

Mayor Campbell was the first one to speak. "Dr. Callahan, is this guy a nutcase? Should we be looking for a former mental patient?"

"No, sir, I don't think so," Danie said. "More likely a psychopath with a history of sexual assault. The murders were most likely premeditated and well planned."

"How could you possibly know that?" Bert Allman, Mt. Pleasant's chief, said. He didn't bother to hide the skepticism in his voice.

Danie was prepared for challenges to her remarks. "As you know, Walsh lived in a very safe neighborhood and was killed in the late afternoon when there were likely to be neighbors around who would have remembered the suspect if he looked the least bit out of place. Detectives Cecchi and Shapiro made a persuasive case that she let her killer in through the front door, which was normally locked. We doubted that she would have let a stranger into her house, so whatever ploy he used to get inside would have taken some planning."

She looked briefly at Mt. Pleasant's chief to see if she was making any headway with her theory. "Like Mrs. Walsh, Rachel Ackerman always locked her doors at night and turned on her alarm, but somehow her killer got into her house without a break-in and probably murdered her while she was in bed. I believe that required some significant planning. Another thing—there were no fingerprints on items we know the killer handled, probably because he wore gloves."

The group seemed satisfied with the answer.

The final question was from the mayor, who had in his hands copies of the photos of Ackerman's body and the disarray in her bedroom. He was furious that such crimes could happen in his city.

"Dr. Callahan," he said, shaking his head in disbelief. "Is there any chance that what he did to this poor Ackerman woman is the apex of his frenzy? That maybe by going to this extreme, he's gotten it—whatever the damn hell *it* is—out of his system?"

Danie thought about his question for a few moments before answering. "Mayor Campbell, these crimes are so unusual. Two weeks ago, when he killed Mrs. Walsh, the scene was not nearly as violent. Today's murder of Rachel Ackerman is a major progression. If he kills again, and I'm quite sure he will try, it may be more outrageous than what happened today. I hope I'm wrong."

She pointed out that the suspect could be employed by a company providing services like pest control, plumbing, lawn care, or even a charity. As she said it, she thought a man with a charity brochure in hand might be just the kind of ploy to gain entry into a wealthy woman's home. But there were too many possibilities.

Mike suggested a utility serviceman, such as phone repair or electrical service. Most people are accustomed to seeing these workmen around the city, and it wouldn't be unusual for them to show up unexpectedly.

"Cable TV is another possibility," Mike said. "They're all over the place. So is the post office."

"Agreed," Danie said. "We need more information. It's just speculation for now."

Billy ended the meeting with a proposal to expand the number of detectives from Charleston PD and Mt. Pleasant PD to coordinate the investigation of the Walsh and Ackerman homicides. Before the mayor left the meeting, Billy pulled him aside for advice on handling the problem that news host Ricky Ramirez had the Ackerman crime scene photos.

After the meeting, Cal was uncharacteristically quiet. If Danie noticed, she didn't say anything about it. Her concern was for Magic. Danie insisted that he deserved a good walk, so Cal drove over to Moultrie Park for some exercise.

"I think the meeting went very well," Danie said as they walked behind Magic. Cal didn't respond immediately. She turned and looked at him, "Don't you think so?"

Cal sighed and wiped the perspiration from his face. "You promise you won't get mad?"

She interpreted his comment to mean he didn't think she did well on her presentation. "Well, I'll wait until you say what's on your mind, and then I'll let you know."

Cal did his best to be diplomatic. "I think you were very persuasive getting the mayor and most of the others to buy into your theory that a serial killer murdered the two women."

Danie looked puzzled. "What's wrong with that?" She abruptly stopped to signal she wasn't going any farther until he answered.

"A strong belief doesn't make it a fact," Cal said. He was surprised at how confident she was about the killer's mindset so early in the investigation. "I wish you had been more tentative about your theory rather than presenting it as though it's the only one."

"So what should I have done?" Danie's irritation was apparent. "Billy asked me to explain why I thought it could be a serial killer—

Cal interrupted. "Yes, and Walter asked you to explain to the mayor and the rest of them the similarities *and differences* between the two murders. He did that so everyone could weigh your theory and come to their own conclusion about whether it was the same guy. You only presented the similarities."

"I think the audience would have come to the same conclusion if I had presented the differences," Danie said.

"What if it turns out these murders are *not* related, and you've steered the entire investigation in the wrong direction? Can you live with that?"

Danie was silent for the rest of their walk. Eventually, Cal suggested they go to Billy's house. Once they were in the car, Danie leaned over and kissed him on the cheek.

"I'm sorry," she said. "I'll fix it."

Chapter 7

DANIE WAS HAPPY WHEN THEY ARRIVED at Billy's home, a meticulously restored oasis of Victorian tranquility on the Ashley River. The circular brick driveway led to a covered porch where two antique rocking chairs rested next to the front door. The covered porch wrapped around the house on one side, all the way back to a large screened-in area overlooking the river and the city of Charleston to the south.

It was a beautiful view at night, especially when all was quiet and the demands of a busy day could easily be forgotten. Cal once told her the story of how Billy, an avid young fisherman, had dreamed of such a place. In the nineties, when an old family friend lost his wife to cancer and wanted to retire to Florida, Billy's dream came true. His friend gave him a good price, happy to sell the house to someone he knew would take care of it.

They let Magic out and went straight to the back porch where Billy and his wife, Lindy, sat with some cold drinks and Biscuit and Bandit, their Georgia Redbone coonhounds, catching the breeze off the river.

KILLER IN THE HOLY CITY

Magic ignored the coonhounds and lay down at Billy's feet. "Smart dog knows who the boss is." Billy patted Magic on the head. Cal laughed as he remembered how Billy used to tease Danie about her "spoiled canine prince" when he heard Danie hired a groomer who came to the house with shampoo and conditioner from the canine equivalent of Lancôme and a behaviorist who tried unsuccessfully—at great expense—to stop him from barking at everybody who walked down their street. Cal hadn't mentioned that Magic's vitamins were formulated at a top-of-the-line compounding pharmacy in Manhattan, and his food was prescription-only from a store in Texas.

"How'd the TV interview go with Ricky Ramirez?" Cal opened a can of cold beer.

"Not bad. It was real short," Billy said with a sly smile.

"I thought Ramirez was a thorn in your side?" Cal said, forgetting for a moment his friend's strength as a strategic thinker.

"Not this time. I had a little chat with his boss. He saw the value of preventing this case from causing people to panic. I told Ramirez's audience that summer often brought an increase in crime and gave a few suggestions on how to avoid becoming a victim. I emphasized that women living alone should never let strangers in their homes without vetting them. Danie, thank you for a wonderful presentation. Mayor Campbell was really impressed."

Billy had offered to take everyone out to dinner, but Lindy overruled him and ordered pizzas so that they could watch the latest *Mission Impossible* DVD while they ate. When the pizza came, their teenagers, Dustin and Sean, ate on the porch with the dogs while the adults went into the family room.

"How's Chloe doing?" Lindy said as she handed out plates and utensils. "She's going to school in Florida, right?"

"Right," Danie said. "Rollins College in Winter Park."

"Whew!" Billy said. "That must have cost a pretty penny."

Cal nodded. "Serious understatement. My mother's helped a lot."

"She has," Danie said. "With tuition and board, but that place is a far cry from the college I went to. A couple weeks ago, Chloe called and said she wanted to go with her girlfriends to Italy for a couple weeks, and listen to this, she needed Louis Vuitton luggage. I don't have any Louis Vuitton luggage."

Billy laughed. "Okay, Daddy, did you get it for her?"

"Not if I want to stay married. I told her to ask Grandma."

It was Danie's turn to laugh. "Cal's mom told her she never had any Louis Vuitton luggage either. Grandma said she could borrow her big Samsonite suitcase."

"I might've been more sympathetic," Cal said, "if her grades were good, but they weren't."

"I wouldn't worry yet," Billy said. "I seem to remember the day when my roommate's father drove all the way to Athens to threaten that he'd pull him out of UGA if he didn't start putting his grades before the football team."

"At least I had a passion for a sport. All Chloe's interested in are parties and guys."

"That's not all bad for a freshman," Lindy said. "Maybe she'll find Mr. Right. That was always the thought I had when I was that age. C'mon, let's eat before the pizza gets cold."

Danie sat next to Cal on the couch with a piece of pepperoni pizza. She did her best to pay attention to the movie but soon started to fiddle with her tablet, searching through online newspaper archives. From the moment she had seen Rachel Ackerman's body, she had the feeling it was similar to a crime she had studied at the Bureau many years before.

It was a serial murder case that, despite its notoriety, had never been successfully resolved. She recalled that there were at least a dozen murders in the series, but the victims were different enough from each other to call into question whether the same killer was responsible for all of them. The first victims were all middle-aged or elderly. When she first saw Rachel Ackerman's corpse, she knew it reminded her of a case from the past. Now she knew which one it was.

Danie found a good summary of the case online. As she read about the scene for the first victim, an attractive fifty-six-year-old divorced woman, her uneasiness grew. The woman had been hit on the head in her kitchen and dragged on a rug to a hallway outside the bathroom—like Margaret Walsh. Her heart beat faster when she read that the woman's son almost fell over a chair that was intentionally placed in front of the door. When she read about the next four victims, she realized that she had to act quickly. She nudged Cal, who was engrossed in the movie and pointed to a page on her tablet.

"What, Danie?" He looked at the tablet without any understanding of why it was important. "Can't it wait until the movie's over?"

Danie shook her head. Cal sighed and took the tablet. She watched his eyes widen as he read about the first five victims.

"Billy," he said. "This is something you really need to see. Do you remember the Boston Strangler case from the sixties?"

"What?" Billy was still transfixed on *Mission Impossible*. "Boston Strangler? Yeah, sure. I remember it."

"Well, the Boston Strangler killed an elderly woman and posed her just like Ackerman. Not only that, he killed his first victim on June 14, 1962, exactly fifty years ago. That was the same day Walsh was murdered, wasn't it?"

"What?" Billy's voice rose as he turned off the movie and came over to the sofa. "Let me see what you're reading."

He took the tablet back to his chair and read the synopsis of the case. When he finished, he passed the tablet back to Cal, took a final gulp of Jack Daniels, and placed the glass on the table in front of him.

Afterward, he folded his hands on his lap, glanced over at Danie, and had only two words to say.

"Oh shit!"

Chapter 8

BILLY WENT IMMEDIATELY INTO ACTION. FIRST, he called Walter and conferenced in Mt. Pleasant's chief, Bert Allman. They quickly agreed that a joint task force was the best way to coordinate the investigation. Not only did they need their best detectives, but they also had to have some very special database expertise and a top-notch criminal profiler. Afterward, Billy and Bert contacted their mayors, delivered the news about the Boston Strangler link, and told them how they wanted to attack the problem.

Mayor LC Campbell told Billy he did not want the FBI involved. The last time Washington had sent one of their people to help the city in a criminal investigation, the agent created a political nightmare for the police and the mayor by leaking sensitive information to the press.

"What can we do to help you, Billy?" Cal asked after the call was over.

Billy frowned. "Danie, I don't know how booked up you are, but is there any chance we could get some of your time as the task force psychologist? I won't have any trouble getting the mayor to sign off on a contract for your work."

The excitement was apparent on Danie's face. "There's nothing in the next few weeks that I can't move around. This case would be great research for me."

"I don't need to get paid," Cal said. "I might have to take a day or two to handle one of my clients, but otherwise, you can count on me, Billy."

"Thanks so much, you guys," Billy said. "If I can't get your hotel expenses fully reimbursed, Lindy and I will gladly put you up."

"And Magic?" Danie said as she looked over at Lindy, who nodded in approval.

Billy cracked a smile. "And Magic, too."

"I'd rather stay at Billy's," Danie said. "It's more like home."

"We'd love to have you with us. It's no problem at all," Billy assured them.

"Danie, how'd they catch the Boston Strangler?" Lindy said. "He died in prison, didn't he?"

"Unfortunately, the Boston Strangler case was never completely solved. A convicted rapist named Albert DeSalvo confessed to the murders, but there was no trial, and yes, he died in prison after another inmate stabbed him."

"Hey," Billy said. "This has been a long day. Let's go to bed. DeSalvo will still be dead tomorrow."

Cal went to bed around eleven-thirty and dozed off within minutes. Danie was right behind him, and soon, the rhythmic sound of his breathing lulled her to sleep and into a dream. She was in a strange house with many floors. She had to find a man, and she was running out of time. She ran from room to room on each floor, but as she opened each door, she found the rooms were empty.

By the time she reached the last floor, she was filled with dread. Blood seeped out from under the door of a room at the far end of the hall. When she reached it, the door opened by itself. A man was lying facedown on the bed. Blood was dripping off the bed and running over the floor. "See if he's breathing," a harsh female voice commanded.

"I can't," she whispered. "I can't!"

She awoke with a jolt. It took a few minutes for her to stop shaking and return to reality. Cal was snoring softly. Danie lay there for a few minutes, fearful she would drift off and fall back into that nightmare.

She slipped out of the four-poster bed, put one of Cal's shirts over her nightgown, and went to the kitchen for a glass of wine. She walked onto the porch where Magic was overjoyed to see her. "Magic!" she whispered as he stood on hind legs and placed his paws on her thighs. She was so bonded to him. Just this little gesture of love relieved some of her anxiety.

One of the things she loved most about Billy's house was the magnificent view of the river. That night it seemed more beautiful than ever. Sporadic moonlight provided a respite from the dark clouds and revealed a gleaming river, which like the city it surrounded, seemed to be at peace—for now.

Permanent moorings held dozens of sailboats, fishing skiffs, and pleasure craft all along the shore to the north and south. In the distance, a small houseboat drifted downriver toward the Battery. On the opposite bank, the flickering lights of North Charleston were plainly visible, and beyond it, the powerful beacons from the Air Force base reflected off the clouds above.

She heard a sound behind her.

"Excuse me," Billy said softly. "Is this the Insomniacs Anonymous meeting?"

Magic growled. "Shush!" Danie said. "It's just Billy."

"I'm sorry," Billy said. "I didn't mean to startle you. Looks like you can't sleep either." He took a swig from his bottle of beer.

"It's been quite a day," she said, "and quite the ending of a very bad month."

He set down his beer and put his arm around her. "I'm sorry I couldn't be there for you and your brother."

"Thanks. I understand."

"I still don't know what all happened that day. Cal told me some of it, but he didn't have time to give me the whole story."

Danie smoothed back the hair that the breeze had blown into her eyes. "I was in the house when he died."

Billy winced. "I didn't know."

She sat on one of the chairs with a view of the river, and Billy sat opposite her. "Johnny had lost his job, and my mother begged me to help him. So, he came to stay with us. He needed to join an AA group, and I helped him find one, but he was still drinking and taking pills."

She took a sip of her wine and put the glass on the table next to her. "We're a family of cops, like your family, and my father is the most successful of us all. You don't get to be the chief of detectives in Cleveland just by knowing the right people. He made the decisions in our family and set the standards.

"My father made no secret of his desire that Johnny would be a police chief someday. He had a career path all planned out for him. Because I was female, he believed I had two careers to choose from—a nurse like my mother or a teacher. And I had to be the very best in whatever I chose. That way, if I was widowed, I would always have a respectable profession to fall back on."

Billy shook his head. "That's not how I was brought up, but Lindy's parents were just like yours."

"I know you never really had a chance to know him, but my brother was really smart. He pursued the things that interested him no matter how trivial or inconsequential they might be. He would've made a great college professor, except for the alcohol and drugs. There was a lot of tension between Johnny and my father. It was a relief not to be in the middle of it after I married Cal and moved to Georgia."

"So what happened the day you found him?"

Weariness flooded over Danie. "He was in a county rehab center when he called and said his roommate was awful, and he was going to check himself out. A few hours later, he showed up at our house completely drunk. He'd hitchhiked from the center and somehow gotten a bottle of vodka on the way.

"He told me he'd go back to rehab, but he wanted to take a shower and clean up first. I was on the phone with Cal, when I heard a shot upstairs. The moment I heard it, I knew what had happened. I just knew it. I got off the phone and ran upstairs. He was slumped over in the bathtub."

Danie tried not to dissolve into tears in front of Billy. "I called 911, but it was too late. He'd put the gun in his mouth and pulled the trigger." Her voice trembled. "There was nothing they could do."

"I'm sorry, Danie."

"I'm not gonna live long enough to get over it."

Billy reached over, put his hand over hers, and spoke softly. "You will, Danie. You have to."

Anger swelled up in her as she spoke, and the tears started to flow. Anger at her failure to save her brother from himself. She tried to control it, to keep it down deep. Like she did all her life. So only she knew where it hid.

"Don't torture yourself over it, Danie," Billy said. "Chances are he would have done it anyway, no matter what you did or said."

Billy was probably right, but it didn't lessen the pain. "I think a part of me died that day, too."

"You have a lot of people in your corner. Me, Lindy. And Cal is a rock." He bent over and wiped away her tears.

After Billy left, Danie placed the empty glass in the kitchen and slowly walked up the steps to the bedroom. She lay down next to Cal, comforted once again by his measured breathing, his familiar smell, and his very presence.

Chapter 9

Charleston Police Department parking lot
11:30 p.m. June 30, 2012

FOR THE PAST WEEK, HE HAD been on an emotional rollercoaster anticipating this day, his mood swinging between giddy overconfidence and a panicky fear of disaster. Now, he was confident he would remain in control.

Despite being up all night, adrenaline kept him going long after his work was done. The first fruits of success weren't something he was going to sleep through. He was so pissed the media had virtually ignored what he did in Mt. Pleasant, but they couldn't possibly ignore him any longer.

Today and tomorrow, news reports would scream about what he did to the old bitch, and he wanted to hear every bloody minute of it. He passed the time listening to the news and checking to see if there were any reporters or media trucks on Meeting Street.

When he passed police headquarters around noon, he saw that SUV again. The Range Rover with the Georgia license plate. It was parked in back of the building along with dozens of other cars. He entered the parking lot and cruised around as if he were looking for a space. He drove closer, glanced inside.

A dog was asleep on the back seat. The windows were down several inches, and the sunroof was half-open. He stopped his car for a moment alongside the Rover, and immediately, the dog was up against the window, snarling with bared teeth. He wished now that he had some hamburger with ground glass to feed him. Well, maybe next time.

This was the second time today he'd seen this car with the Chatham County, Georgia plate. What were a man, a woman, and a dog from Savannah doing with the Charleston police?

This morning while he was standing in the crowd outside the house, watching the police, he saw the man drive up in the Rover and park on the street. He walked quickly to the door where a cop briefly talked to him and let him inside. The blonde babe with him took the dog for a short walk, put it back in the car, and walked to the house a few minutes later. The same cop at the door smiled at her and let her inside, too.

From his perspective, she could definitely make a man smile. Tall, lean, with a very nice ass he wished he could get into bed. For a moment or two, he wondered how he might start up a conversation with her, but then he came to his senses. This hot blonde was not on his side. She was with the cops in some way or another, even though she didn't look like one.

The couple wore casual clothes, and they had a fucking dog with them. Now, with someone from Georgia at the crime scene and meeting with police, it had to be about the murders. He had to find out who they were and why they were here. If they were a threat, he would have to find a way to neutralize it.

They were not going to stop him. Not ever.

Chapter 10

Autopsy Room, Medical University of South Carolina
9:15 a.m. Sunday, July 1, 2012

RAPE, MANUAL STRANGULATION, AND A HALF-DOZEN other subjects were on Cal's mind as the Range Rover raced to Ackerman's autopsy. It was always better to see evidence first-hand rather than read a report that might be written several days or even weeks after the event. So much could be overlooked and was open to individual interpretation.

The Medical University of South Carolina had grown so large in recent years he almost got lost in the maze of new buildings. Even on a Sunday morning, he had trouble finding the right place to park for the autopsy.

He wished now that despite last night's excitement about a Boston Strangler copycat, he had listened to his voicemail. A little after nine p.m., Dr. Thacker left a message that the autopsy would begin at eight Sunday morning—a message he didn't get until after eight this morning. Since it was a courtesy to let him observe, he was embarrassed to be an hour and fifteen minutes late.

Dr. Charlotte Thacker was a tiny, suntanned brunette who looked to be in her mid-thirties. Cal was surprised they didn't have an older, more experienced pathologist for this autopsy, but Billy said she was one of their superstars.

He apologized profusely, but she understood that her voice message was delivered late on a Saturday night. Cal didn't have to explain what his key interests were in this autopsy. Thacker knew instinctively what questions Cal would have.

"The hyoid bone is definitely broken," Thacker said as she pointed to Ackerman's neck. "I may change my mind if we find something unexpected, but right now it appears she was manually strangled, and not by that pillowcase tied around her neck."

"That's how it looked to me at the scene, but I wanted to be certain," Cal said. "How bizarre."

She glanced up at him and nodded. "Very strange, indeed. Maybe it was overkill or some symbolic gesture, like the lacerations in and around the vagina. We took oral, anal, and vaginal swabs of course, but we haven't processed them yet. As I examined the genital area, I didn't see any seminal fluid, but we'll know for sure later."

The analysis of Ackerman's stomach contents would be critical. If the lasagna had been her dinner—which, according to her maid, she would have eaten around six o'clock—it would be helpful in determining the time of death. If she had died in the early-morning hours, the lasagna would no longer be in her stomach.

Every autopsy has a series of steps that are necessary—but mind-numbingly boring, like weighing the organs. During some of these procedures, Cal's mind wandered to what had happened to this poor woman in the last hours of her life. He had been thinking about the empty bottle of expensive wine, which was not there when the maid left Friday afternoon.

With that in mind, he wondered what her blood-alcohol level would show. He made a mental note to ask Joe Asher, the lead detective, several questions related to the wine bottle. He couldn't imagine a house like that not having a place to store bottles of wine. Joe should check to see if there were other bottles of Silver Oak or high-end vintage wines somewhere in the house. If there was no special wine collection in the house, had there been any progress on finding out who had bought that bottle? Did he check her credit cards or even the trash for the receipt? He hoped Joe and his partner had called the owners of local liquor stores to see if they ever carried the older vintages of the expensive Silver Oak.

He grappled with the possibilities in the hours leading up to Ackerman's murder. Suppose she had a visitor that evening and brought out her expensive wine and best crystal. Did she have a glass or two, or did the visitor drink the whole bottle? If she shared some with a friend, why was there only one glass in the dishwasher?

If she and the visitor finished off the bottle, then it was likely the visitor was the killer. Who else would wipe off the fingerprints? Another possibility was that she did have a visitor, but after the visitor had left, she placed the bottle on the kitchen counter. Later, the killer finished the wine and wiped off the fingerprints. In Cal's mind, this wine bottle was a key factor in understanding what went on before the murder.

The coroner's deputy estimated that Ackerman's time of death was probably in the early-morning hours. A normal visitor should have been gone long before that time. If the visitor was, in fact, the killer, why didn't he kill her earlier in the evening instead of waiting until she went to bed?

Cal had been leaning toward a theory that a friend of Mrs. Ackerman had stopped by. Ackerman served wine, and when her visitor left, she put the unfinished bottle on the counter. Perhaps she was a little tipsy and forgot to lock the door and set the alarm after the visitor left, which made it easy for him to get in.

The more he thought about that idea, the less likely it seemed. How could the killer have anticipated that she would have a visitor and forget to lock the door? Then again, maybe he came to the house with the intention of breaking in but found the door unlocked.

How the killer got into the house was the same question that plagued the Walsh case. No sign of burglary, but Ackerman's maid suggested another possibility. Only the front door, which opened directly onto the sidewalk, and the wrought-iron gate across the driveway entrance were normally locked during the day. The door to the ground-floor porch was usually left unlocked until after the maid left, but the maid didn't know what time Mrs. Ackerman locked the porch door.

It wasn't impossible to get over the wrought-iron fence that surrounded the property, so perhaps the killer climbed over the fence, got in through the unlocked porch door, and hid in the house until the maid, and possibly a visitor, had gone. That theory sat much better in his mind—well, at least for a minute or two. So many unanswered questions and possibilities made his head spin.

Cal looked at his watch. He had been there for over an hour and planned to leave in the next few minutes, but not before he had the opportunity to thank Dr. Thacker for letting him observe and apologize again for being late. Though she would receive all the police reports on the case, Cal took a few minutes to share with her some of the details that made the case so unusual. It was his way to make sure he gave her a complete picture.

"Don't worry about being a little late," she said. "Incidentally, I really appreciate your time. I don't often get the benefit of working with someone with your experience. As soon as we put together the results, I'll personally get them over to you."

MARILYN J. BARDSLEY AND MARK GADO

"Thanks, Doctor," Cal said. "It's been a pleasure."

A few minutes later, as he walked to his car, Cal regretted his parting remark. After all, the butchered body of Rachel Ackerman lay before them like a piece of slaughtered meat. How could it be "a pleasure"? But in the very next moment, Cal realized he was over-thinking this. After all, medical examiners look at dead people all day long.

It had to be a pleasure to have someone alive in the room for a change.

Chapter 11

"WE MAY HAVE OUR FIRST SUSPECT," Billy said with some enthusiasm as Detective Joe Asher walked in, joined by Danie. "Listen to this. Uniform picked up a man yesterday who threatened a female neighbor living in his apartment building. No assault or physical contact, but the woman was worried about the way he's been acting lately."

Billy looked at the patrol report. "The complaint came from a Mrs. Billings, a widow in her sixties, who lives in a rundown building off Hanover Street. She reported that a tenant had been acting weird ever since the story on Margaret Walsh's murder appeared in the newspapers. Billings noticed he never left the apartment during the day. He'd only go out after midnight and come back before dawn. She didn't think he had a job because he always dressed exactly the same: blue jeans and a gray sweatshirt. He wouldn't shave for weeks on end and 'stunk like a pail of garbage.' I gave all the info to Joe, and he's been busy digging up the background on this guy. It looks like he's supposed to be under supervised release up in New York somewhere."

Joe sipped his coffee and then brought Billy and Danie up to date. "Billings said that the day after the Walsh murder, she saw him put a woman's bloody stocking in the trash. He had scratches on his face that he tried to hide by pulling up the hood on his sweatshirt. When she read about the murder in the papers, she thought maybe there was a connection. So, she watched him closely, wrote down the times he left the apartment, and when he came home.

"His name is Lester Beach," Joe said.

"Yesterday, Billings called us again," Billy said, "and this time, I spoke with her. She told me that early yesterday morning, she saw Lester stumble into the lobby of her building, really drunk. He was carrying a knapsack and drinking from a wine bottle. Hanging out of his backpack was some women's underwear. Once he was in his apartment, she went into the lobby and picked up a bra he'd dropped. She held onto the bra until the police showed up and then gave it to them."

"Okay," Danie said, "so what did he do to get himself picked up?"

"Ah, I'm getting to that," Billy said. "While this guy was in the parking lot, another woman who lives in the building scolded him for being drunk. He told her he was going to strangle her and cut off her breasts. Scared the crap out of her, so she ran into the building and called the police. Patrol units took Beach into custody, and he eventually wound up in the loony bin over in Summerville. I'd like both of you to go over there and interview him. I'm not saying he's our man, but we should check him out anyway."

While they drove to Summerville, Joe and Danie caught up on their lives since they had last met several years earlier. After Joe had told her the story about how he met his wife, an emergency room nurse, when he brought in an assault victim to the medical center, he asked how Danie had met Cal.

The question brought a flood of wonderful memories. "Well, I was at a seminar in Atlanta where Cal was giving a presentation on the value of gunshot residue as evidence in murder trials. I was impressed with how smart he was." She didn't mention she thought he was one of the most attractive men she'd ever met and immediately planned how she could get to know him better.

"After his presentation, I told him I'd like to share his research with some of my friends at the Bureau, and he suggested we get together for drinks later." She canceled her flight back to Quantico that afternoon and ended up staying over the weekend. A smile spread across her face as she remembered what a wonderful weekend it was.

Joe noted the expression on her face. "And then?"

"Oh, we really hit it off, and one thing led to another. I got a position in Atlanta, and we eventually decided to get married."

"Nice story," he said. "With a happy ending."

She smiled. "Thanks. But what about today? How do you want to handle this?"

Joe suggested he do the initial interview with Lester, and Danie would participate if the situation called for it.

"Jump in any time, Doc," Joe said. "It's okay, believe me. Sometimes, these interviews go much better when it's a boy-girl team rather than two men asking a lot of questions."

"What about his background? I read what Billy gave me about his life, but what do we really know about him?"

"A lot," he said. Joe was an ardent researcher. He believed in accumulating as much information as possible about a suspect before he sat down for an interview. It was the only way to know if the suspect was telling the truth. Joe called every jurisdiction that had had contact with Lester over the years and learned he was born and raised in the Adirondacks in upstate New York. His mother died from syphilis when he was six. His father died a few months later when he fell off a mowing tractor, blind drunk, and the damn thing dragged him into a gulley. His grandmother, a religious zealot who was obsessed with Scripture, took the boy in. She forced him to memorize Bible passages every day—or she wouldn't feed him.

To make matters worse, she made Lester sleep on the dirt floor in the basement where there was no light or even a bed. According to a social worker, he would sit in an empty room for hours, staring at the wall, or wander from room to room with his head tilted to the ceiling, as if he were listening to voices.

"Sounds like schizophrenia to me, Joe."

"Yeah," Joe agreed. "He's been locked up many times and committed more than once for a mental evaluation. 'Peeping Tom' offenses, public lewdness, assaults on women. You name it; he's done it. And everyone I spoke to said he's clever and very violent."

A probation officer told Joe that Lester was under the delusion that God talked to him and helped him when he got into trouble. Thanks to his grandmother, he could recite scripture at will and was quick to use it to defend himself.

"What's the rule on commitment in South Carolina?"

"Under state law, we file a petition in probate court for involuntary commitment. If they approve, and they usually do, we have fifteen days to complete a mental evaluation."

Danie and Joe pulled into the parking lot of the state hospital in Summerville shortly before 11:45 a.m. The hospital was a drab, three-story brick building, typical of many government facilities. A few minutes after they signed in, a stern woman wearing thick-rimmed glasses showed up and introduced herself as Nurse Harris. She was about fifty, overweight, and wore a sparkling white uniform.

"Please come with me." She motioned for them to follow her down the nearest hallway. "You want to see Mr. Beach, is that right?"

"Yes, ma'am," Joe said. "Lester Beach."

When they reached the first door, the nurse slid her entry card, which hung by a chain from her neck, into a reader on the wall. The door swung open, and they walked through. A long, narrow hallway led to another door, which also required an entry card. Once it opened, they entered a wider junction, which had three passageways in different directions. A sign on the wall read WARD 7, EAST.

"That's us," the nurse said. "W7E."

As they came to the end of the passage, she pointed to an open archway. "Almost there. You'll see an interview room at the other end. Lester Beach is in there with an attendant waiting for you."

They stepped into the ward, which, like the previous one, had an identical series of doors but these had no windows, only large sliding metal bars with immense locks on both ends. The large fluorescent lights that hung from the ceiling on metal chains were dim and only offered a patch of light directly under each fixture. A big, metal table and chair sat at the end of the hallway. An old, black wall phone hung on a piece of plywood behind them, and next to it, a faded list of phone numbers had been hastily written on the wall. A loud pounding, which sounded like someone trying to break down a door, echoed through the ward. Nurse Harris led the way to the interview room.

"Here we are," she said as they entered. "Rules allow a thirty-minute visit. If you need assistance, press that red button on the wall." Before the nurse and the attendant left, she pointed to a large round disk near the doorframe. Under the button, someone had written the word EMERGENCY in big block letters. In the center of the windowless room, sitting at a folding aluminum table, was a young man slouched in his metal chair with his arms crossed on his chest. His eyes seemed vacant, and he did not blink.

"Lester Beach?" Joe said.

The man didn't move.

After what Joe had said about Lester, Danie expected someone much different. He was maybe six feet tall with a medium build. His dark brown hair looked like it hadn't ever met a comb, and he'd grown a couple days of dark stubble. Even though he was a bit unkempt, he was somewhat attractive in a boyish way. His legs were strapped together at the ankles and knees.

"Lester?" Joe said again.

The man's eyes flinched, and he seemed to come out of a daydream. There were two chairs where Danie and Joe sat next to each other facing him across the table.

"Who's asking?" Lester said.

He wore a white T-shirt with no sleeves. On his right bicep was a tattoo of a woman's face; a long dagger went through the top of the head. A tattoo showing a chain made of thorns wrapped around the left bicep, and the fading ink of a black cross on his chest peeked out from the top edge of his shirt. One of his fingers was bleeding from where he had chewed his nails down to almost nothing. All his fingers were red and swollen.

"I'm Detective Asher, and this is Dr. Callahan. We'd like to talk—"

"I'm not sick. Why the fucking doctor?" Suddenly, his eyes widened, his voice wavered, and he sat up straight in the chair.

"—to you about something that happened last week near your building."

Relief swept visibly across Lester's face. "Oh? That bitch on the third floor? I told her to stop bothering me."

"Well, I don't know about that, but you scared her when you threatened her," Joe said.

"I don't make empty threats."

"Lester," Danie said, "we'd like to ask you about—"

"The Bible warns us: 'Send one of your number to get your brother,'" he shouted. "'The rest of you will be kept in prison, so that your words may be tested to see if you are telling the truth. If you are not, then as surely as Pharaoh lives, you are spies!'"

Danie continued, ignoring his loud outburst, "—last week outside your apartment."

"Let me tell you something, Doc." He looked directly at Danie. "I don't bother nobody." His body stiffened.

Danie did what she could to soothe him with a sympathetic tone and a pleasant smile. "I understand, Lester, but we'd like you to help us if you can. We just want to get some information."

"Why?" His tone shifted slightly.

"Well," Joe said, "we're not out to hurt anybody. We're just trying to get to the truth. What's wrong with that?"

"The truth?" Lester said. "That's all I ask for, too. I just want the truth of why I'm here. What have I done, Lord?" He raised his arms up and looked at the ceiling. "In fact, the law requires that nearly everything be cleansed with blood, and without the shedding of blood there is no forgiveness!"

"Lester," Joe said. "Let me ask you a question."

"What's stopping you?"

"A few weeks ago, you came home very late at night. I think it was the night of June fourteenth. Do you remember that?"

"I come home late every night."

"The night of June fourteenth. A Thursday."

He placed his hands over his eyes. "How the fuck am I supposed to know where I was three weeks ago? Are you kidding me?"

"On this particular night, you might have thrown some clothes into the garbage bin in the alley behind your building."

"Yeah?" Lester tilted his head as if he was trying to remember the event.

"You know, in the trash. A woman's clothes?"

He clasped his hands together and folded them on top of his head. "Let me think." He remained in that position for what seemed like an eternity without making a sound. Then his lips parted into a wide smile that bared his teeth. It was an unsettling look.

"Oh, yeah," he said as if he had a revelation. "I know what you mean. You got those clothes, right?" He shook his head back and forth slowly. "Cops! They're everywhere, man."

"Yes, the clothes," Joe said. "Where did you get them? Can you tell us?"

"You promise you won't tell?"

"Yeah," Joe said. "We promise, Lester."

Lester was enjoying this game. He glanced to his left and right as if to see if anyone was listening. "I stole 'em," he whispered.

"Where from?" Joe said, hoping for a real answer.

"I thought you were a detective. Figure it out."

For a moment, it appeared as though the volatile young man was becoming bored with his games. He broke into loud, condescending laughter for a few seconds and as suddenly it began, the laughter stopped.

"Can you remember exactly where you got them?" Danie said. "It's important to us."

He narrowed his eyes at Danie. "You ever fuck any of your patients, Doc?" Lester licked his top lip and let his smile grow wider.

Having a reservoir of experience with sex offenders, Danie was no stranger to attempts at intimidation. She found the best way to deal with it was to proceed as if it was normal conversation.

"Oh, come on, Lester, you know I'm not allowed to do that," she said. "What about the clothes? I'll bet it's a great story. Where did you get them?"

He laughed. "What's it to you? What do I get out of it?"

"If you don't want to tell us, that's fine," Joe said. "But we wanna ask you about another night when you came home late."

"Not for anything, but why are you crucifying me?" He lifted his arms up far over his head with his palms facing out. "You understand, O Lord; remember me and care for me," he shouted. "Avenge me on my persecutors. You are long-suffering—do not take me away; think of how I suffer reproach for your sake."

Joe ignored the outburst. "Yesterday morning, you came home drunk and fell on the floor in the lobby. Do you remember that?"

"How can I remember it if I was drunk?"

"Witnesses say you left a brassiere in the hall, and they saw scratches on your face," Joe said.

"Witnesses, Detective? Don't tell me you're relying on that fucking slut on the second floor? That Mrs. Billings? Is that who we're talking about?"

"Lester, do you know Rachel Ackerman?"

"Never heard of her," he said. "Is she a slut, too?"

"No, she was murdered, Lester," Danie said.

"Murdered?" Beach shouted. "Is this about those women that were killed? The one off Pitt Street in Mt. Pleasant? Well, I'm in the clear on that one. I don't even know where Pitt fucking Street is!"

Lester knew Pitt Street was near the scene of a murder, which meant he knew of the Walsh killing.

"We're just asking questions, that's all," Joe said.

"Yeah, sure. That's how it starts. Then before you know it, I'm layin' on a cot in the state pen with a fucking needle in my arm! I never killed nobody!"

"We're not saying you did, Lester," Joe said.

"'Be strong and courageous,'" he said. "'Do not be afraid or terrified because of them, for the Lord your God goes with you; he will never leave you nor forsake you.'"

"Deuteronomy thirty-one," Danie said. "I'm familiar with that quote."

He looked at her with surprise. "I don't even know those women."

"You don't have to know somebody in order to kill them," Danie said.

"I do," Lester said. "But you guys still have the bra you found on the floor, right? Why don't you try it on the dead woman and see if it fits? Remember OJ? If it doesn't fit, you must acquit."

"That's not funny, Lester," Danie said.

"I'm not a funny guy."

"What about the clothes in—"

"The clothes! The clothes! So fucking what? I like to steal women's clothes. You wanna lock me up for that? Go ahead. Can you see the headlines? Man gets ten to fifteen for stealing a bra. Maybe they'll give you a promotion for that, Detective."

"No one reported the theft, Lester."

"Not every crime is reported. I thought you knew that."

"We don't have a lot of time, Lester," Danie said.

"I stole those clothes from some woman who lives on River Street. She was walking back from a laundry, I think. She got in a couple of shots at me, too. Scratched my face up, the bitch. Go ask her. She'll tell you."

"Do you know her name?"

"Do you think I stop to ask someone their fucking name when I'm robbing them? She should be easy to find, though."

"Why's that?" Joe said.

"The bitch only got one arm."

Joe glanced over at Danie. It was time to go. It didn't seem they were going to get anything more from Beach. The thirty minutes were almost up.

"Lester," Joe said, "we gotta go now. But we may come back to ask you a few more questions. Is that okay with you?"

"As long as you bring the hot doctor with you."

"I'll try," Joe said.

"And Doc, wear something that's low-cut in the front. You look like you have a nice rack."

"We'll let you know if we want to talk to you again, Lester."

He placed his palms on the table and spoke in a whisper.

"Call me Les," he said. "Doc, let me ask you a question."

"Go ahead," Danie said.

"You seem like an honest person," he said. "Is it an act?"

"I like to think I'm honest," Danie said. "We want you to be as well, Lester."

"You may be asking too much."

They left Lester sitting at the table as an attendant came through the opposite door and asked him to stand. As they began the walk down the corridor, she saw the attendants place leather restraints around his arms.

"Come back soon, Doc!" he yelled from the room. "Don't be a stranger!"

Danie and Joe got into the car and drove out of the parking lot. She immediately rolled down the window for some fresh air.

"What a shithead." Joe gently shook his head.

"Yeah. Really." Danie was slightly ashamed to admit she felt fear during the interview, especially since Joe had seemed to take it all quite calmly. It was the cop in him, she thought; but Lester scared her.

What kind of person would kill women in the way Rachel Ackerman and Margaret Walsh had been murdered? She tried to imagine the killer inside their homes as he hid in the dark, waiting for his moment, waiting for the right time to strike. The killer knew what he wanted. He had to be a violent and angry man; there was no doubt about that—a person filled with hatred and contempt for women, someone who didn't mind preying on the weak and defenseless. She thought about all those things. Then Danie tried to imagine Lester being that man.

She didn't have to try very hard.

Chapter 12

Charleston Police Department
12:15 p.m.

"You remember that old Irish toast, 'May your soul already be in heaven an hour before the devil knows you're dead?'" Billy said to Bert Allman. "Just pray that we're completely ready when the world learns about the Boston Strangler connection."

"So far, so good," Bert said with some optimism. "When I came in, there were only two media vans outside on the street, and a couple of bored-looking reporters in the lobby waiting for the desk sergeant's briefing. The rest are probably at the coffee shop."

Billy had spent his morning organizing a task force operation. He had Walter and Bert select the team members and marshal the administrative and technical resources. Billy had contacted Clarence Hightower, an old friend and a King Street bar owner, who owned numerous commercial real estate properties in the city and was always eager to help the police department.

Billy understood it was not a good idea to have a command center at headquarters where too many civilian employees refused to understand the need for confidentiality. Hightower offered him a few options, and Billy chose a vacant, two-story office building on

East Bay Street near Wentworth that was outside the busy down-town area. It had privacy, easy access to the street, and its own parking garage.

Investigators and technicians spent the entire morning bringing in equipment and setting up the networks. When Cal, Danie, and Joe returned, Billy told them about the plan and said the command center should be set up by the end of the day.

"Danie," Billy said, "I was thinking that maybe you and Joe could interview Rachel Ackerman's pain-in-the-ass son, Greg Ackerman, and his son today. Afterward, let's all meet at the command center around 1800 hours."

Cal was glad that there was time for lunch and a few moments to relax. The task force meeting was hours away. As Cal and Danie walked over to the hotel near the PD, Danie seemed weary.

"You all right?"

"Sure," Danie said. "Just a bit hectic, I guess." She didn't want to worry him about why she didn't get much sleep last night.

"So, tell me about Lester. What kind of guy is he?"

Danie went through the morning's tense meeting with Lester Beach at Summerville. "He scares me," Danie said with an involuntary shudder.

"You've seen worse."

"I don't know about that."

"Really? Is he capable of pulling off something this complex?"

"Lester is capable of anything. He's weird, and his behavior is psychotic."

Cal was beginning to believe Lester might be a viable suspect. Danie wasn't sure because there was so little to tie Lester to either killing.

When the waitress brought the food to the table, Danie's appetite was gone. She took a few bites, leaving the cheeseburger to sit on the plate like a rock while she pushed the fries around with a fork. At the end of their lunch, Cal boxed up Danie's uneaten burger for Magic and went back to the command center.

Later, on the way over to Greg Ackerman's home, Danie and Joe theorized why the Ackerman murder scene had been devoid of fingerprints. Danie said it was part of the killer's MO. She believed the absence of DNA meant the murderer was sophisticated about police procedure.

"He's smart," Joe said. "No doubt about it."

"And in control," Danie said. "Notice that he's trying to stage a scene to copy past sex-motivated murders, and yet, no bodily fluids and no DNA evidence. He exercises self-discipline in a way the original Boston Strangler didn't. One of the big unknowns in my mind is how he chooses his victims. Is it random? Or is there a purpose?"

"How did the Boston Strangler choose his victims?" Joe said.

"Don't really know. He may have stalked his victims, or he may have selected whoever let him into her apartment." She paused. "By the way, Joe, why did Billy call Greg Ackerman a pain in the ass?"

He laughed for a moment. "'Cause he is. Greg is one of those people who think the cops are always wrong, and he's always right. He's got something to say about everything if you know what I mean."

Greg Ackerman's house was rather modest, and nothing like his mother's mansion. As they exited the car, a paunchy middle-aged man in jeans and a sweaty T-shirt emerged from the front door.

"What is it this time, Detective? It's Sunday, ya know," he said.

"Nice to see you again, Mr. Ackerman," Joe said. "This is my colleague, Dr. Danielle Callahan. We only have a few questions, if you don't mind."

They followed Greg into his family room, which was a drinking man's room. Antique mugs and other vessels made of pewter, tin, silver, and copper covered a thick, wooden mantel over the fireplace. More of the collection sat on several shelves on three of the four walls. A handsome wooden bar in the style of an English pub took up the length of one wall. Joe sat on a barrel stool while Greg went to the bar to retrieve a bottle.

"Help yourself." He poured some whiskey into a glass, lit a cigarette, and took a long drag.

"Greg," Joe said, "I'd like to ask a few questions about your mother's social life. Do you know if she was seeing anyone?"

The question caught him by surprise. "My mother?"

Joe nodded. "We have to ask."

"Not with her personality. What man…" He paused. "I would have known. At least, I think I would have known. My mother wasn't always forthcoming with me."

"On the night she died, it seems your mother might have been drinking an expensive wine called Silver Oak. Are you familiar with that?"

"Do I look like a wine guy? She drank wine once in a while. She heard it was good for her health."

"It's a very expensive bottle," Danie said. "We were thinking that maybe a visitor brought it over that night or that she brought it out of her cellar for someone special."

"I really don't know." Greg seemed annoyed by the questions.

"When was the last time you spoke with your mother?" Joe said.

"The day before it happened. On the phone around noon." He took a quick swallow of whiskey. "I already told you that. Don't you guys take notes?"

"Was it a long conversation?"

"I don't remember. Look, we had our differences. The divorce was very hard on all of us, and it divided the family into separate camps. Mother never got over it. She kept to herself, nursing her anger and wanted to be alone in that mausoleum and watch the television all day. Just herself, that damn house, and the fucking TV."

They spoke for almost half an hour, searching for a lead into what happened on the night of June thirtieth, but Greg could not come up with anything that was helpful. He said his mother was very security conscious because she lived in such a big tourist area, and he didn't believe for a minute that his mother would ever willfully let a stranger into the house, especially at night.

"For God's sake, you should be looking at some of the people who walk around that neighborhood, especially late at night. One of 'em probably broke in, and when he saw an old woman, he figured he had an easy mark. That's what I think. I mean, how many detectives do you have working?"

Joe interrupted. "Did she keep cash in the house?"

Greg said that he had no idea, although she had a safe in her bedroom closet that might have had some cash.

"Hey, Dad." A tall, young man with a muscular build and short, dark hair came in from the outside patio, can of cola in hand. Greg introduced him as his twenty-two-year-old son, Leland.

"Please call me Lee." He sat in a chair next to Greg. "Is there anything I can do? I want to help."

"Well," Danie said. "Would you know if your grandmother was involved with anyone?"

"That I don't know."

"She kept to herself, we understand."

Lee glanced at his father. "Yes, she did. She only wanted a few people in the family around her. I think it was because Grandma never got over the humiliation of Grandpa going off with a young woman." He paused for a moment. "Grandma could be pretty tough on people, but she wasn't that way to me."

"Do you know if she routinely left any doors open in the house?"

"I think she usually left the door to the first-floor veranda open during the day. In the evening, it was different. She'd lock the door to the porch when it got dark. She was—"

Greg pointed to his son. "He was her favorite."

"—kind of cautious that way. I can't believe she would leave a window or a door open at night. Do you have any ideas?"

"We're working on it," Joe said. "Believe me."

Lee took a deep breath. "I can't believe anyone would want to do something so horrible to her. She never hurt anybody. I just can't believe…" His voice trailed off.

Danie was sympathetic. "Well, sometimes this kind of thing may be a burglary that went wrong or something similar. Your father said she drank wine occasionally. Was it only when she had company?"

"Yes, she did drink wine, but not often as far as I know. There are a lot of bottles in that wine vault my grandfather bought years ago."

"Was she worried about anything lately or having trouble with anyone?"

"Not that I know of. She wasn't an easy person to work for, but the guys who did the yard and her maid were used to it. She may have yelled at them, but she paid them well."

"Did she mention any friend who might have visited her recently?" Joe said.

"I don't really know her friends. Mostly family came to the house."

"When's the last time you spoke with her?"

"Well, let's see. I hadn't spoken to Grandma since the week before it happened. That would have been on June twenty-third."

"In person?"

"Yes. I went to visit during the afternoon. Had a sandwich there. Stayed for a while and left. I just can't get over it. God! So awful."

"June twenty-third?" Danie said.

"Yes. It was the last time I ever spoke to her. I'm positive."

"Why?"

"It was my birthday. She called and asked me to stop by so she could give me a present." He pointed to an expensive-looking sports watch on his wrist. "I'll always treasure it."

"Oh, yeah," Greg said. "I remember that day. He showed me the watch. I forgot all about it."

"I miss her," Lee said. "I hope you get the sick bastard who did this to her!" Tears welled up in his eyes as he reached for a tissue on the desk. He seemed embarrassed and tried to hide it.

"I'm sure we will." Joe got off the stool, indicating to Danie it was time to end the interview.

"Try harder!" Greg frowned and took a swallow of whiskey.

Joe ignored the remark. "I want to tell you how sorry we are about your loss. And thanks for talking with us."

"I wish I could do something to help you." Lee walked with them to the door. "She was the one person in the family that I really felt close to, and now she's gone. I wish I'd spent more time with her. Maybe I could've prevented it from happening."

Lee's comment struck a chord with Danie. Lee probably felt the same kind of guilt about not doing enough to protect his grandmother that she felt about her brother's suicide.

Once they were outside, Danie said. "I don't think we got anything particularly valuable from either of them, do you?"

"Well, it wasn't a complete waste of time. We know when the son and grandson last spoke to the victim." He got into the car. "It was something that had to be done, anyway. I'll write the report later, and we can chalk up another completed interview."

Danie and Joe got to the new task force command center just as Walter was updating everyone on the investigation. They settled into their seats while the chatter toned down and Johnson's booming voice took over.

"One of the most important details of the case we have learned…"

The rear door swung open with a bang. A uniformed officer entered the room. He scanned the audience until his eyes settled on Billy.

"Chief?" he said.

He approached Billy and whispered something into his ear.

"Okay, thanks," he said to the officer, who practically ran out the door. Billy pushed his chair back and stood up. His voice demanded attention.

"Dispatch over at headquarters just got a call. Husband came home, found his wife murdered on his yacht at the City Marina."

Chapter 13

Charleston City Marina
5 p.m. Sunday, July 1, 2012

Billy, with Cal and Danie as passengers, made a ferocious turn into the marina parking lot and came to an abrupt stop at the end of a wooden pier. Several patrol units had already arrived and set up yellow crime scene tape. A cop walked toward the car.

"Officer Gleason, what do we have?"

"Dead woman," the young cop said, "and it ain't pretty. She's lying on the bed naked, clothes ripped off. Something tied around her neck. Looks like she's been DOA for a few days, Chief."

"Have we notified the coroner?"

"Yes, sir. My partner called it in. They're on the way."

"Okay," Billy said. "You know the drill. Find out who else is on those boats. Let's start the neighborhood interviews. Detectives are responding, too."

An unmarked police unit barreled into the parking lot and screeched to a halt. Three plainclothes officers, including Joe Asher and his partner, RK, jumped out and sprinted down the dock. Police radios crackled with the sound of impatient voices bantering details back and forth. Within seconds, an ambulance pulled into the lot and headed to the famous fifteen-hundred-foot long Megadock.

Cal glanced over at Danie, who had a strange look on her face. "The third body?"

"It could be like Helen Blake," Danie said.

"Helen Blake?" Cal said.

"The Strangler's third victim." Danie took a deep breath. Her heart was racing. "Killed fifty years ago on June thirtieth, but found two days later."

The Charleston City Marina was an opulent country club for boats. The more Danie saw of the obvious wealth of its inhabitants, the more she dreaded the possibility that this was the scene of another murder by the Boston copycat. She raced down the pier with Billy to the dock where many huge, luxurious yachts were moored. With their gleaming hulls, expansive decks, and sparkling chrome rails, they were the very best of Charleston's elite boating community.

Out of breath and not knowing what to expect, Danie arrived alongside a sleek modern yacht in the midst of the marina's largest boats. It was well over a hundred feet of glistening white fiberglass with an expanse of windows that stretched like an elongated teardrop around the main deck cabin. Inscribed above the striking contemporary window, in bold, black letters, was *Victoria's Delight*.

As Cal walked the length of the yacht, he noticed all the outside lighting fixtures were on. They had probably had been on since the murder. He followed Billy and Danie up a stairwell to a spacious area outside the main salon. The dark, wooden floor sparkled with a varnish that looked like it had been applied yesterday. He saw a large dining table with eight armchairs, all draped with beige canvas covers.

Across the deck was a good-sized bar with four barstools, all covered. Cal imagined that if he owned this boat, he'd plant himself on one of those barstools every night and watch the boats on the

Ashley River until his eyes crossed. Why on earth own a yacht like this if you weren't going to sit outside in June?

Billy led them through the sliding glass door into a luxurious salon. Just inside was another full bar, where Cal imagined the owner might sip his martinis while lounging on the cream-colored leather sofa. Opposite it was a long coffee table with an open fashion magazine on top and a single wine glass, partially filled. He looked around the elegant room, his gaze drawn to the writing desk. Its single drawer was on the floor, and several pieces of stationery, two pens, and a few paperclips lay beside it.

"You know, Billy," Danie pointed to the drawer, "I could understand an intruder looking at the owner's personal papers, but blank sheets of paper, pens, and paper clips?" The drawers in Rachel Ackerman's bedroom were still fresh in her mind.

At the far end of the room on a mahogany-paneled wall, Cal recognized a magnificent John Stobart oil painting of nineteenth-century Charleston. The accent lights over the painting were on, as were the lamps next to the sofa. The murder had happened at night before the victim would have turned them off.

As they walked forward, he saw a formal dining room with a long table inlaid with exotic woods and upholstered armchairs and a kitchen beyond. Billy stopped to talk to the officer who guarded the hall stairway down to the next deck. Well before they reached the stairs, Cal's nose told him the victim was down below.

"Chief, she's in the master suite immediately to the left. Her name was Victoria. Here's something for you," the officer said, offering them an open jar of Vicks VapoRub.

"I never get used to the smell," Billy said, putting some of the Vicks under his nose.

"Me either," Danie said, dipping her finger into the jar.

He entered the master suite, immediately drawn to the spectacle of the darkened, bloating mass of flesh. The dead woman lay face down. She was completely nude, and her legs were spread apart. Much of the shimmering gold-silk duvet cover was stained with the fluids of decomposition.

Once Billy had taken in all he needed to of the scene, he went up to the main deck and spoke to the officer at the top of the stairs. "I'm gonna talk to the victim's husband."

"He's on the top deck, making phone calls to his wife's family in England."

"Can I come with you?" Danie said, wiping the Vicks ointment from under her nose with a tissue. "I'd like to hear what he has to say."

"Sure." Billy took the tissue Danie offered him. "Cal, you staying down there?"

"I'll just be a few minutes." Cal put on the latex gloves he always carried in the pocket of his sport coat. "I may come back again before they move the body if that's okay. I don't want to get in the way of the crime scene work."

"Do what you need to do," Billy said.

Under Victoria's reddish-blonde hair, he could see a black, lacy fabric with what looked like a stocking tied under it. He gently lifted up her hair to get a better look. Pantyhose had been wound around her neck and tied tightly in back. Over the hosiery was a black brassiere tied under her chin. While the strangulation details were slightly different from the other two victims, Cal no longer had any doubts the same killer was responsible for all three murders.

During his years as a medical examiner, he had trained himself to study the entire death scene and not just the victim. Now, with three murders, that in his mind were clearly linked, he sought to put the circumstances of each one in context. Danie was right after all.

Victoria had put up a fight. Several of her fingernails were broken. The accent pillows from the bed were scattered about the room, and the duvet cover was halfway off the mattress. Her turquoise silk dress had been torn apart and lay on the bed and floor in at least three pieces. He didn't see burglary as a motive as he noticed the jewelry she had been wearing. A gold necklace was also on the floor, and only one of her long, gold earrings was still on her earlobe. The silk dress and the gold jewelry meant to him that either she had been out earlier in the evening or she was expecting company. All the lights in lower deck hall, master suite, and the bathroom were on.

Until he had information to the contrary, Cal favored the theory that Victoria was dressed up because she had been expecting a male visitor rather than the possibility she had returned from an evening event and been attacked once she was back on her yacht. Victoria, presumably, had turned on every exterior light and many of the interior lamps.

The yacht must have been quite a sight at night, all lit up—one that would impress a visitor but wouldn't encourage a random criminal attack. Then, in the salon, there was the open fashion magazine and the wine glass on the coffee table. Since the husband had found her in an advanced state of decomposition, he must have been away for a few days at least.

With her husband away, she had invited a man to her yacht, reading her magazine with a glass of wine while she waited for him. Perhaps then, wanting to show him the rest of the yacht or have sex with him in her bedroom, she went downstairs voluntarily with her killer. There were no signs of a struggle except in the master suite.

Rachel Ackerman, on the other hand, had been in her bed and eaten some ice cream before she was killed. Those details fit with the coroner's estimated time of death as late night or early morning hours. If this woman and Ackerman were murdered on the same day, it seemed to him that Victoria was the first of the two to die.

From what Cal knew about the first victim, Margaret Walsh, she had also expected a visitor and unlocked her front door to let him in. After he had killed Walsh, he waited until it was dark and left the scene at a time when he was less likely to be seen.

It would make sense if he did the same thing after killing Victoria. He probably didn't expect that she would have turned on every exterior light on the boat, which would have put him at risk for being seen, so perhaps he waited awhile until the docks were quiet before he made his exit. If Victoria's murder happened the way Cal theorized it did, it would explain why Ackerman was in bed at the time of her death. However, the way the killer entered her house was still a mystery.

Cal tried to analyze the three crime scenes together. On each side of Victoria's built-in king-size bed in the center of the room was a door. One was slightly ajar and appeared to be a closet. The other opened to a large, brightly lit bathroom, where he found every drawer and cabinet had been emptied onto the floor.

In Walsh's house, the killer had disturbed only a few items. Here on the yacht, the contents of a desk drawer in the salon had been carefully removed, but only the bathroom drawers had been dumped on the floor, whereas Ackerman's bedroom looked like the handiwork of a maniac. There was a pattern in the three murders: the disarray had been progressively more extreme.

Cal wanted to examine the room a bit longer, but he heard Master Police Officer Delores Goodall giving instructions upstairs in her distinctive New England accent to her crime scene techs. It was time for him to get out of the way. He briefly looked at the other staterooms on the lower deck, but there were no lights on and no sign they had been disturbed.

When Billy and Danie climbed up to the sun deck, the techs had just finished up. Joe and RK were already getting information from the victim's husband. Billy motioned for Joe to come over to talk.

"How's he holding up?" Billy said.

"Considering what happened, he's taking it very well."

"Do you think he's involved?"

"At this point, I don't think so, Chief," Joe said. "He's been very cooperative. He gave us a file right out of his briefcase with his itinerary, hotel bills, boarding passes, all kinds of receipts. We'll check it out, but all the documentation had him leaving for Malaysia June sixth and returning today from India via London."

Billy was willing to go along with Joe's theory about the husband's innocence for the time being. "I'd like to talk to the poor guy. What's his name?"

"Harry Howells," Joe said. "His wife was Victoria Trowbridge-Howells. British citizen."

Danie followed Billy and Joe through the sun deck over to the sofas where Harry Howells and RK were sitting. She guessed Harry to be at least sixty years old and a good fifty pounds overweight. His thinning hair and heavy eyebrows had been dyed a shade too dark, creating an unnatural contrast between his jowly white skin and dark brown hair. The effect was a bit jarring, but she didn't attach much importance to it. Despite his unbecoming hair color, Harry was an attractive man for his age.

Billy expressed his condolences to Harry and promised he would do everything in his power to bring Victoria's killer to justice.

He introduced Danie as a former FBI profiler assisting Charleston PD and afterward, excused himself on behalf of the work he had ahead of him. When they sat down, RK started to bring her up to speed on what they had learned.

"Mr. Howells…"

"I told you to call me Harry. Every time I hear 'Mister Howells,' I think of my father—and them ain't such good thoughts."

RK cleared his throat and continued. "Harry tried to call his wife's cell phone several times over the past few days but got no answer. He flew in from a business trip in Asia and took a limo from the airport directly here. After he had found his wife in their bedroom, he called 911 immediately."

Harry looked disgusted. "I didn't think nothing of her not answering my calls, 'cause it happened before. Lots of times. Ditzy broad always forgetting to charge the goddamn thing or not taking it with her."

They paused to absorb Harry's remark.

"Harry," Joe said, "before the chief came, we asked about any potential enemies you or your wife may have, anyone who might want to harm her."

"Victoria didn't have no enemies. Unless one of those young punks she fucks—" Harry stopped for a moment, looked over at Danie, patted her knee, and said, "Sorry, honey," and then turned back to the detectives. "She don't really know nobody but these studs. You ever find her phone, check 'em out."

RK looked up from his note taking. "Do you have any of their names?"

"Nah. Randy McDevitt, 'cross the dock on the Catalina 445, might. He probably seen a few of them, maybe even talked to them."

"Harry," Joe said, "how did you find out about her infidelities?"

He paused a few moments, a look of resignation on his face. "I started paying attention to my credit card bill earlier this year when we was in Naples, Florida. Most of her charges were, ya know, for clothes and her hair, but when I was away on business, she'd run up some pretty hefty bills in the bar at the Ritz. Victoria hardly ate nothing. That's how she stayed so thin. She drank—couple glasses of wine, even three maybe—but no way she drank that much—even at them prices at the Ritz—to get bills that high. She was buying drinks for someone else. No big deal by itself, but when she goes and takes rooms for the night instead of going back to the marina, I knew something was up. Then when we was back here in June, and I was away, she did the same damn thing. Big bills at the bar and then for a room."

"Did you ever talk to her about it?" Joe said.

"Nah! How'd ya talk about something like that? She'd just lie to me. Here I am knocking myself out every goddamned day making money so she can live like a queen. And that's what I get for it. I decided after that to take her with me on trips."

"Harry," Danie said, "could you tell me something about your business?"

"Sure, doll. What's your name again?"

"Danielle Callahan."

"I bet you're wondering how some high school dropout from Erie, Pennsylvania made enough money to live like this."

Harry had read her mind. "No, sir. I mean, Harry. International business travel just sounds so glamorous."

"Sure, honey. Sounds dandy to someone who don't got to do it. I'll tell you what I do, Danielle. Every time you go into stores like Neiman and Saks, just about anything you buy now is made in shitholes like Bangladesh that don't pay nothing to the slobs working fifteen hours a day, seven days a week. The stores do the contracts, but I'm the guy who goes there to make sure things get made right for the store. You wouldn't believe the kind of shit that goes on in some of these places. They'll rob you blind."

"Did you have to go away a lot?" Danie said.

"Usually for a month at a time. Come home for several weeks, sometimes more," Harry said. "This was our home. We used to have a condo in Naples, but I sold it a couple years ago."

"When was the last time you spoke to her?" RK said.

Harry had to think about that. He pulled out a phone and studied it. "She called me on June twenty-eighth to find out if I was still coming home today. I was at the airport in Dhaka. That's Bangladesh. After that, all I got was her voicemail." His voice wavered, his eyes focused on the floor. "Now I know why."

"Harry," Joe said, "when you got on the boat this afternoon, how did you find out what happened?"

"The boat was unlocked," Harry said. "So I knew she was home, and there was lights on in the salon and on the deck. Victoria was pretty good about locking the boat when she went out. I brought my two suitcases in and went into the kitchen to get a cold beer. I called out for her, but she didn't answer. I figured she was taking a nap or maybe a shower, so I sat down and started on the beer. But right away, I smelled something really bad. I waited a bit, though. Maybe I was afraid of what I'd find, I don't know. I decided to go downstairs where the smell was even worse. I knew something was wrong. That's when I saw her on the bed…"

Harry abruptly got up. "Hey, I gotta take a piss."

During the next fifteen minutes, they could hear repeated retching coming from the bathroom. When Harry returned, his face was all red, and his eyes were noticeably puffy.

"Harry, we know how tough today has been," RK said. "But we need to have you come over to the station and make a statement. Also, if you can give us the numbers of her cell phone and credit cards, we'll try to reconstruct what she was doing and who she was talking to while you were gone."

He nodded. "Can you give me a few minutes alone?"

"Okay, Harry," RK said. "I'll stay over here by the stairs in case you need me."

Danie watched him closely. Harry looked beaten. From what she could see, his world had collapsed. His mean words were just bluster, a tough guy trying unsuccessfully to cover his wounds. If he had killed his wife, then he was a truly talented actor, but Danie didn't buy it. This was a guy who was grieving.

After the interview with Harry, Danie caught up with Cal who was explaining his theory to Billy about Victoria inviting a man aboard the yacht. A man who could have been the killer. "I think Cal's right," she said.

"Billy," Danie said, "Our copycat has struck again." She went on to describe the similarities to the other two murders. "It looks to me like Victoria died before Rachel Ackerman, perhaps by just a few hours. I'll see if there's any evidence to back that up, but just the fact that she was found a day or so after she died fits in neatly with the Boston case." Danie explained the connection to the Helen Blake murder, the Boston Strangler's third victim. "And most importantly, Victoria was killed on the same day as Blake exactly fifty years ago. It's no accident, Billy."

"I was afraid of that," Billy said. "You were right, Danie."

"I think it's the only conclusion we can make based on the evidence," she said. "Especially the timing. It can't be a coincidence."

"I agree completely," Cal added.

KILLER IN THE HOLY CITY

As the techs processed the rest of the crime scene, Joe and RK spoke to neighbors and deck hands who had gathered on the dock. When they were done, they exchanged information with each other.

"Anything?" Joe said.

"Nah," RK said. "One guy, Ken Bristow, said he worked on *Victoria's Delight* from time to time. But he hasn't been on board since maybe the first week in June."

"Did you believe him?"

"Yeah, Joe. He's just a kid."

Joe smiled. He almost never believed anyone. It was just the way he was. He had learned to listen to everyone but verify everything. People had too many opportunities to be less than truthful during a criminal investigation, especially in the beginning, when police weren't aware of all the facts. He made a mental note to find out what Bristow was doing the past few days.

While Billy and Cal waited for Harry to join them, a few reporters carrying large cameras and some lighting equipment, pushed their way through the crowd.

"For God's sake," Billy moaned. "Here we go."

104   Visit CRIMESCAPE.COM for more action-packed original fiction!

Chapter 14

"THE KILLER IS FOLLOWING THE BOSTON Strangler's calendar," Billy said at the podium while he studied the task force members gathered before him. "In exactly forty-nine days, another Charleston woman will die unless we catch this bastard."

He paused a moment to let the warning sink in.

"I want you to understand that you're on this task force because of your areas of expertise. This is your time to shine."

Billy turned the podium over to Walter Johnson, the commanding officer.

Walter stood before them, broad-shouldered and ramrod straight. "Last evening, we brought the mayors, the chiefs, and the solicitor up to speed. They fully understand the urgency of our mission. This morning, you will get everything you need to know about the Boston case, the recent murders, and the links between the two cases. By this evening, I expect each of you to be an expert."

The task force members watched their plans for their Fourth of July baseball games, picnics, and fishing trips fade away. No one who knew Walter would dare disappoint his expectations.

KILLER IN THE HOLY CITY

"You already know that our killer is a publicity hound, and he's selected one of our strongest supporters to be his mouthpiece—Ricky Ramirez, WCBD-TV's evening news anchor."

The group laughed.

"And another of our greatest defenders, Council Member Troy Driggers—"

The audience collectively groaned.

"—has also volunteered to oversee our progress and report to the community every chance he gets."

He paused for a moment. "Listen closely if you value your career here. The media will distort, second-guess, and fabricate what we're doing, but they will get absolutely nothing from you. Or from your wife, your friends, or the guy next door. There will be zero tolerance for leaks. Hear me?"

He tapped his pen on the podium, looking some of the detectives in the eye.

"The press isn't going to limit its questions to you," he said. "They'll go after your friends, your Aunt Patty, and worse, your pals who didn't make the task force."

Two officers in the front row started to laugh nervously—until Walter glared at them.

Walter then introduced Danie as the task force psychologist. There was a low grumbling in the audience when she came up to the podium. Very few of the officers had ever set eyes on her, and most of them knew nothing about her. Experienced cops were wary of inviting in outsiders.

He raised his voice so everyone in the back of the room could hear him clearly. "Hey, you remember Marcy Scott in Atlanta? The six-year-old who was found floating in the Chattahoochee River last year? The cops were convinced it was an isolated murder until their chief asked Dr. Danie to help. Without her, they wouldn't have been able to link that killer to murders in five states."

Again, there was a murmur from the group as they whispered among themselves. Walter let it continue for a couple of minutes. The mention of the Marcy Scott case brought forth an explosion of horrific memories in Danie's mind. Images of all those murdered little girls would haunt her for the rest of her life. Her only moment of relief was the day that her months of exhaustive research pointed to the devilishly clever interstate truck driver now on death row in Florida.

"I could go on with the examples of cases that probably wouldn't be solved today without Dr. Callahan," Walter said, "but we don't have time. We've got one tough challenge ahead of us, and we're real fortunate to have her. Any questions?"

"Yeah," one of the veteran detectives said without taking the trouble to clear the skepticism from his voice. "Exactly what is she going to do?"

Walter was ready. "She'll put together a profile, of course. When one of you guys dig up someone good—and the situation calls for it, she'll interview him—thoroughly."

Next, a young, female officer asked how the city of Boston had reacted when they learned about the Strangler. "What happens when our citizens find out we're dealing with a serial killer?" she said.

Danie explained that many residents armed themselves with baseball bats, knives, and even handguns. The streets were deserted at night. Stores, restaurants, and theaters lost a lot of business, and it got worse as time went on. She described how the newspapers had reported nearly every detail, including the crime scenes, forensic evidence, and even the autopsy reports.

Some of the press revealed the victim's injuries and sexual assaults, leaked from the medical examiner's office. With each killing, the panic had intensified until it felt like the entire city was under siege. She told them there was no reason to believe that the people of Charleston would behave any differently.

"Something you should prepare yourself for," Danie warned, "is that as that case stretched out over months and then years, the police were called lazy, stupid, incompetent, and worse. Newspaper editors demanded resignations from just about everyone in City Hall."

There was a noticeable sigh from the audience. They all knew how unsympathetic the public could be when a killer wasn't caught quickly.

"For a while," Danie continued, "just about every police officer in the Boston area was assigned to the investigation in one way or another. Hundreds of leads poured in and tracking each one down took a massive amount of manpower. Every sex offender released from state prisons in Massachusetts and nearby states in the previous two years had to be accounted for. Mental patients with sexual histories had to have their whereabouts verified on the days of the murders. You can just imagine how much work that entailed."

She took a moment to take a sip from the bottle of water she had brought with her.

"Unfortunately, the press made every murder with even a slight resemblance seem like the Boston Strangler. Let's face it, hysteria sells newspapers. Perhaps we'll be lucky. We have much more technology than the Boston cops had fifty years ago. Even though semen had been found on a few of Strangler's victims, it was decades before DNA science. Like our killer, they had no fingerprints and assumed he wore gloves. Police had several promising suspects but never enough evidence for a prosecution."

Danie leaned forward with both hands on the sides of the podium. "Please take note of another very important similarity between these three recent murders and their counterparts in 1962. There's no sign of forced entry. At least two of our victims, like those in Boston, seemed to have voluntarily let the killer into their homes. Either they knew the killer, or they felt safe enough to let a stranger inside.

"In Boston, there was evidence that the killer sometimes went door to door in an apartment building until he found a victim. That's not what happened here. The neighbors of these three murder victims said positively that no stranger had been canvassing their streets around the time of the deaths."

When Danie finished speaking, Walter took over again. He told them that most of what the investigators had analyzed so far were records of sex offenders and mental patients with a sexual history. Danie, he said, had suggested that investigators check area media outlets to see if the killer had sent one of them Margaret Walsh's driver's license, the only item missing from her home. They discovered that it had, in fact, been delivered to WCBD-TV, the same TV station that received Ackerman's death photos. The employee who handled the station's community mail had recently returned from vacation. She was puzzled about the driver's license, not knowing that it belonged to the murder victim. It was only when she asked her supervisor what she should do with it that the station contacted the Mt. Pleasant Police.

"I've contacted the station manager," Walter said. "He told me that if any more evidence showed up on their premises or on the cell phone of any of their employees, it would be handed over to us immediately and confidentially. I'm cautiously optimistic he'll keep his word."

The task force burst into laughter. While they didn't know the station manager, they all knew the news anchor who worked for him: Ricky Ramirez, the brash young man who hosted the six o'clock news and was no friend of law enforcement.

Walter smiled and waved his hand to quiet them down.

"This killer is no dummy," he said. "Think about it. Of all the newsmen in the greater Charleston area, he sends his stuff to the one who's the most hostile to us."

While Walter handed out work assignments, the Callahans moved to a table at the back of the room. Danie studied the detailed Boston crime scene photos she'd received from her Bureau friend in Quantico.

Cal watched the expression on her face. It meant she was on to something.

"Cal, look at this." Danie showed him a photo of one of the Boston victims. "The way the killer posed Ackerman's body is virtually identical to the way the Strangler posed Ida Irga—"

He looked closely at the old photo. "Who's Ida Irga? Refresh my memory."

"She was the fourth Boston victim, and she was murdered in mid-August. I don't know what to make of this. As the third victim, Ackerman is a very real deviation from the Boston case."

"Take me through it," Cal said. "I don't know all these details of the Strangler's victims."

"Okay. We've had three victims who were killed either on or very close to the dates of the first three Boston victims. Margaret Walsh was the first, and she was posed like Anna Slesers, the first Boston victim. So far, it appears as though Victoria Howells was the second victim, and her body was posed like Helen Blake, the second Boston victim, on June thirtieth.

"Now, we would expect that Rachel Ackerman, who appears to have been the third victim, would be posed like Nina Nichols, the third Boston victim. But she's not. We found Ackerman posed like Ida Irga, the fourth Boston victim."

Cal shrugged. "So what? Why is that important?"

"Because this killer has gone to great lengths to copy the Boston Strangler. Now, all of a sudden, he throws us a big curveball. Yeah, maybe he screwed up, but my gut tells me something different." So many possibilities flooded her mind.

"Ida Irga was killed in August," she said. "By posing Ackerman like Ida Irga, maybe he's telling us that he's going to kill again next month."

Cal looked at the Ackerman photos again. "I think you're reading too much into this. What if he just hated Ackerman? She wasn't a real lovable lady."

"Good point, or maybe his fantasy was controlling him, and he didn't care that it was different from Boston's third victim."

"By the way, in the Boston case, did the killer ransack the crime scene more and more with each victim?" He told her about his theory and reminded her about the mess the killer had made of Victoria's bathroom.

"Come to think of it, in Helen Blake's apartment, her killer searched through all the drawers and even left one on the floor," Danie said.

"What about the third victim, Nina Nichols?"

"The scene was completely torn apart," she said. "Drawers emptied, clothes thrown around." Police assumed he was searching for something, but nobody figured out what it was."

"Sounds like Ackerman's bedroom to me."

While Walter continued the work assignments, Billy and Mt. Pleasant Chief Bert Allman joined Danie and Cal at the back of the conference room, along with Joe Asher and RK. Cal and Danie filled them in on her discovery about how Ackerman's body was like the fourth Strangler victim.

"The Strangler again?" Bert said. "I have to tell you that some of the task force members aren't convinced of your theory. They see the similarities, but they're not as sure as you guys seem to be. He's dead, right? The original killer."

"That depends on who you think the killer was, or if it was even one man," Danie said. "Most people think Albert DeSalvo was the Boston Strangler. He was charged in the Measuring Man case and the Green Man rapes but never with any of the Strangler killings."

"Measuring Man? What the hell is that?" Billy said.

"He'd pose as a talent scout for a fake modeling agency, talk his way into a woman's apartment, and convince her that she was pretty enough to be a professional model. Then he'd take her measurements and say he'd send them to the agency. This went on a couple of years before the Strangler murders. DeSalvo served eleven months of a two-year sentence for assault and battery and got out in April of 1962."

"I've heard of worse crimes," Bert said.

"There's more. DeSalvo finally admitted to being the Green Man—the one who was going around Massachusetts and nearby states raping women. He usually wore a green uniform and posed as a maintenance worker sent to fix something in his victim's apartment."

"And DeSalvo was eventually murdered in prison, correct?" Bert said.

"Yes, in 1973. Stabbed to death in his cell. Never did find out who did it, but he had already confessed to being the Boston Strangler."

"So what does it all mean to our case, Danie?" Billy folded his arms in front of his chest as if to signal the conversation needed to come to a conclusion.

Danie picked up her coffee cup and cradled it with both hands. "It means our killer knows the Boston case very well. That's all that matters. The next murder is due on August 19, and we have seven weeks to stop it."

Chapter 15

Planters Inn, Charleston
3:15 p.m.

LATER THAT AFTERNOON, DANIE, JOE, AND RK drove over to Charleston's elegant Planters Inn, where Victoria often went for dinner and drinks at the bar of the hotel's Peninsula Grill and at least on one occasion, had stayed overnight. The Planters Inn was a beautifully preserved architectural jewel at the intersection of North Market Street and Meeting Street—a location that overlooked the Old City Market, ideal for tourists with money. It was annually voted as one of the finest hotels in the South.

They first stopped at the Peninsula Grill's Champagne Bar to interview Andy Greene, the bartender who had been working on Wednesday, June twenty-seventh, the last time Victoria had stayed overnight at the hotel. They were a few minutes early for the interview, and the bar was empty, so they sat at one of the tables. The décor was sophisticated. The black-lacquered wood of the cabinetry contrasted with the salmon and black granite surface of the bar. Classical music emanated softly from unseen speakers. Danie picked up the small drink menu on the table and laughed.

"Eighteen dollars for a glass of cabernet keeps the riff raff out."

As Danie examined the luxurious furnishings, she could understand why Victoria would feel comfortable at the Champagne Bar. She was among people of her social class here.

A young man came through the restaurant into the bar and made eye contact with her. He smiled pleasantly as he approached. Greene agreed to come in well before work so that they had ample time for the interview. He seemed to her like a personable young man with a sweet, boyish face. He mentioned that like many of the younger staff members, he was working to pay his college tuition while his girlfriend's salary paid the household expenses.

"Sounds like a good deal to me," RK said.

"You bet," Greene said. "She's an excellent web designer. Makes very good money." Suddenly, the smile vanished from his face, which Danie interpreted as Greene remembering the solemn reason they were there to interview him.

"I was so shocked to hear about Mrs. Howells," he said. "Let's go sit at a table in the dining room, where it will be more private. The restaurant doesn't open until five-thirty, but the bar could get busy earlier."

He showed them to a table in the restaurant where the only sound was the waiters setting up for dinner. The walls in the sumptuous supper club were covered with a shimmering oyster-colored velvet, illuminated by distinctive copper and chrome chandeliers.

Joe started right in. "How long had Mrs. Howells been coming here?"

Greene gave the question some thought. "Since early June of this year. She spent the winter in Florida."

"About how often did she come to the Peninsula?"

"I work here five nights a week at the bar, so you might want to talk to Tony Shaffel. He works with me on the weekends, and he's mostly by himself on Monday and Tuesday nights. On the nights I worked, I'd say she was here maybe two or three times a week. She'd come in around six-thirty and sit at the bar and order dinner and a glass of wine."

"How much did she drink? Did she ever seem inebriated to you?"

"I think the most I ever saw her drink was three glasses of wine, and that was over a period of several hours."

"Did she ever say why she came to the Peninsula so often?"

"I never asked her, and she never told me why, but I came to some conclusions on my own. This is a pretty safe place to drink at night. We bartenders watch out for women customers who are by themselves. When she paid her bill, I'd ask her if she wanted a cab, and if she did, I'd have the doorman call one for her."

"Do you think safety was the main reason she came here?"

"Well, I think she was lonely, too. Her husband was gone a lot, and she didn't have any friends in Charleston as far as I knew."

"Did she ever flirt with you?"

Greene looked uncomfortable. "Once or twice."

"How about with Tony or some of the waiters?"

"I don't want to give you the wrong impression. Her being dead and all."

"Don't worry about that. We need to know these things. How about Tony? Did she come on to Tony?"

Greene seemed reluctant to say anymore. "Yeah."

"What about the other men who work here?"

"Fred. He's a waiter," Greene said in a low voice. "Don't tell him I told you. He's married."

"Did you screw her?"

Greene looked down at the table. "I never did anything with her except think about it."

"What about Tony and Fred?"

"I don't think so, but if they did, they wouldn't tell anybody."

"Did Mrs. Howells make friends with any of the male customers in the bar?" Danie asked.

"She struck up conversations with a number of men at the bar—and with women, too."

"Did you ever see her leave with one of the men?"

"Not that I ever saw. But on June twenty-seventh, she and the doctor sitting next to her got very friendly. He was drinking martinis, and she had several glasses of wine and a martini. Bad combination, particularly since she didn't order dinner that night."

"Did they leave together?" Danie asked.

"She paid her bill and left the bar maybe ten minutes before he did, but no cab that night."

"Tell me some more about this doctor. What did he look like?" Joe said.

"I'm not very good with ages, but I would have guessed the doctor was around fifty. His hair was completely gray. He was distinguished-looking and dressed very well. Killer tie. It was a Wednesday night, so the bar wasn't real crowded. He mentioned he was a neurologist and in town for a meeting."

"Did he tell you his name? Maybe signed a credit card for his drinks?" Joe said.

"Shoot! Mrs. Howells did mention his last name once, but it slips my mind. He paid cash for his drinks, and Mrs. Howells always used a credit card."

When Joe asked some additional questions, Danie excused herself to interview the clerk at the front desk of the hotel.

The man at the desk said he'd been on duty when Victoria booked her room for the night of June twenty-seventh. When Danie showed him her photo, he remembered her because she wanted a suite and didn't care what it cost. The best was the Proprietor's Suite, which went for five hundred dollars a night. He assumed she was a rich woman who had too much to drink. She appeared to be alone and had no luggage.

Just after five-thirty, Danie and the two detectives went back to the command center. The first thing RK did was enter the information about the doctor Victoria met into the task force database. A few minutes later, Mt. Pleasant Detective Ira Shapiro called and asked if the neurologist was Clay Etheridge. The description the bartender gave had matched Etheridge perfectly. RK said the bartender couldn't remember the doctor's name but thought he would recognize it if he heard it again.

"Wait a second, Ira. I want to put you on speaker so Joe and Danie can hear this."

"Hey, Ira," Joe said. "What's up?"

Ira laughed. "That doctor with Victoria Howells could be someone we've been trying to locate. While there are other people in this country named Clay Etheridge and even some doctors have the last name Etheridge, we couldn't find a neurologist named Clay Etheridge."

"Hold on for a minute, Ira," Joe said. "RK, would you call the bartender and see if he recognizes the name Clay Etheridge?"

"Sure." RK took out his phone and searched for the number.

"Go on, Ira. What'd your suspect do?" Joe said.

"All the women Etheridge contacted had the same story. He would approach them at social gatherings and charity fundraisers, strike up a conversation, flatter them about their looks, then take a call on his cell, and leave abruptly. A few days later, he'd call the women and ask to drop by that evening. Two of them let him come over."

"Did he assault them?" Joe said.

"No," Ira said. "At least one of them admitted he seduced her, promising he would call the next day to continue their relationship. Well, neither of the women ever heard from him again, and when they tried to find him, they realized he wasn't who he said he was. It's hard to say how many more women actually fell for him. They were probably embarrassed about having let him into their beds."

"I'll bet we had some here, too," Joe said. "But I don't think we'd follow-up on a complaint like that."

"Neither would we," Ira said. "The only reason we got those calls was because of the murders. So we looked into it."

"I wonder if this guy is somehow connected to Victoria's murder," Danie said. "Remember the Measuring Man from the Boston case?"

"The one who told pretty women he was a talent scout for a modeling agency?" Joe smiled. "Got to give the guy some credit for ingenuity." He paused for a few seconds. "He never raped any of those girls, did he?"

"No, he didn't," Danie said. "But DeSalvo's tricking women into letting him touch their breasts and hips was technically assault and battery. This was the first stage in him evolving into the Green Man rapist."

RK returned to the group with a cola in his hand.

"What'd you find out?" Joe said.

"I gave the bartender three very different names," he said. "And asked if the doctor was one of them. He recognized 'Etheridge.' The good doctor paid cash for all of his drinks and left the bar a few minutes after Victoria."

"Ah, discretion. I love it," Ira said. "Don't let the help see you leaving together."

"I'd like to look into this a bit," Danie said. "Maybe Victoria hooking up with this Etheridge character is just a coincidence, but I hate coincidences. Especially one that takes place a few days before she's killed. Ira, could you ask the women who called about Etheridge if they would speak to me?"

"Sure, Danie. Let me make a few calls."

"I'm putting Etheridge's name into the database. Let's see if the doc made any friends in Charleston," RK said.

"I've got news, people," Billy said loudly as he entered the room. "Listen up!"

Everyone froze in place.

"Summerville PD just called," he announced. "An hour ago, while he was being taken to his shrink, Lester Beach overpowered a guard, killed him with his own weapon, and escaped in a vehicle he carjacked from the parking lot."

Danie's chest tightened. It suddenly became hard to breathe.

"Our boy Lester Beach is now wanted for at least one murder."

Chapter 16

Charleston Police Department
9:15 a.m. Tuesday, July 3, 2012

DANIE SHIVERED.

She couldn't get Lester out of her mind. Was he coming for her? Cal had tried to convince her to return to Savannah, but she'd insisted on staying in Charleston. She needed to see the case through to the end. While half the local police forces in Charleston County were looking for Lester Beach, the work of the task force continued on just as urgently.

A Sony digital recorder lay on the desk in front of RK. Kenneth Bristow, the young man who had worked on Victoria Howells's yacht, had called the night before. RK remembered him from the interview on the dock on the day Victoria's body was found.

"Listen to this," RK said as he started the recorder.

"I saw him with her on the *Delight* at least two or three times, almost up to the day she was killed," Bristow said.

"What's his name, Kenneth?"

"Well, this guy is as slick as they come—tells people he went to law school, but then decided he didn't want to be a lawyer. He tells bullshit stories, so I don't believe anything he says. And he's got one hell of a temper. Hey, man, whatever you do, don't tell him I talked to you. I don't like this guy, and I don't want him coming after me. He's mean as a fucking snake."

"What's his name?"

"I saw him beat the shit out this guy one time. It only took him like a minute. He really hurt this dude, and it was totally uncalled for. He's a shithead who—"

"Kenneth, what's his fucking name?"

"Dwayne Deveraux. Promise you won't tell him I said anything?"

"We won't tell him. Don't worry. We don't work that way. Where can I find this Dwayne Deveraux?"

"He works for a mortgage company downtown. I don't know which one."

RK switched the recorder off.

"Interesting?" he said. "I already researched Deveraux, and he has a rap sheet with us. Been locked up three times for assault. Two were girlfriends, one DWI, and one drug possession. Back in '04, he was arrested in Atlanta on a murder charge. He whacked some drunk in a fight outside a bar. Hit him with a pipe. The guy died a few days later. But Deveraux was acquitted at trial. Self-defense."

"Did you find out where he works?" Cal said.

"Coastal Empire Mortgage over on King Street. I already told his boss we'd be over this morning for a little talk and not to warn Deveraux we're coming. Incidentally, Deveraux graduated from the University of Georgia's law school. According to his boss, he's a valuable employee."

"Let's go see him. Cal, you wanna ride along?" Joe said.

"Sounds good to me."

"Sure," RK said. "If anything goes wrong, we'll already have a doctor at the scene."

Cal smiled. "I don't know what good I would be. All my patients are usually dead."

Coastal Empire Mortgage took up most of the block on King Street. With its restored antique gas lanterns and Boston ferns around the leaded glass doors, it looked like an inviting place to do business. Inside the lobby, a prim middle-aged receptionist, in fine Charleston style, graciously offered to help them. Joe asked for Dwayne Deveraux.

"Is he expecting you? I didn't have any appointments for him this morning."

"We discussed our visit with Mr. McFarland this morning."

His explanation seemed to satisfy her curiosity. "Whom shall I tell him is here?"

Joe showed his badge. "Detectives from Charleston PD."

The look of surprise on her face was only momentary. "Please take a seat, if you wish." She gestured to the sumptuous tan leather sofa and chairs in the ostentatious lobby.

"Thank you, ma'am," Joe said.

She went through an arched mahogany doorway into a long hall and disappeared for a couple of minutes. "Please follow me," she said when she returned.

The slate flooring of the lobby turned into plush maroon carpeting as they followed her through the doorway. Along the hallway were framed prints of historic sailing ships and antebellum Charleston. Several open offices on each side of the hallway held prospective clients discussing business with the company representatives. When they turned the corner, there were two offices at each end of the short hallway.

"That's Mr. McFarland's office," she said. "Over here to the right is Mr. Deveraux's. He'll be with you in a moment."

"Really nice digs. Not quite what I expected." RK and Joe sat in the two chairs facing the huge wooden desk.

Cal sat on a sofa along the wall. He noted that Deveraux's desk was exceptionally neat, almost to a fault. It had a highly polished top, but no stacks of paper, no photos, no open files, not even a coffee cup. Just a lamp, a telephone, and a shallow rectangular outbox with a couple of folders in it. He decided that Deveraux was either a control freak when it came to orderliness or he didn't have much work to do.

As Cal was wondering what to make of the absence of any personal effects, a tall man with dark brown hair entered from a side door. Dwayne Deveraux was a good-looking, powerfully built man in his late twenties, maybe early thirties. He was well dressed in a gray suit, white shirt, and conservative tie.

"Gentlemen," he said with a winning smile, "you must be here about Mrs. Howells. Terrible thing. I should have contacted you sooner, right after I heard about the tragedy. I've just been so busy."

Joe, never one for meaningless small talk, said, "I understand you and Mrs. Howells had an intimate relationship."

Deveraux looked genuinely surprised. "Intimate? No, Detective, not at all. We had a few conversations at a restaurant near the City Marina. She was thinking about buying some property. We talked maybe three or four times, but that's all. And I bought her a couple glasses of wine."

Joe's expression didn't hide his skepticism. "We have several witnesses who saw you on her boat the night she died. Why don't you tell us about that?"

"What night are you talking about? I was only on her boat twice, and I don't remember which nights. I was only trying to make her more comfortable about real estate and financing."

"Only twice?" Joe said. "We have more than one witness who saw you on her boat a number of times."

"Mrs. Howells had many male friends. Perhaps you are aware of that."

"Ever hit her?"

Deveraux was taken aback by the abrupt change in tone. "Hit her? Of course not." He looked at Joe as though he was crazy for even suggesting such a thing.

"Come on now, Deveraux," Joe said. "We've seen your rap sheet. You've beat up women before."

Deveraux folded his arms across his chest. "Those girls were lying. I'm more careful now about the caliber of women I go out with."

"Where were you the night she was killed?"

"You still haven't told me when she died. What I heard on the news was that she had been dead for days before her husband found her. I don't know what happened or when."

"She was killed on the night of Friday, June twenty-ninth, or in the early morning hours of Saturday, June thirtieth. Were you with her?" RK said.

Deveraux paused. "I don't remember."

"Well, try to remember," Joe said. "It was only a few days ago."

Deveraux opened the top drawer of his desk and pulled out a small planning diary. He flipped it open and shook his head. "I don't have anything for the twenty-ninth or the thirtieth. If I'd had plans, it would be in here."

"I wouldn't expect you to put Mrs. Howells on your calendar if you planned to kill her," RK said.

"Deveraux, we'd like you to come over to headquarters for a formal statement," Joe said.

He froze. "All right, Detective. No problem. Just let me tell my boss."

While Deveraux was out, Joe roamed around his office. "I think he just lied through his teeth about Victoria."

"You know," Cal said, "this is just the type of guy who could persuade women to let him into their homes."

"And he's a lawyer." Joe looked down the hallway. "So you already know he's full of crap."

After they had left the mortgage company with Deveraux following in his own car, Joe called Danie and asked her if she would talk to Deveraux under the pretext of adding to the victim's profile.

"Sure thing," Danie said. "Any chance of talking to the girlfriends he roughed up?"

"RK's working on that. We're trying to contact them. Deveraux is pulling in behind me now," he said.

Ten minutes later, Danie entered the interrogation room where Deveraux was sitting at a desk, his hands folded on his lap, and his legs crossed. Danie introduced herself. "Danielle Callahan."

"What a pleasure to meet you," he said with a broad smile. "Do they call you Ellie or Danie?"

"Dr. Callahan will be just fine, Mr. Deveraux." Danie had his number right away; he was the guy who always had to ask a professional woman her first name so he could establish dominance over her.

"Dr. Callahan it is, then." He winked. "I'll be glad to help you put your profile of Mrs. Howells together. A lawyer has to be reasonably competent in psychology, don't you think?"

Danie sat down at the table next to Joe, across from Deveraux. "Excellent, Mr. Deveraux. Let's start with when and where you first met Mrs. Howells."

He nodded. "To the best of my recollection, I met her in early June at a restaurant next to the marina where her boat is docked. She struck me as a lonely woman. Her husband was away on business much of the time, and she seemed starved for companionship."

"That's what I've heard. Can you tell me how many times you and Mrs. Howells talked?"

"Three, maybe four times at the most."

"What kinds of things did you talk about?"

He explained that locally he was known for his knowledge in real estate financing. "She was interested in buying a house on Isle of Palms using the money her former husband gave her in their divorce settlement. She had heard that I was the best person to talk to."

Danie suppressed a smile. "And where did you get together? Was it at your office or on her boat?"

"A couple of times on her boat." He hesitated for a moment and then added, "We always sat outside on the deck."

"Why always on the deck?"

"I was the one who insisted on sitting on the deck."

"And why was that, Mr. Deveraux?"

He took a few moments to answer. "Her husband is very wealthy. If he imagined I was having an intimate relationship with his wife, he could hurt my career."

"So it wasn't your sense of propriety, but rather a concern for your reputation. Is that correct?"

"Dr. Callahan, I don't know if you're aware of this, but Mrs. Howells was not exactly the soul of discretion. She had a rather unfortunate reputation around the City Marina."

"I'm sorry, Mr. Deveraux, I'm new to this case. What exactly did she do to create this reputation?"

Another hesitation. "I don't like to say bad things about the dead."

"Let's pretend she's alive, then," Danie said.

Deveraux wasn't sure how to react. "Well, let me be candid. She slept around—a lot."

"And you didn't want people to think you were sleeping with her?"

"Exactly. That's why I insisted that all our conversations take place on the deck."

Danie looked confused. "But your fingerprints were found in a number of areas inside the boat, including the master suite, where she was killed." She knew it wasn't true but wanted to gauge his reaction.

With his eyes fixed on the table in front of him, Deveraux repeatedly twisted his large college ring on his right hand. "Oh yes, I forgot. The first time I was on her boat, she showed me all around, inside and outside. It was clear to me she wanted sex that night. I never went inside after that one tour."

"When you sat on her boat, did you always sit in the same place?"

"Let me think for a moment. Yes, we always sat on the main deck."

"The aft deck or the forward one?"

"Is that important? It's the area just outside the...the parlor, I guess you'd call it. It's the first place you reach after you climb the stairs to get onto the boat."

Danie laughed. "I wondered what you thought about the bright red-and-green Chinese-print upholstery on all the furniture in that area."

He laughed with her. "Oh, that. It was horrible. Not my taste at all. I assumed her husband picked it up on one of his business trips."

"The discretion you exercised makes perfect sense, Mr. Deveraux. I mean, after what you did to two of the women you dated, you'll have to be careful in the future."

Danie saw instantly that she had hit a nerve. Deveraux paused for a moment to recover his confidence.

"Those girls were liars. I was too young and naïve then to understand how much damage they could do to my reputation."

Danie made a show of going through her notes. Deveraux shifted his weight several times in his chair, crossing and uncrossing his legs.

"I'm confused," Danie said. "The two women I'm talking about filed charges here against you in the past twelve months. Did you assault other women when you lived in Georgia?"

Deveraux's discomfort suddenly turned to defensive anger. "Look, if you want the truth, Victoria was no better than a good-looking, expensively dressed old whore. She wanted men eating out of her hand because she thought she was so beautiful. So classy with that upper-class British accent. Stupid, old broad."

"Why do you think she was killed?" Danie said. "You have more insight into her personality than anyone else I've spoken to. What did she do that would have made someone want to kill her?"

Deveraux didn't answer right away. "Some men just hate women. It gets all bottled up inside and eats at them until they do something about it. Then they feel like a man again."

Danie's eyebrows rose at his explanation. It almost seemed like a confession. "Interesting," she said. "So, you think it's not something Mrs. Howells did that got her killed but simply because she happened to meet up with the wrong guy."

"Just a guess on my part. I'm not a psychiatrist. Let's face it, she was an unpaid whore. Hard to have any respect for someone like that."

Danie had heard enough. Abruptly, she thanked Deveraux for the information and left the room. She met Joe in the hallway.

"I have a very bad feeling about him," she said. "Did you catch the part when he claimed that when he was on Victoria's yacht, they sat outside on the aft deck? Remember how it was all covered up with canvas?"

"Yeah, I remember that," Joe said.

"Well, out of curiosity, I lifted some of the coverings to see what the furniture looked like. It was all done in cream and blue. There were no red-and-green Chinese prints."

"Why would he lie about such a trivial thing?" Joe said.

"Exactly," Danie said. "Why?"

Chapter 17

"OH, JESUS," BILLY MOANED. "THAT'S ALL I need. A psychic rammed down my throat by the guy who wants to be the next mayor."

Billy had more important things on his mind. The task force's workload was growing rapidly, and Billy expected it to explode if the media linked the recent murders with the Strangler. For reasons unknown, the Charleston killer had chosen to leak photos of his crimes to one television station.

Billy detested the TV news anchor, Ricky Ramirez, but grudgingly gave him credit for being a pit bull of an investigative reporter. He understood why the TV station promoted the young man. His in-your-face style and exclusives had lifted the station's ratings to new heights and captured the young audience advertisers loved. What Billy disliked the most about Ramirez was that his success came from cultivating alliances with politicians like the shamelessly ambitious and influential Charleston City Council Member Troy Driggers.

As much as Billy disliked Ramirez, he hated Driggers with a passion. Driggers was using his political capital to mount an effort to defeat Mayor LC Campbell in the next election. Billy figured

Ramirez had already shared the photos taken by the killer with Driggers, and if that were true, it gave them a fine opportunity to undermine the mayor.

Billy pulled Cal aside for some advice. "You're not gonna believe this, but the most powerful man on the city council wants me to bring in a psychic from Philadelphia to work on the case."

"What? You're not going to, are you?"

"The son of a bitch won't leave me alone, Cal. I can't throw him out of my office. He's got a lot of friends at City Hall, and he's buddies with Ramirez. And let's face it, if he becomes mayor, I don't wanna poison our relationship."

Billy explained that he had resisted Driggers at first, but after reading a Philly newspaper clipping about the psychic, he became more optimistic. Her name was Gertrude Rose Kellner. According to the story, she had provided vital clues to the Philly PD, which had led directly to the apprehension of a murderer. She told reporters that she had long suspected the killer was a former cop who had turned bad and was getting even for some old hostilities he had suffered many years ago. Kellner said she'd had visions in which she saw the killer's face and a police badge pinned to his chest.

"I got no choice. I have to bring in this psychic and give it a try. If I don't, Driggers will say he tried to help us, but we refused and let the killings continue."

"That's bullshit," Cal said. He hated to see his friend knuckle under to the demands of a politician.

"I know it. You know it. But I can't afford to have the public think we didn't do everything we could to solve the case. Driggers has the pulpit right now, not me. He's on the fucking TV every night, building his case for becoming the next mayor. He's got Ramirez on speed dial, for God's sake."

"I don't put much faith in psychics, Billy."

"What about Danie? Does she?"

"She's open-minded, but, honestly, I didn't know of any murder case where a psychic has been of value until today."

Billy insisted Cal ride with him to pick up Kellner, who'd taken the long bus trip down from Philly. They jumped into the chief's massive Crown Victoria sedan and zoomed out of the parking lot like it was the starting gate of the Daytona 500.

"I have to tell you, Cal, when I read this story about Kellner, I was impressed." Billy held the clipping in one hand and the steering wheel with the other. "You know, I don't normally believe in this crap, but even the detectives up in Philly said there was no way she could have known that a former cop was the primary suspect. Let's give it a try. What harm can come from it?"

"We can waste time, that's what," Cal said as Billy came within inches of side-swiping a FedEx delivery van.

Cal gripped the dashboard. "Where'd you learn to fucking drive?"

"Got my license from Walmart. Thought you knew that," Billy said. "Mt. Pleasant's chief, you know Bert Allman, is convinced we should give her a chance. He's a good man. Been on the job thirty years, and he takes these things seriously."

"Okay. We're here to help. Whatever you decide to do, Danie and I are for it. Say, you aren't taking this psychic to the command center, are you?"

"Hell no, Cal. As far as she knows, there isn't any command center. I asked Danie to meet us over at the PD."

They pulled up to the bus depot, where a small, stout woman stood smoking a cigarette in a long, gold-colored holder. She quickly glanced from side to side while she nudged her glasses up to the bridge of her nose. A ridiculously large, multi-colored cloth bag hung over her shoulder. When she took a drag on the cigarette, dozens of thin, silver bracelets slid down her wrist into the crook of her elbow. A massive crest of flaming red hair rested on top of her head. Her eyes were surrounded by bright blue shadow and thick black liner. The moment Cal saw her, he knew.

"This just has to be our girl," he said.

As they pulled to the curb, Billy powered the window down.

"Hello, Miss Kellner?"

"Well, it's about time!" she said. "I've been standing here for all of five minutes. People will think I'm working the street, for heaven's sake! Open the trunk!"

Billy popped the trunk while Cal gave her a hand with her luggage. She couldn't have been more than five-feet tall. Before he could lift the large piece of luggage, she grabbed the handle and dragged it over to the rear of the car. With one sweep, she picked up the suitcase and flung it into the trunk.

"Howdy! Let's go!" She jumped into the rear seat in one fluid motion.

Once they had sped away from the bus station, Cal introduced Billy and himself. "We're happy to have you on board, ma'am," Billy said.

"Everybody calls me Rosa," she said as she adjusted her glasses. Each time she moved her hand, the silver bracelets clanged together, making a sound very much like a loud wind chime.

"You can call me Cal."

"Dr. Cal, you married?" Rosa said.

A psychic would know that Cal thought, but he decided to be agreeable.

"Yes, happily. You'll meet my better half when we get over to the PD. My wife, Dr. Danielle Callahan, is over there. How much do you know about the murders, by the way?"

"Not much."

Cal glanced at her in the rear mirror and saw she was looking at him. He noticed her eyes were bright blue behind those over-sized glasses.

"How long you been married, handsome?" Rosa said.

"Me?" said Billy. "About twenty years."

"I was talking to Dr. Cal, Chief."

"Well, I just assumed..." Billy said, and they all laughed.

Billy drove down Rutledge Avenue toward headquarters, dodging rush-hour traffic, and keeping the windows open to lessen the impact of cigarette smoke.

When Billy and Cal reached headquarters, their plan was to introduce Rosa to Danie and give the psychic some limited details of the murders. Whatever revelations she might have, Cal reasoned, Rosa should have them on her own, not as the result of any information provided by the police or anyone else. If the task force wanted to give her more than that, the decision was up to them.

As he entered the squad room, Danie was sitting at a large desk with hundreds of photos around her stacked into neat, separate piles.

Danie smiled as she got up from behind the desk. "This must be Miss Kellner."

"Call me Rosa. Everyone does." She extended her hand as the bracelets performed their noisy dance on her wrist. "You have so much to do here, Dr. Danie. I don't want to bother you now. I'll come back later when we can talk."

"No, that's all right," Danie said. "We can go over a few things whenever you like. But how do you work? What can we do to help you?"

"Normally, I look at some evidence or an article of clothing and get a reading there. Maybe go to the scene, see what hits me. I don't know, Dr. Danie. I have no control over it. Sometimes I might get a strong feeling. Other times, it's like a gentle nudge. Police reports are always helpful. If I could see some of those, it might steer me in the right direction."

"I'm sure," Cal said, but the cynic in him thought differently.

For the next twenty minutes, Billy, Cal, and Danie gave her a brief overview of the murders. During that time, Rosa rummaged around in her giant handbag and muttered to herself.

"God damn it! I can never find anything in this stupid bag!" Her hand emerged, grasping a broken piece of what must have once been a very large cookie that had settled to the bottom of the bag.

"I knew I had some left," she said triumphantly. "Want some?" She held the crumbling cookie out to them. They shook their heads in unison.

"Well," Billy said, "I think we should get you settled in first and maybe start fresh tomorrow.

Danie looked down at the pile of photos on the desk, fixated on the photograph that was closest to her. She had her index finger pressed on its image and twirled the photo from side to side with her thumb. Cal knew that look. There was something there, and she wanted to tell him, but couldn't.

"Sergeant?" Billy barked into the nearest phone. "I'm bringing Miss Kellner down to you. Get an officer to take her over to the Hampton Inn on Meeting Street and get her situated. Report back to me later."

"We'll see you soon, Rosa," Danie said. "Go get checked in, have something to eat, and we'll get together tomorrow."

After Cal had delivered Rosa, he returned to Danie and asked her what she had found.

Danie looked carefully at each photo of Victoria's bedroom, hoping that a clue would somehow jump off the bloody images, hit her over the head like a sledgehammer, and solve the case. It didn't happen.

"I don't know yet," Danie said. "I…I have a feeling we're on the wrong path here, Cal. But I'm not exactly sure why. But it's something. I can feel it. There's something missing, but I don't know what."

"The wrong path?" Cal said. "I thought you had a handle on this?"

Danie rested her hand on the back of her head. "I did too."

Danie studied the gruesome images of the dead women, each with her own family and her own dreams. What was going to happen? Who would be next? For the first time, she felt a weight upon her shoulders, a weight that Billy must feel, that any cop must surely feel during moments like this. If they were not successful, someone else would die at the hands of a monster who had no conscience and no soul. For the first time in a long while, she prayed.

Her thoughts were interrupted by the vibration of her phone. She answered and recognized the voice immediately. There was no mistaking it.

"You should give yourself up, Lester."

"Not now. I'm having fun. I miss you."

"You killed that guard at the hospital. Do you think the police are going to ignore that?"

"Why not? I have," he said.

"Why did you kill those women, Lester?"

"I'll come into your bed one night soon, Doc. Before you know what's happening, I'll have your hands tied behind your back. Then I'll rip your clothes off. I'll lick your back up to your neck while my hands are on your ass. I'll put you on your belly and spread your legs. Do you like that, Doc?"

"The cops will find you, Lester."

"The cops! The cops!" he shouted. "What the fuck can they do? They couldn't even convict OJ. 'The Lord is my strength and my song. He has become my salvation. Shouts of joy and victory resound in the tents of the righteous!'"

Danie was silent.

He laughed. "By the way, you know where I ate last night? The Peninsula Grill. I think it's overpriced, though. And the lobster was overcooked. I complained to the waiter about it."

"The Peninsula Grill?" The thought of him even mentioning the restaurant was frightening. How did he know she had been there yesterday? Then it dawned on her that maybe he knew Victoria frequented the bar and asked one of the bartenders if the police had interviewed them.

"Actually, a friend of mine bought me dinner. Go ask him. His name is Stanley Higgins. A fine gentleman. And generous, too."

"Lester…"

"You know, when we get together, you'll never want another man after me. You ever been fucked by a killer, Doc? We know how to treat a woman. I'm gonna take some photos of you, too. I'll share them later with that asshole reporter from the TV. Oh, I forgot to tell you one thing."

"What?"

"I like to bite."

Danie heard the line go dead.

She took a deep breath, cleared her throat, and walked over to Billy's office where he was talking with Cal about how to test the psychic's ability. The two men stopped talking the minute she stood at the door. The expression on her face betrayed her state of mind.

"What happened?" Cal said. "You okay?"

"Grab a seat, Danie," Billy said. She sat in the chief's chair.

She did her best to describe the entire conversation with Lester without letting them know how much the phone call had rattled her.

"Higgins?" Billy said. "Who the hell is Stanley Higgins?"

"I don't know," Danie said. "He never elaborated."

Billy picked up the phone and instructed a detective to research the name in the department database system. "The minute you get anything, call me back."

Cal was worried about Danie. "Can you remember anything else he said to you?"

Danie went through the call from beginning to end as Billy took notes. She told them about the Peninsula Grill and maybe that was the connection with Victoria. In twenty minutes, the detective called back. Billy answered and wrote down the information on his desk pad.

"All right, Detective," Billy said. "Good work. Yeah, go ahead and do that and keep me posted."

Cal was impatient. "Okay, so who the hell is this Higgins?"

"Lester never had dinner with him," Billy said, "and he's not a friend. Stanley Higgins is a teacher over at the College of Charleston. Yesterday morning, he went to get gas and found that two of his credit cards were missing from his wallet. He doesn't know how it happened, but the only time the wallet was out of his possession was yesterday around noontime. He was exercising over at the Bluefish Club on Concord Street, and he put his clothes in a locker, but he didn't have his lock with him. He made a report to the PD yesterday."

"So Lester got into the club somehow and took the cards?" Cal said.

"Looks that way," Billy said. "One card was definitely used at the Peninsula like he said. We checked."

"Well, he's probably dumped the cards by now," Danie said.

"Maybe not. Thieves will use a stolen card till it's turned down."

"But Higgins canceled the cards, right?" Cal said.

"We're calling right now and trying to get their cooperation to keep the card alive. We'll be notified immediately when and where it's used. We'll be able to track Beach that way."

"That's great," Cal said.

"Danie, any ideas about Lester other than how he knew you were at the Peninsula?" Billy said.

"I don't know. Maybe he doesn't really know. He never actually said that. Could it have been a coincidence?"

"Maybe."

"He's clearly a psychopath," Danie said, "and he gets a kick out of scaring women."

"Well, I think we're finished for the day," Billy said. "I think we all need a break." He placed a hand on Danie's shoulder. "Especially you."

Chapter 18

Blind Tiger Pub
6:45 p.m.

"HERE'S WHERE YOU'LL FIND ME WHEN the job gets to be too much," Billy said as he parked in front of the Blind Tiger pub on Broad Street. "I've been coming through these doors since I was in uniform twenty years ago. This place will make you feel better, Danie. I promise."

The L-shaped bar, an ancient piece of wood finished to smooth perfection by long-gone craftsmen, extended almost the length of the room. A well-used brass rail, where tired feet could always rest, ran along the bottom. Above the faded mirrors behind the bar, rows of beer bottles were lined up on top of wooden cabinets. Next to the cabinets, dozens of bottles of various sizes, shapes, and brands of liquor were positioned on shelves. The room, paneled in a dark, mellow wood, accentuated the tavern's antiquity and warmth.

They settled in seats at the center of the bar, which was relatively quiet since most of the customers were sitting outside in their courtyard. Danie sat next to Billy and Cal stood between them. The bartender, a young man with a neatly trimmed goatee, recognized Billy and came over to get their order.

"Hey, Chief," he said. "What can I get for you?"

"Oscar, these are friends of mine, Dr. Calvin Callahan and Dr. Danie Callahan."

"Welcome to the Tiger."

"Oscar, gimme a Jack straight up," Billy said.

Danie asked for a martini on the rocks. Cal ordered a Sam Adams. Like Billy, he realized that Danie needed to unwind. When the drinks arrived, Danie couldn't wait to take that first sip. "Aaaah, that's so good." She was finally beginning to relax. "The Blind Tiger is an odd name for a saloon. What does it mean?"

Billy relished the chance to tell the story. "Charleston was a wild and wicked place a couple hundred years ago, filled with sailors, pirates, and crooks from all over the world. And it stayed that way for generations, even during the Civil War years. The governor back then, a rambunctious, one-eyed farmer named Ben 'Pitchfork' Tillman wanted to clean up the city, so he put a lot of Prohibition-like controls on booze. Naturally, private clubs opened up. Here, the owners told people they had to pay admission to see a real tiger, but there was no damn tiger. Only booze."

"And people left blind drunk!" Danie said.

Billy laughed. "Right. So this place became the Blind Tiger."

"Hey, you guys see this?" Oscar moved the TV he kept on the bar to where they could see it and turned up the volume. The familiar face of TV lawyer Nancy Grace was on the screen. The caption under her image read "The Charleston Strangler." Grace was talking about the murders. The guest was an older man with white hair and eyebrows, sporting a pair of black, thick-rimmed glasses. He had a ruddy face but was quick with a smile. The caption identified him as Detective Seamus Powers.

Billy let out a deep sigh. "It was bound to happen, I guess." He took another swig of his Jack Daniels.

"Good thing you're prepared for this," Cal said.

"So the Boston Strangler case," Grace said in a voice dripping with skepticism, "that mesmerized the nation back in the early sixties may have a connection to what's happening now in Charleston?"

"Yeah," the man answered. "I was with the Boston PD for twenty years. I worked on dozens of homicides during my career. There are a lot of similarities between the Strangler case and these Charleston murders. I think—"

Grace interrupted. "Well, like what? Specifically, what makes you think that, Detective?"

"Look, Nancy, I've seen enough homicides to know when there are certain things that have to be more than coincidence. For example, in the Boston case, the bodies of the victims were always posed in a sexually provocative manner. My book, *The Boston Strangler File*, details how Albert DeSalvo, the Boston killer..."

Nancy Grace quickly cut off his book promotion. "And that's the same as in Charleston? Because we don't really know the details of these killings. The police down there aren't saying much of anything. You told me you're on your way to Charleston. Is this something you're doing on your own?"

"No, Nancy, our police commissioner asked me to offer my help and professional expertise to the Charleston PD in any capacity..."

Billy slammed his hand on the bar. "He couldn't have worked on the case because he wasn't even on the job yet. Who's he kidding?"

"The Boston Strangler case is already fifty years old," Cal said. "He just wants to plug his damn book."

Billy's phone rang. He quickly reached for it and checked the number.

"Chief Murphy here." He got up from his seat and retreated to a quiet corner of the room.

After a brief conversation, Billy returned and dropped his phone on the bar.

"I got news for you," he said in a low voice and then took a long gulp of his Jack and placed the glass on the bar. "That was the mayor. You see that knucklehead up there on TV?"

"Yeah?" Cal said.

"He'll be in my office tomorrow morning. The mayor wants me to meet with him and see what he has to say."

"How are you gonna handle Powers?"

"I got it figured out. Me and Walter will see if there's anything useful this guy knows, buy a copy of his book, and then we'll send him home. No big deal. The mayor will go along with whatever we decide."

On the TV, Seamus Powers was winning the talking contest with Nancy Grace.

"Hey, Oscar," Billy said. "Give us another round. I think I'm gonna need it."

He leaned over to Cal. "We've got to find the connection between the two cases. I mean, what in God's name does a psycho in Charleston have to do with an ancient murder case in Boston? Does this Powers bastard just want some fame? He strikes me as one of those kinda people, don't he?"

Cal looked up at the TV again. Powers was still talking non-stop. "Yeah," Cal said, staring at Seamus Powers, "I know just what you mean."

"On the bright side, what more can happen?" Billy took a swallow of Jack. "First, a crazy killer. Then a flaky psychic shoved down my throat, a psychopath stalking my best friend's wife, and a blast from Boston's past to tell me how to do my job. I'm just one lucky guy today."

Chapter 19

Rachel Ackerman's residence
9:30 a.m. Wednesday, July 4, 2012

ROSA WAITED PATIENTLY TO SEE THE desk sergeant while she munched on a cookie in one hand and fanned herself with a magazine in the other. Dressed up for the Fourth, she wore a loose-fitting white peasant blouse and bright blue, ruffled floor-length skirt. Around her neck were multiple strands of red, white, and blue beads, and she wore matching bracelets on her wrists. Despite her effort to style her red hair festively, it still looked suspiciously like a cheap hairpiece.

"Ready to go, Rosa?" Billy said. Rachel Ackerman's daughter, Camilla, had been kind enough to let investigators take another look at the crime scene. Billy thought it was a good opportunity for Rosa to prove her psychic powers. She gobbled up the remaining cookie with one bite and stood up.

"Yes, sir!" she said. They walked out to the car where the Callahans were waiting, and Rosa lumbered into the back seat.

"So, you guys have been married for a long time, right?" Rosa said to Danie.

Danie smiled. "Oh, yes. A long time."

Cal was only half-listening to the conversation, since sitting in the front seat with Billy driving had its own pressures.

"He's quite a catch." Rosa winked at Danie.

Rosa was enamored with Cal. Well, that was fine. Cal was an attractive man, and women sometimes flirted with him, even in her presence. She had learned long ago to take it in stride. What mattered to her was what Rosa could learn at the crime scene. She had never seen a psychic in action. Last night at Billy's house, she'd done some research on psychics who assisted police investigations and was surprised to learn how many people believed they could see events that others couldn't.

"Well," Rosa said, "maybe if I could see some police reports, just to get an idea as to what happened, the condition of the body and so forth. That might help me better understand the situation."

"Maybe later." Cal glanced at Danie with a look that implied it would never happen.

When Rosa first saw the Ackerman mansion, her jaw dropped. The arched windows over the wide, elegant entrance reminded her of a cathedral.

"Who lives here?" Rosa said. "God?"

Billy rapped gently on the massive oak door using the brass swing handle. Even from where he stood, Cal could hear a distinct echo from the inside. In a few moments, the door swung open.

A slim, attractive woman with auburn hair tied stylishly behind her head appeared. Her short black dress displayed a nicely proportioned figure. As Billy introduced the Callahans and Rosa, Camilla greeted each one politely.

Billy asked if they could examine her mother's bedroom. "Yes, that's fine. Anything to help, really."

Billy motioned for everyone to follow him up the fabulous marble staircase that curved gracefully to the second floor.

"These stairs probably cost more than my entire house," Rosa announced.

The door to Rachel Ackerman's bedroom was open. Danie saw that the room had been restored to its original condition. The thick velvet drapes were tied back, letting the morning sun brighten the room. The carpet was spotless, and the bed was made up with a beautiful flowered duvet. She was relieved that the oppressive heat of the murder room had been eradicated by air conditioning and a ceiling fan.

Rosa wandered around the room for a few minutes. She went to the closet, examined the windows and the bed, and then tilted her head to the ceiling slightly as if she were trying to hear something and then brought her finger to her lips. Billy tried to talk to her, but she stopped him.

"Please," she said. "Just one moment."

Cal retreated to a corner of the room with Billy, choosing to give Rosa a free hand.

"I feel very cold here," Rosa said with eyes closed. "Very cold." She extended her arms in front of her with palms turned up. "She let him in," she whispered. "He's very smart, this person. Meticulous. I see a... a... very small room. I taste something." She smacked her lips together and made an expression of disgust. "I taste something bitter. Ugly. It was in this room. He was on the floor here." She pointed to the nearby closet and closed her eyes again. "On his belly. He played with something." She paused for a moment. "Did you find coins in this room?"

Danie gave Cal a look.

"He cleaned up after himself," Rosa blurted out. "He cleaned a glass. I don't know why." Before anyone could answer, she held up her hands again. "He was all over this room. He went in there."

She pointed to the highboy which had its drawers searched. "And there!" She placed her hand on one of the end tables. "But he took nothing," she said as she roamed around the room, stopping every few feet as if she was listening to voices inside her head.

"He's a liar," she said. "A schemer. And full of hate. But he's very cunning, like a… a…"

"A fox?" Billy offered.

"No!" Rosa snapped. "Like a jackal!"

"Can you see his face?" Danie asked.

"He spent a lot of time in this room. Things were moved. Rearranged. I don't know why. The images come and go, and I don't want to give the wrong impression, but it's very confusing." It seemed as though her vision had come to an end, but then Rosa started shaking. Slowly, she was drawn to the front of the bed, stopping directly over the exact spot where Rachel was found lying on her back, each leg draped over a chair with a pillowcase wrapped around her neck. Rosa's mouth opened as though she was going to scream, but only a strangled gurgle escaped her lips. The shaking became more pronounced, and she started to lose her balance.

Cal rushed to steady her and helped her to a nearby chair. She collapsed like a deflated balloon.

"I'm trying hard, but there's no more."

"I think we can call it a day," Cal said. "Rosa, do you want some water?"

Tears ran down her cheeks as she nodded feebly and crossed herself. "Dear Lord…"

Danie reached in her briefcase for the small bottle of water she always carried and gave it to Rosa. "Yes, no more today."

The water seemed to revive Rosa. A few minutes later, she pulled a hand towel from her bag and wiped her face. "I need a cigarette, for God's sake." She pulled out a crumpled pack of Virginia Slims, placed a cigarette in her mouth, and began the mandatory search for a match.

"Rosa," Cal said, "maybe you should go outside for that smoke. I don't think Camilla would like the idea of smoke in her mother's bedroom."

"Oh, sure, sure. No problem." Rosa found the matches and walked over to the glass doors that led to an expansive terrace, went outside, and lit up. While Cal and Billy waited in the bedroom, Danie joined Rosa who was already puffing away.

"Are you all right, Rosa? You were very upset in there," she said.

"I'm okay, Doctor. I don't know where it comes from. It just happens, you know?"

"Do you actually see images? Or is more like impressions?"

"Both." Rosa took another drag on the cigarette. "I first noticed my gift when I was a teenager. I would be able to see certain things others couldn't. Like I knew the names of strangers on a bus or in the supermarket. At first, I wasn't scared of it at all."

"You couldn't see who did this murder?"

"Then, one day, I passed someone on the street, and I saw a dark aura around this man in my neighborhood, almost like a halo."

Danie was beginning to understand Rosa liked to finish her thoughts before she answered questions.

"And that scared you?"

Rosa shrugged her shoulders. "No, not right then. The next day scared me. I heard that he died. And he wasn't the only one. It happened many times after that."

Danie was impressed. No one knew about the stacks of pennies in the closet except the police and the killer. This detail was never reported in the press and never discussed outside the inner circle of investigators. It had to signify something. "Rosa, can you actually see who killed Rachel Ackerman?"

"I wish I could. I'm sorry, Dr. Danie, but it doesn't work like that. I can't demand something of the gift. It sort of tells me. I'm just a listener if you know what I mean."

"I think I understand," Danie said, unable to hide her disappointment.

"But, there was just one more thing." Rosa glanced through the terrace doors into the room. She covered her mouth with a hand. "I don't know if I should say this. I didn't want to say it in front of everyone, you know." She paused. "The chief and all."

"Please tell me, Rosa. Anything would be helpful."

Rosa extinguished the cigarette with her fingers, rolling out the residual tobacco over the terrace rails. She placed a trembling hand on Danie's shoulder and whispered into her ear.

"He knows who you are," she whispered. "Be very careful!"

She took one last look at the death scene and hurried downstairs.

Chapter 20

At headquarters, Danie was still thinking about Rosa's warning when she felt the phone vibrating in her pocket. She instinctively answered it.

"Hi, Doc," the voice said. "How you be?"

It was *him*. Lester gave her the creeps, and now that he was on the loose, he freaked her out even more.

"Lester, what do you want?"

"Just thought I'd call and see how you're making out."

"That's bullshit! Go to hell!" Everyone in the conference room froze in place. "We're gonna get you. Count on it." She signaled for Joe to come closer. Then she grabbed a pen and wrote *Lester* on the back of a manila folder. Joe quickly punched in a number on his own phone.

"I thought shrinks understood people," Lester said. "You should try harder."

Joe wrote some words on the blackboard at the front of the room. "Tracking now," he wrote. "Keep him on!"

"When you kill someone, Lester," Danie said, "the police stop trying to understand you. Turn yourself in."

"For what? I haven't done anything."

"You killed that hospital guard."

"Oh yeah," he said. "I forgot."

"You should surrender."

"I always wanted to give myself up to you, Doc." He laughed. "And here, I thought I wasn't getting through to you. You probably fuck like an animal." He made some strange guttural sounds.

"Lester—"

"I wanna take a video of you and me. That's what I have planned for you, Doc. Tie you up and listen to you beg for a while. I'll put it online. You'll be famous."

Danie tried to get an admission from him. "Did you have to kill those women?"

"For God's sake! How many times do I have to tell you that I didn't kill those bitches? 'Do not be afraid; you will not suffer shame. Do not fear disgrace; you will not be humiliated.'" he screamed.

Danie looked at Joe, who gave the thumbs-up signal to show that Lester's call was successfully being tracked. She followed Cal and Joe out of the room and down the steps. RK and Billy were already sprinting through the parking area to the chief's police unit.

"Lester, let me ask you something," Danie said.

"I'm all ears."

"Why mimic the Boston Strangler? What does he have to do with this case? Can you tell me that?"

"It's been nice talking to you, Doc. I hope we can chat again."

"I want to help you, Lester—"

"Yeah, help me get a needle in my arm."

"Let's make a deal. You come in, and we'll talk about—"

"Are you fucking crazy, Doc? Do you know what the cops will do to me? I'll be shot on sight. That's not gonna happen to me. I got to go now, girl."

MARILYN J. BARDSLEY AND MARK GADO

"Lester, call me tomorrow. Maybe we can work things out."

"Yeah, sure. We'll have coffee. But you can skip the dessert. Bring me a bullet-proof vest instead."

The connection went dead.

"Did he hang up?" Joe said.

"Yup. Damn!"

Joe and Danie jumped into the chief's Crown Victoria and charged out of the lot onto East Bay Street at full speed. RK and Cal got into another unmarked car directly behind them.

"Sprint tracking said he's in the area of Broad and Legare near St. John's Church," Joe said. "It's a cell tower right off Meeting. We're not gonna be able to tell the exact spot where the call originated, but we can get pretty close. I called over some additional units to cruise the area. They all have a description of Lester, so maybe we can spot him. Hurry up, Chief!"

"Don't you worry. We'll be there in a few minutes."

They raced down East Bay toward the church where mid-day traffic blocked their way. Thanks to the screeching siren, and Billy's tendency to drive like a New York cabbie, a path opened in the left lane. At Broad Street, they made a quick right. Billy shut down the siren and slowed to a crawl.

"Okay, the target tower is right over there behind those buildings." He pointed to a row of homes on the right. "That means the call had to come from somewhere in this area. My guys are talking to Sprint security right now to find out the limits of the tower and to get a better idea of the perimeter. Let's just cruise around. Maybe we'll spot him. Danie, you check the sidewalk, I'll keep an eye on the street."

They scanned the pedestrians on the sidewalks and drivers of oncoming vehicles. It had only been several minutes since the phone call so Lester could still be somewhere in the area. If he was on foot, he couldn't be too far away. If he was in a car, though, he might be on the interstate ramp out of downtown already or speeding over the Ravenel Bridge.

They had no way of knowing. Billy had several other units join in the search and directed central to broadcast a description of Lester so every police officer in the city would be on alert. They circled St. John's, went up to Queen Street, over to State Street, and cruised through Broad again. There were hundreds of pedestrians on the sidewalks, and the streets were thick with traffic.

"It's gonna be tough," Joe said. "Too many people out. He could be anywhere."

They carefully drove up and down streets and alleys, Billy checking streets from City Hall down to the Calhoun Mansion without seeing anyone suspicious.

They began to relax. He drove north on King Street, where men, women, and children were strolling the sidewalks, going to lunch, or simply enjoying the holiday. Just as they passed the intersection of Market, Danie saw a man about to cross the street. At the moment, he was about to step off the curb, the man glanced at the traffic, and Danie caught a glimpse of his face. He was smiling.

"There he is!" she shouted, pointing across the street.

"Where? Where?" Joe yelled.

"Over there! With the blue shirt and the white cap! See him, Joe?"

He looked up and down the street. "No, damn it! Which corner?"

"There!" Danie pointed again to the northwest corner. "He just turned away. Did you see him, Joe?"

"Yeah. White hat, blue shirt, walking away. He made us for sure. Chief, make a U-turn. We can still get him!"

Billy switched on the red lights and hit the siren. He did the best he could to make the turn while avoiding oncoming traffic. He jammed the accelerator to the floor, spinning the rear wheels as the massive car struggled to gain traction.

"Watch out, Billy!" Joe yelled.

At that moment, a city bus traveling in the opposite direction smashed directly into the right front fender.

"Damn!" Billy yelled. The car came to an abrupt halt with its front bumper buried into the left wheel well of the bus.

"I'm going after him!" Joe said as he jumped from the car. Danie looked down the street and saw the silhouette of a man running. He was already halfway down the block. Billy got on the radio as RK jumped from his car and ran after his partner.

"Central, we just had a sighting of the suspect at Meeting and Broad," Billy said clearly but urgently on the radio. "Send all available units to the area forthwith. Suspect is on foot running south on King with officer in pursuit. He's wearing a blue shirt and a white baseball cap, dark pants. This unit was also in a PDO accident with a city vehicle. Send a tow."

With that, Billy yelled, "Let's go!" and bolted from the front seat. Billy and Danie trotted after Joe who was running full speed chasing Lester. Within seconds, they heard sirens in the distance in all directions.

"Hey!" the bus driver yelled out from his window. "Where y'all going? What about my bus?"

"Watch my car!" Billy shouted back at him as Joe's voice came over loud and clear on the portable radio.

"Central, suspect last seen heading south on King near Clifford. Officer needs assistance!" Joe sounded out of breath already.

"Central to responding units. Plain clothes officer in pursuit reports suspect last seen on King near Clifford."

"Sector 3 responding!"

"Sector 2 on the way!"

When Billy and Danie reached the location, they slowed to a walk. Several police units sped by, lights on and sirens blaring. They rested at the next intersection while Billy called headquarters on his phone.

"I don't wanna hear it," he shouted. "Tell them to keep looking!"

After he had hung up, he turned to Danie. "Let's start back to the car," he said. They haven't found him yet. Joe and RK are over on Meeting Street. They think Lester was headed there when they last saw him. But no luck yet."

"He's smart," Cal said. "I wouldn't be surprised if he caught a cab already."

"Central, have units check local cab companies," Billy said into his radio. "See if they picked up anyone with that description in the last few minutes."

When Joe returned from the foot chase, he said he lost visual contact with Lester as soon as he reached Clifford Street. For the next hour, police units saturated the downtown area, checked public transportation, and stopped dozens of cars and possible suspects.

"I don't know what the hell happened to him, Danie," he said. "He could have reached Meeting and just slipped into the crowd. And to tell the truth, if he did that, we probably would have missed him."

"The moment you lose visual contact," RK said, "it's over. It's just too easy to get away."

Billy had to return to the accident scene while everyone else got a ride back to headquarters with a uniformed unit. By the time they arrived, no one could hide their feelings of disappointment. Lester had slipped through their fingers.

"Joe, let's get Sprint back on the line and see what else they got," RK said. "Maybe Lester made more calls. You never know."

Billy walked into the room, out of breath and sweating profusely. "Looks like he's in the wind," he said. "And we got nothing to show except a crippled bus and banged-up police unit. I'm gonna hear about that from the damn press, I bet."

"Nobody got hurt," Joe said. "So what's the big deal?"

Danie was exhausted. The stress was overpowering, and running around the city in suffocating heat and humidity made it worse. Trying not to make it obvious, she pulled up a desk chair and unceremoniously plopped down in it.

"You all right, Danie?" Joe said. "Here's a bottle of cold water."

She smiled. One of the things she liked about Joe was his compassion. Though he could be tough and hard-nosed, he could also be attentive and caring.

"Yeah, thanks," she said. "Just worn out, I guess. How do you guys do this all the time?"

He laughed. "Well, not every day is like this."

"Yeah," RK said from across the room, "just half of them."

Danie looked at her watch. In a few hours she would be at a podium for the press conference. Fortunately, the lightweight summer suit she bought for the occasion wasn't badly rumpled by the running, but sweat and humidity had done plenty of damage to her hairdo and makeup. She promised herself that as soon as she had some water, she would summon the energy to get up out of the chair and make herself look presentable.

"I'm going to the ladies' room," she said.

A short distance down the narrow hallway was a door with the word "WOMEN" painted in bold black letters. Inside was a typical police station bathroom: a toilet, a sink, and a mirror. Spartan but utilitarian. As she placed her purse on the sink, her phone rang.

"Hello?"

"You almost had me," he said softly.

Danie had sort of expected he would call her again. "It's only a matter of time," she said.

"You'll have to try harder then."

"Where are you?"

"Far enough away so the fucking cops can't reach me."

"They'll catch you. It's what they do."

"I doubt it. I saw you and your boyfriend in the car before you saw me." He laughed. "I figured they'd be looking for a guy with a blue shirt and a white cap. I mean, police work is so basic, ain't it? So I ducked into a store and bought me a nice new suit, compliments of the generous Mr. Higgins. He's the gift that keeps on giving, I tell you. Then I went out into the street and just went about my business. I counted seven police cars—"

"Your days are numbered, Lester."

"It just goes to show you how thin the line is between you and me, Doc. I mean, I put on a fucking jacket and a tie and all of a sudden, I'm just like everyone else. Think about that. It should be a little scary to you."

"Don't call me anymore."

"Awww. Don't be that way, Doc. After all, we have a date, and I'm getting hungry for you. Very hungry."

"Lester?"

Nothing but silence.

"Lester?"

Danie switched off the phone and dropped it into her purse. She glanced at the mirror over the sink and brushed the damp strands of hair away from her face. The ceiling light was dim, but she could see that her eyeliner was smeared, leaving a dark shadow under her lashes. Rummaging through her purse, she finally found some tissues to clean her face. As she did, she looked into the mirror at the dim reflection. It seemed foreign for a moment as if it were someone else, a stranger even. She stared into the woman's eyes, searching for recognition, hoping for something familiar.

No need to panic, she told herself.

It was only fear.

Chapter 21

Charleston Police Department
4 p.m. Wednesday, July 4

THE INVASION HAD BEGUN.

As Danie and Cal approached police headquarters on Lockwood Drive, they saw a convoy of satellite trucks, media vans, and an army of reporters outside the building. Nancy Grace's interview with Seamus Powers had been enough to ignite a national curiosity about the Charleston case. Early that morning, a flood of phone calls had poured in from newsrooms wanting to know about the links to the Boston case. Inside the building, dozens of reporters clamored for information. They shouted questions in rapid succession without waiting for any answers and demanded to interview the chief.

"They're coming out of the walls," Billy said.

"It seems that way, partner." Cal had seen it before in Atlanta and knew the feeling well. Today's objective was to control the revelations caused by the Grace interview. Earlier in the day, Billy had politely declined Seamus Powers's condescending offer to help.

It had taken several early morning hours for the Charleston PD spokeswoman and her counterpart from Mt. Pleasant to prepare their joint press release. The final version noted that the three recent homicides were linked to one another and may have some similarities to the fifty-year-old Boston Strangler case.

The objective was to guarantee that the investigation was their departments' top priority. The strangler story was finally ready for prime time. Billy and Bert agreed there was no point in unnecessarily alarming the public but on the other hand, if there was a serial killer active in the Charleston area, they felt an obligation to be as forthcoming as possible.

No one wanted to face specific questions at a press conference, but if they had any hope of controlling the flow of information, it was necessary. Mayor Campbell gave the order to notify the media he would hold one at four o'clock. Soon after, Campbell's office received a request for a CNN interview, which was quickly followed by similar requests from all the major networks. When the press conference began, Billy and Bert Allman stood together at the podium with Charleston Mayor Campbell, Mt. Pleasant Mayor Jesse Featherston, Walter, and Danie. After Mayor Campbell had introduced the group to the press, he turned the floor over to Billy.

"Good afternoon," Billy said. "Three women were recently murdered in our community. Margaret Walsh, a Mt. Pleasant widow, was found dead inside her home on the night of June fourteenth. The body of Mrs. Rachel Ackerman of Charleston, a retired teacher, was discovered in her home on June thirtieth. And, the body of Victoria Trowbridge-Howells, wife of businessman Harold Howells, was found on the family's yacht at the Charleston City Marina on July first.

"The same person may have committed all three homicides. As a result, we have convened a task force of top Charleston and Mt. Pleasant detectives, forensic technicians, and crime experts. The task force is headed by Deputy Chief Walter Johnson. I want to assure the people of our city that bringing this killer to justice is our highest priority."

As he spoke, Billy watched a tall, skinny woman with unusually short, jet-black hair elbow her way through the crowd to a spot just in front of the podium. Over the years, he had spoken to all the female reporters in Charleston and many from other South Carolina cities. This reporter was not one of them, and the way she pushed to the front of the crowd suggested that she was unfamiliar with southern manners.

Just as Billy was turning over the podium to Bert Allman, the woman loudly interrupted. "Why are you hiding the fact that the women were raped and mutilated?"

Billy tried not to sigh or roll his eyes. Ambitious reporters, he thought, could cause so many problems.

"All we're able to tell you at this time, ma'am, is that all three women were strangled. We have—"

The reporter's face contorted in anger. "What about the bodies being intentionally posed after death? Why are you covering that up?"

"Ma'am, if you'll be patient, we'll tell you as much as we can without compromising the investigation."

"Was it a burglary gone wrong?" someone shouted from the back of the room.

"We don't believe that it was," Billy said. He added that there was no evidence of forced entry and no evidence that anything was taken by the killer.

Chief Bert Allman spoke. "There's a very important point we would like to make. As far as we can tell, the victims were comfortable enough with this individual to let him into their homes. It's also possible he gained access through an unsecured door or window. We urge everyone in our community to be extra cautious.

Keep your doors and windows locked. If you have an alarm system, make sure you use it.

"Above all, do not let people into your home that you do not know well, no matter how innocent or respectable they appear. If someone comes to your door and tells you he has been sent by one of the utility companies to repair wiring, or a faulty gas connection, or to upgrade your Internet service, or whatever, do not let him inside until you get confirmation from the company that supposedly sent him.

"This killer may present himself as trustworthy and polite. If someone—"

"How do you know the killer is a man and not a woman?" the woman with jet-black hair demanded.

"Let me just say this," Bert said. "If a stranger wants access to your home and he doesn't check out with the company that he says sent him, please contact us right away."

The reporter persisted. "Wouldn't a woman be more likely to let another woman into her house, even if she didn't know her?"

"Maybe," Bert said, "but we are confident that the killer is male."

Another reporter raised his hand. "Chief, is there any chance the Boston Strangler has come to Charleston?"

"We don't think so. If the Boston Strangler were still alive, he would have to be seventy or older. It doesn't make it impossible, just highly unlikely."

"What about a copycat?"

"Maybe," he said. "We're looking into it."

"What if Albert DeSalvo faked his death?" one reporter asked. "Is there any proof he isn't alive?"

"To answer your questions about any of the connections with the Boston case, I want to introduce a former FBI profiler who has worked on many homicide cases and has agreed to assist in our investigation, Dr. Danielle Callahan."

Danie, nervous but confident, stepped up to the podium to address the last question.

"For those of you who are not familiar with the Boston Strangler case, Albert DeSalvo was a burglar and rapist who confessed to being the Boston Strangler. He never went to trial for those murders, but he was imprisoned for life because of his many sexual assaults. He was later murdered by another inmate."

The local Fox reporter signaled that he had a question. "Dr. Callahan, the joint statement by the police indicated that even though there were some similarities to the Boston crimes, there were also significant differences. What would those differences be?"

Danie was grateful for such an easy question. "Well, one striking difference is that the Boston Strangler victims all lived in apartment buildings in the city and surrounding suburbs. Police suspected that the killer might have posed as a maintenance worker to get into the victims' apartments.

"However, in the Charleston cases, two of the women lived in their own homes, where the ruse of a being a repairman sent by the apartment superintendent wouldn't work. The other woman lived on a yacht at the Charleston City Marina.

"Another difference is that the victims of the Boston Strangler were middle-class women of modest means. The three women in the Charleston case were well-to-do. For the most part, they were less likely to be victims of crimes. They lived in neighborhoods that were safer than most. They had alarm systems and weren't normally exposed to criminals and drug dealers in their daily lives."

"Considering nothing was stolen," the Fox reporter continued, "do you think the women's status was what made them targets?"

"I'll let Chief Murphy take that question." Danie stepped aside.

"We don't know at this point," Billy said. "There has been some media speculation on this, but it is not grounded in any evidence that we have."

The aggressive female reporter wasn't giving up. Her voice rose an octave. "You still haven't said they were raped and sexually posed."

"A number of things rumored in the press are essentially speculation, and that's all," Billy said trying to hide his annoyance. "Ma'am, I'm afraid I can't comment on your specific question at this time."

The woman became visibly angry and stormed out of the room without another word. She had never identified the news organization she represented, but somehow Billy knew they could expect less-than-objective coverage.

Billy answered a few more questions and then turned the podium back to Mayor Campbell. A career politician in his seventies, Campbell was adept at handling the press. He told the reporters that the two police departments were the best in the region and that both he and Mayor Featherston had full confidence that they would catch the killer.

After the conference, Billy spoke to the local press and then decided it was time to head home. The camera lights were turned off, and the reporters shut down their tablets and laptops.

"How about we pick up some pizza on the way home?" he said to the Callahans.

"That works for me," Danie said.

As soon as they arrived at Billy's house, Billy and Cal set up their laptops on chairs on either side of the large-screen TV in the family room. That way everyone could view the coverage on the networks at one time and hop from station to station. The case was the top story on most of the cable news shows. The presentation was the same on each newscast: snippets from the day's press conference, obituary photos of the victims, a summary of the Boston case, and the inevitable concerns from "experts" that the killer must be caught before he killed again in mid-August. Only one of the cable stations took a different tack.

"Do you think the police in Charleston are up to the task?" The news anchor put on his best serious look.

"I never say a bad word about my fellow cops," the former New York City police official said when the network put him on a split screen. "But you gotta understand what it's like down there in the South. It's a good-old-boy place. You get ahead with who you know, not what you know."

"Probably very racist," the host said.

"Oh, yeah," the man replied. "They get their fun harassing blacks any time they can. You talk about intimidation; they're the experts in that. Confederate flags all over the place. I heard that even their K9s—that's what they call police dogs—are racist. But you got to understand that the people there have a terrible education."

The anchor quickly keyed off his guest's comment. "Do you think that if Charleston increased the educational requirements for police, that they wouldn't be so racist?"

Billy hit the remote.

"I can't take it," he said. "Of course, these assholes never heard of Reuben Greenberg, our chief for more than twenty years, who was a black Orthodox Jew. Undereducated? He had three master's degrees from Berkeley, graduated from the FBI Academy, and was a professor at three state universities. All this racism bullshit makes me mad as hell."

Billy's phone rang.

"Hey, Walter, what's up? That's just great. I'll be sure to watch it. Thanks for the warning."

Danie poured some more wine for Lindy and herself. "I take it that was the deputy chief."

"Ricky Ramirez is going to interview Troy Driggers on his show this evening."

"That's the councilman gunning for the mayor's job?" Cal looked up from the glow of his computer.

"One and the same, partner."

"I thought Campbell was a very popular mayor," Cal said. "Does this Driggers guy even have a chance in the next election?"

"Don't underestimate Troy Driggers," Billy said. "This guy is going to be mayor someday. Mark my words, he'll do whatever it takes. He's just waiting for the right opening, and this damn case might be it."

He turned to the Ramirez show on the large screen TV, which was already showing clips from the morning press conference.

As soon as the clips were over, Ramirez told the audience he was grateful Driggers was able to appear on such short notice. Driggers had a full head of dark brown hair cut in a classic Ivy League style, with a touch of gray at the temples. His facial features were just a bit too large to be considered handsome, but they were distinctive: dark, bushy eyebrows, a well-shaped square jaw, and a wide smile with perfectly capped teeth. His plain white shirt and dark suit coat were the backdrop for a traditional tie of red and gold stripes.

"Nice dresser," Danie said. "Really nice dresser."

"That's about all that's nice," Lindy said. "He's everything I hate in a politician."

"Mr. Driggers," Ramirez said, "I can always count on you for an unvarnished opinion. Are you satisfied with the handling of this strangler case?"

The big smile on Driggers's face that had continued through Ramirez's flattering introduction was quickly replaced by a frown.

"Our city is in crisis," he pronounced each word slowly. "I'm sorry to say I don't see the quality of leadership in the administration that will end this crisis anytime soon."

"Sir, are you referring to Mayor Campbell or Chief Murphy?"

Driggers tilted his head and folded his hands together. "Well, both of them are responsible for this dangerous situation. First, it took almost a month for the police to 'fess up to the fact that we had a deranged killer preying on the women of our city. Then, through their negligence, the main suspect broke out of a supposedly high-security facility for the criminally insane and killed a guard. This guy is still running around loose.

"In just a few weeks, another woman may die. If this great city cannot keep our women and children safe from homicidal lunatics, then we have the wrong leaders. Period."

"What do you suggest, Mr. Driggers?" Ramirez often posed questions that fit Driggers's political ambitions.

He smiled in a confident way. "Well," he said, "let's face it. The public needs accountability. I'm going to propose to the council that we set a date. If the killer isn't caught by then, both the mayor and the chief of police should tender their resignations."

Billy hit the remote again, and the screen went dark. "I can't stand to listen to *him* anymore either. He knows damn well that the county runs that hospital where they had Lester. The PD has nothing to do with that place, nor does the mayor."

"Is there anything you want us to do to help?"

"I don't think so, Cal, but thanks. I'm going back to my office. I need to think and discuss some things with Walter. Who, by the way, may just be the next Reuben Greenberg. Racist police force, my ass!"

Chapter 22

He stood up, very pleased with himself, and slightly drunk.

Off came his tie and suit jacket so he could be comfortable for the rest of the show. He flopped back into the chair and sat mesmerized while fragmented clips of the press conference appeared on the small screen. For the next hour, he flipped through the channels, riveted by the non-stop coverage of what he had done.

He had finally claimed the undivided attention of the press. Here he was, at the top of the news on every network. They had all kinds of titles for him: The Charleston Strangler, The Boston Strangler of the South, The Boston Strangler Reincarnated. It was all quite flattering. Time to celebrate. He emptied his glass and opened the other bottle of wine.

The scene at police headquarters was chaotic, to say the least. He was amazed at the number of press vans and satellite trucks parked in front of the building. Towering antennas and satellite dishes were spread out everywhere, on the lawns, in the street, and on the sidewalks. Dozens of frantic reporters roamed through the parking lot, cell phones pressed to their ears and urgent looks on their faces, all driven by the fear that one of their competitors might get a morsel of information they didn't have. A pack of fucking vultures, he thought. They eat their own.

Fox's Greta Van Susteren showed the entire press conference. When it came to the reporters' questions, he laughed at their stupidity, but then good-looking Dr. Callahan took the podium and his smile faded. Greta called her "a talented former FBI profiler and the hero of the Marcy Scott case in Atlanta." He didn't know that. Then one of the big-name serial killer experts, who knew her well, said if anybody could identify the killer; it would be her.

He wished he had known that earlier, but no big deal. No matter how good she was, he was still much smarter, of that he was sure. He was no ordinary killer, and things were far more complicated than she could ever imagine, FBI profiler or not.

But as he listened to what she said, his view of her shifted dramatically. He became convinced that, in time, she would become more dangerous, and he would be wise not underestimate her. He had come too far and accomplished too much to have it threatened by this mercenary bitch who had no idea of who she was up against. What gave her the right to interfere with his plans, his life, and his future? His self-confidence turned into apprehension, and his elation changed quickly to anger.

He poured more wine into his glass as he wondered what he should do about her. That was the question. Maybe give her a warning, a signal that she should abandon this case and go back to Savannah. Or maybe it should be something a bit more dramatic.

More personal.

Chapter 23

North Charleston
11:00 a.m. July 5, 2012

WAS DWAYNE DEVERAUX THE KILLER OR just a sadistic liar?

Danie found elements of his personality disturbing. Like his false sense of propriety about Victoria's morals. Hard to believe that he thought that beating up his girlfriends put him on higher ground than Victoria. So what if she was a lonely woman who was trying to relive her youth? The task force had quickly produced dozens of possible suspects for Danie to examine, but so far only Lester, Deveraux, and possibly the mysterious Dr. Etheridge had the potential to be the real killer.

There were two women who might help her get a better fix on Deveraux's character but finding them took more time than she expected. Both women had complained to the police about his assaults, but neither had pressed charges. Danie couldn't help but wonder why.

One of the young women, Patricia Simmons, had married and left the Charleston area, so RK and Danie went to her parents' home and talked to her father. He said she refused to be interviewed because she was going through a difficult pregnancy and didn't want to relive her painful relationship with Deveraux. His wife was with their daughter, helping her prepare for the birth of her child.

"Was your daughter living here when she was dating Deveraux?" RK said.

"No," he said. "For two years, she rented a room in Charleston near to the Wendy's where she worked. She didn't have no car. One day, Mama gets a call from the manager saying Patty come to work all bruised up. Patty said she fell down the stairs, but the Wendy's lady didn't believe it. I took off work and brought her home. Both her eyes was all black. And she was so scared and crying. First, she didn't want to tell me who done it. Afraid I'd take my shotgun to the bastard. Ain't nobody gonna hurt my baby like that and get away with it."

"Is that when she talked to the police?" RK said.

"No, damn it!" Simmons said. "She was too scared. I told her anything ever happens like this again, I'll shoot his balls off. And I meant it. Next day, she puts all this make-up on her eyes and begs me to drive her back to the Wendy's.

"What does she do? She goes back with that man again. She tells Mama how sorry he is, and how he loves her, and all kinds of crap like that. A week later, she calls Mama crying. He got mad at her again. This time, it's for wearing lipstick to work. Ever hear of anything like that? So what does this bastard do? He puts his gun in her mouth and tells her if she ever cheats on him, he'll kill her."

"What'd you do?" Danie said.

"I picked Patty up from work and took her right to the police station. I told her that if she don't report him, I would. Then we went to the Wendy's again, and I talked to her boss. A real nice lady. I told them what I done and what I was gonna do."

"Did you ever meet Deveraux?"

"Just once, about a week after Patty left, when he come here looking for her, mad as hell. Said she stole money from him. That was a lie. Patty never stole nothing. Not ever. I went in the house and got my shotgun. He left right away."

"Did Patty ever go back to him?" RK said.

"Getting her away from the bastard is the best thing I ever done for her," Simmons said. "I took her to my sister's in Myrtle Beach. Now she's married to a decent guy. Owns a gas station with one of them little stores in it. She's gonna give us our first grandbaby if all goes well."

"I'm glad things worked out so well, Mr. Simmons," Danie said.

"That S.O.B. sure has another side to him than what he showed to us," Danie said to RK when they got outside. "Thank God her father got her away from Deveraux before there was a tragedy."

"That's an understatement," RK said. "By the way, we found the other woman Deveraux assaulted. Her name's Ruby Middleton. She lives with her mother here in North Charleston, and we can go talk to her now if you want."

"Sure, let's go."

RK made the call, and they were on the way.

The trip didn't take long. Right after they passed the Mark Cross Expressway, they made a series of turns into a residential area west of Rivers Avenue. Ruby Middleton's home was in a dreary neighborhood. The houses on this short street looked almost exactly the same. They were rectangular boxes with roofs, small windows in random places, one small door in front, and one on the side. Middleton's home was no exception. The tiny front porch was propped up by sagging metal poles, and broken cinder blocks stood where steps used to be.

When RK knocked at the door, the curtain in a nearby window parted. Seconds later, a woman who could have been a model at one time opened the door. It was hard for Danie to guess her age because her heavily made-up face bore the ravages of too much time in the sun. On the other hand, her figure, generously displayed in hot pink short shorts and a matching halter, would have made any teenage girl jealous.

"Mrs. Middleton? I'm Detective Rod Karlovec, Charleston PD, and this is Dr. Danielle Callahan."

She took the cigarette out of her mouth, flicked the ash on the porch, and smiled. "My God, if Charleston is hiring cops as handsome as you are, I'll have to find some way to get myself arrested. Come on in, sweetheart, and you, too, dear. I'm Gloria, Ruby's mother."

The two large fans and ancient window air conditioner almost made the temperature bearable, but the smell of cigarette smoke was overpowering.

"Have a seat," Gloria said, pointing to a large couch and armchair. The furnishings looked expensive, surprising considering the poor condition of the house. Danie guessed she was renting and brought the furniture from another home.

"What can I get you to drink, Detective? I have beer, whiskey, vodka, lemonade, cola."

"Thank you, ma'am, but I'm not real thirsty right now."

"And you, dear?"

"I'm fine, thank you, Mrs. Middleton."

"Ruby's in the bedroom, trying to get our little two-year-old, Samantha, to take a nap. Maybe we can talk a bit about this Deveraux before she comes in."

"Did you ever meet him?" RK said.

"Oh yes," she said with emphasis, crushing her cigarette out. "Ruby came home with him right around the holidays last year. Between Christmas and New Year's, it was. We weren't living in this dump then. We had a place in town. I was impressed with Mr. Deveraux. He was very polite, handsome, and educated. He had a good job, and he drove a Lexus. He seemed so much better than anyone else Ruby brought home. My mother was here at the time. He brought with him some real good barbecue from Charleston for our dinner. Stayed and talked with us for about an hour, played with little Samantha, and then he and Ruby went out for the evening. I really wanted Ruby to have a good husband, but I knew it was hopeless."

"Mrs. Middleton," Danie said, "why did you think it was hopeless for Ruby?"

She sighed and lit another cigarette. "Ruby is such a sweet girl, but she is a child, and she'll always be a child. The social worker calls Ruby 'developmentally delayed.' The good Lord was generous to Ruby when it came to looks but not when it came to brains."

The bedroom door opened, and a cute little girl with curly blonde hair ran into the room.

"Samantha, girl! You're supposed to be taking a nap," Gloria said. "Now be a good girl and go back to the bedroom."

"No!" she said emphatically and cracked a big smile.

Gloria put down her cigarette and scooped her up. "This is my granddaughter, Samantha. Now say 'hello' to the nice visitors."

Samantha laughed. "No!" Then she giggled again, wiggled down from her grandmother's lap, and turned toward the bedroom. "Mommy!" she squealed.

Into the room walked a beautiful girl wearing a pink sleeveless shift and sandals. Her long, dirty-blonde hair fell over her shoulders in graceful curls, and her skin was a perfect, radiant pink. Her most extraordinary feature was her large, blue eyes and long, dark lashes. She was no more than five foot three and could hardly weigh more than a hundred pounds. Ruby could have passed for fifteen or six-teen years old, even though she was twenty.

"Ruby," Gloria said. "This is Dr. Callahan and Detective Kar-lovec. What do you say?"

With a smile that could have graced an angel, Ruby said, "Ma'am, I am so happy to make your acquaintance, and sir, I am so happy to make your acquaintance."

There was something very mechanical about Ruby's greeting. "Ruby, darling, why don't you take Samantha back to the bedroom and try to make her take her nap."

"Yes, ma'am." She picked Samantha up and returned to the bedroom.

"What a lovely daughter and granddaughter you have," Danie said.

Gloria didn't answer right away. She seemed to be on the verge of tears. "Yes, they are. Thank you." She paused for a few moments to compose herself. "Ruby is both God's gift to me and punishment for my sins. When I'm too old to take care of her, my prayer is that Samantha will be able to look after her."

"Mrs. Middleton, would you prefer that we come back another time?" Danie said.

"No," she said. "Not really." She sat down in a chair in the corner of the room. "Someone has to tell the story."

"Mrs. Middleton," RK said. "Clearly, Mr. Deveraux did some-thing that made you take Ruby to the police station. Please tell us what he did."

"If I tell you, how can you protect Ruby and my granddaughter? I just don't want some police or court record that will hurt the two people I love the most."

"I give you my word that Ruby and Samantha will be protected," RK said.

Gloria thought about that. "Okay, I'll tell you exactly the way it happened." She crushed out a burnt-up cigarette and lit another.

"A couple of weeks after I met Deveraux, he came to me, Ruby in tow, and asked my permission to have Ruby and Samantha live with him in a fancy mobile home he'd rented just outside North Charleston. I deluded myself into believing that maybe Ruby's beauty and sweet personality and Samantha's charm would be enough for this man to marry her. Even though my mother was totally against it, I gave Deveraux my permission.

"At first, things seemed okay. Ruby and Samantha were happy. But then I started to notice things. Deveraux wasn't really living there. He still lived in Charleston. Later, neither Ruby nor Samantha seemed happy anymore. She became withdrawn, and Ruby was depressed, but she wouldn't talk about it.

"Well, one day Ruby asked if I would take care of Samantha for the weekend because she wanted to go to Miami with Deveraux on a business trip. After she had left, I started to comb Samantha's hair, and I noticed there were these round crusts in several places on top of Samantha's head. She cried when I touched them. I took her to my doctor because I thought she had an infection. I went into a tizzy when he told me what had happened to Samantha."

"What did he say?" RK said.

Gloria's eyes teared up. She took a tissue from the table and wiped her eyes. "He said the scabs on Samantha's scalp weren't an infection but burns from drops of acid that had been put in four different places. It was clear to him that it was child abuse. By law, he said, he had to report it. I begged him to hold off for a day or two until I could find out what happened. He was also Ruby's doctor, and he understood that she was slow."

Danie was stunned. It took her a few moments to find the right words. "Are you saying that Deveraux did this?"

"I didn't know. Ruby was smart enough to cover up something that was wrong," Gloria said. "If she, for some misguided reason, put acid on Samantha's scalp, then I had to face the reality that Ruby could not bring up Samantha by herself. If Deveraux did it, I wasn't sure what I'd do."

"How did you find out who did it?" RK said.

"I went over to Ruby's mobile home Monday after she and Deveraux had come back from Florida. I took Samantha with me. Ruby was by herself. I told her that I just found burns on Samantha's scalp and asked Ruby what they were. Finally, I got the story out of her. Deveraux had two men over several times the week before, and they took turns having sex with Ruby. One of them wanted to teach Samantha about sex, so he took off his pants and had Samantha play with his—you know what." She started to cough and drank some of the cola next to her."

Danie took a deep breath and sat down in a chair facing Gloria. "My God, this must have been devastating. What did Ruby do to protect Samantha?" she said.

Gloria's hand trembled as she lit another cigarette. "Ruby was so angry that she told Deveraux she was going to take Samantha and come back here. He went into a rage and stormed out. Later he came back with a small bottle. He grabbed Samantha, took an eyedropper, and put drops of that acid on her head. Ruby said Samantha screamed in pain. He told Ruby that if she ever tried to leave him, he'd take the acid and ruin her face and Samantha's. They're terrified of him.

"Then I learned he took her to Miami because he wanted her to have sex with an old man who was going to put money into some real estate scheme. When she refused, Deveraux dragged her into another room and beat her. They came back the next day, but he was still furious. He beat her again, stripped off her clothes, and stuck a pistol in her mouth. He said he'd use it if she didn't do what she was told."

"That's when you took her to the police station?" Danie said.

Gloria hesitated. She was clearly nervous about answering Danie's question and bought a little time to think. "To be perfectly honest, I was afraid the police would learn the whole story and the county would take Samantha away. I knew the police weren't going to let me do all the talking and Ruby isn't smart enough to know what to say and what not to." She looked closely at both Danie and RK, trying to gauge their reactions.

"You did take Ruby to the police, though," RK said. "I have their report."

"Yes," Gloria admitted. "There had to be a record of his abuse, but I made sure that it was limited to him hitting Ruby. I just wanted that bastard out of her life. I don't have the money to fight a man in court who's a lawyer. We didn't press charges."

RK thanked Mrs. Middleton for her cooperation and advised her to call immediately if Deveraux tried to contact her daughter again.

On the way back to the car, Danie was worried. The assaults on Ruby and Samantha upset her so much, it was impossible to get them out of her mind. She tried to place herself in Gloria's position and wondered what she would do. Eventually, she admitted there was a huge gap between what she would have wanted to do and what she could have actually done. Of one thing she was sure: Deveraux was a sadistic monster.

When they returned to the command post, RK briefed Billy, Joe, and Cal.

"What a piece of shit this guy is," Billy said.

"Chief, it's gonna take a little time," Joe said. "We need subpoenas for the phone and bank records. I'll call the solicitor's office in the morning and see if we can get a rush. In the meantime, RK has an in with a local bank." He turned to RK, who was sitting at his desk writing everything down.

"Yeah," RK said. "I can give him a call and see if we can take an unofficial look just for our own knowledge. We'll still need the subpoena later, Joe."

"Understood. Do we know his phone carrier?"

"What's his cell number? We can get it from that," Billy said.

"I'll do it," RK said as headed down to the record room.

"Let's see what this son of a bitch has been doing for the last six months," Billy said. "We'll track his calls, his credit cards, and his ATM transactions every waking minute until we know when he even took a goddamned leak."

Chapter 24

Charleston County, South Carolina
Friday, July 6, 2016

No sleep.

Danie never slept well when she was away from home, even at a friend's house. No matter how exhausting the day had been, falling asleep took forever, and staying asleep was difficult at best. After she finally dozed off, she would wake up at odd hours. It was always something: the bed was not comfortable, or she heard noise from the boats on the river or the dogs barking. She was grateful Billy and Lindy had welcomed them into their home. It was so much better than being in a hotel, especially with Magic. However, she respected Lindy's rules for her own pets, which meant Magic slept on the porch with Bandit and Biscuit. At home, when Magic cuddled up to her at night, he had a calming effect and helped her sleep. She missed not having him by her side.

Being away from home generated stress, even though her career frequently required it. The more she traveled, the more she discovered how important her routine was to her happiness. At home, she awoke at six a.m., and ten minutes later, she was running on her treadmill, watching cable news.

Afterward, she would go back to the bedroom and gently remove Magic without waking up Cal. While Magic roamed around the backyard, she would have her coffee and toast and make a list of what she had to do that day. She wished that someday she wouldn't have to travel so much. Each day, she would go home to Cal and prepare dinner with him, talk about the day over a glass of wine, and play with their wonderful puppy.

More than the strain of being away from home, she felt the pressure of the clock ticking until the next murder and the realization they were no closer to the killer than the day they had arrived in Charleston. The tip line provided dozens of leads that had to be chased down but yielded nothing of real value so far.

Dr. Etheridge, with his curious habit of seducing women, was still under investigation. Some on the task force thought Deveraux was the best suspect, but others were convinced that Lester Beach was the killer.

Danie was at the command center reviewing reports on the most promising leads when Joe called. He said that nine women had complained about Dr. Etheridge's behavior and one said he had tried to force himself on her. Billy wanted all nine women interviewed, and there were just two left. Would she be able to talk to them today and urge them to make a statement?

The first woman was a thirty-nine-year-old teacher, Norma Hollis, who had met the elusive Dr. Etheridge during an educational seminar at a Marriott hotel in November of 2011. Hollis lived in a small complex with perhaps two dozen apartments in three separate brick buildings. The grounds were neatly landscaped, and parking was conveniently located in front of each building.

A few seconds after Danie knocked, a female voice called out, "Who is it?"

"Hello," Danie said. "My name is Dr. Callahan. May I speak with you, Ms. Hollis?"

"About what?"

"I'm with the police department. It's about your call concerning Dr. Etheridge." She heard the sound of the turning lock.

"Oh yes, I remember." There was a pause, but the door didn't open. "That was a week ago. And what kind of doctor are you with the police department anyway? They have doctors?"

"I'm a psychologist, Ms. Hollis. I'm helping the Charleston Police Department on a special case."

When the door finally opened, Hollis held it in front of her like a shield.

Danie showed her identification. "Okay, come on in," Hollis said.

Danie didn't know if this was always how Ms. Hollis was, or she'd been careful due to the news reports.

The apartment was neat and organized. Hollis locked the door and pointed to a sofa that sat in the middle of a living room opposite a loveseat and a bamboo coffee table. Hollis had an easy smile and friendly demeanor that made Danie feel as if she had known her for years.

"I'm working with the police department on an investigation," Danie said, "and they asked me to talk with you about this Dr. Etheridge—"

"Doctor? The hell he is."

"—and your relationship with him."

"Listen, I had no real relationship with him." She sat on the loveseat, lit a cigarette from the open Marlboro pack, and put it between her lips. "He's a bastard, whatever his name is. And it's not Dr. Etheridge at all. He can't be a medical doctor, can he?"

"We don't know for sure yet."

"You married, Doc?"

"Yes." Danie was a bit surprised at the question.

"Happy?"

"Very. My husband is a good man."

Hollis took a deep drag on her cigarette and slowly exhaled. "That's nice to hear. Especially today. So much crap going on. Nobody wants to stay married. Women have kids left and right, and they're not even married."

Danie nodded her head in agreement. "Times have changed," she said. "What happened when you met him last year?"

"I'm a schoolteacher in Charleston. During the year, we have seminars on trends in the educational system and things like that. During a break, he came over to me, and we had a brief conversation. He said his name was Dr. Etheridge, but to tell you the truth, I never thought to ask him if he was a medical doctor or a dentist or what, you know?"

"So what did he say to you?"

She rolled her eyes. "What did he say? What do all men say? 'You're cute. You're hot.' And we fall for it every time!" She laughed easily. "You've heard the same line, Doc. Am I right?"

Danie couldn't help but laugh. "I guess I have. Did you leave the seminar with him?"

"Nope. He got a call from somebody. Said it was his assistant. Whoever the hell it was, he spoke on the phone for a few seconds and said he had to go. I talked to him that night in the hotel bar for maybe twenty minutes. That was all."

"When did you next hear from him?"

"A few weeks later, I don't know. Maybe a month? I got a call from Etheridge, and he said, 'Remember me?' He told me he was impressed with me and said, 'Can we go out to dinner?' I said sure.

I was kinda surprised in a way because I had almost forgotten about him."

"How did he behave?"

"We went downtown to a very nice restaurant. We eat, we drink. He's a good talker, and I'm not gonna lie, he's a handsome guy. I was attracted to him. And the fact that I thought he was a doctor—a neurologist, he told me. Well, you know what I mean."

"Sure. I understand."

She took a deep breath. "Well, pretty soon we're in a hotel room, and he's stripping off my clothes. What the hell. I slept with him. But I don't want you to think I do this all the time. I don't."

"It's okay, don't worry."

"Look, I was divorced last year; I had a rough break-up. A real mess. I was looking for someone new, you know. Someone better than what I had. And to tell the truth, I wanted sex, okay?"

"Did you see him after that night?"

Hollis took another drag on the cigarette and then dropped it into the ashtray.

"No. That was the only time. I was very disappointed that he never called again. I kept wondering what I might have said or done that turned him off. I kinda hoped that we could keep the relation-ship going." She paused for a moment and then smiled. "And he was great in bed, too."

"Look, Ms. Hollis—"

"Call me Norma."

"Okay, Norma, the police need you to give a formal statement. Are you willing to do that?"

"Well, I've been thinking." She looked away for a moment and brushed her hair back from her face. "Look, I don't want my name plastered all over the papers, you know. Then everyone will know

I slept with the guy on a first date. I mean, what damage was really done? It's not like he raped me. Yeah, I had too much to drink, but I would have slept with him if I'd been stone cold sober."

"I know how you feel, Norma. But you know what happened to these women who were murdered, right? I'm not saying it was Etheridge who did it, but he should be checked out."

"But will the press find out my name?"

"Ask for Detective Rod Karlovec, they call him RK. Tell him how you feel. He's been assigned to your case. I'm sure he'll do everything he can to keep it confidential. Can you come in today?"

Norma wiped her forehand with her free hand. "Yeah, I guess so."

"Good, they'll be waiting for you." Danie gave her the address of the command center. She stood up and walked to the door. "Everything is going to be okay, Norma. Try not to worry."

Danie looked forward to comparing Hollis's experience with Lisa DiAngelo's in Mt. Pleasant, the second name Joe provided. After she crossed the Ravenel Bridge and got onto Coleman Boulevard, Danie drove through some very quiet neighborhoods until she reached Simmons Street. She passed Ocean Grove Cemetery and turned onto a street flanked by stately palm trees.

Lisa DiAngelo, a forty-two-year-old divorced nurse who worked at the VA Medical Center, planned to move back to New York to be closer to her family. She told police she met Dr. Etheridge at the Medical University of South Carolina, where she attended an awards presentation for a prominent surgeon in Charleston. Etheridge claimed to know the surgeon and spoke very highly of him. About a month later, Etheridge had called her. They went to dinner several times. During the last date, she said, he tried to rape her.

When Danie reached DiAngelo's house, she parked the car in the empty driveway which led to a two-car garage and a stone walkway. The path curved to a large front door with a bulky brass knocker on a metal plate. The lawn had not been mowed recently and the weeds had already grown slightly taller than the grass. Danie thought Lisa DiAngelo might not be home and assumed she worked during the day. That would explain why the police could not get in touch with her. Across the narrow street, two children rode their colorful bicycles on the sidewalk and up their own driveway. In the distance, music played on a loud radio. A single car drove slowly past the house.

The front porch had an overhead supported by several handsome wooden columns. There sat an old rocker, made from tree branches, nestled into the farthest corner next to a rattan coffee table. An empty teacup lay on the floor next to the chair, and a vase containing faded flowers rested on the railing near the door. She knocked on the door and waited for a reply. No answer.

She knocked again.

Danie peeked through the window next to the door but saw no movement. She saw a sofa, two chairs, and a table in the living room. In the mailbox attached to the siding, several days of mail of assorted sizes and shapes were stuffed into the box.

She decided to leave a note. As she reached into her bag and grabbed the pad, Danie dropped the pen to the floor. When she bent over to pick it up, the window to her right shattered into a thousand pieces. Danie thought she heard a car backfire. At the same time, she saw a small sedan idling at the end of the driveway. The two children across the street who were riding bicycles froze in place and stared directly at her.

"What the hell?" Danie said.

She instinctively ducked down and in that fraction of a second, another explosion and a small hole appeared in the door a few inches from her head. She hit the porch floor hard, scraping her knees on the rough floor. Her left cheek rubbed on the wood planks, but she still managed to get an unobstructed view of the street. The car that was idling at the end of the driveway pulled away quickly with its tires screeching. Danie never saw the driver and couldn't tell what kind of car it was. It disappeared in a few seconds, and the neighborhood seemed peaceful once again.

She heard a dog bark. Then another. The kids across the street had dropped their bikes on the sidewalk and sprinted into their homes. A man who had left his home next door ran toward her. Danie didn't know if she was wounded, but she didn't feel any pain. She was just too scared to move.

"Hey, are you all right, lady?" the man said as he jumped onto the porch. "Are you okay? Damnedest thing I ever saw. The guy in that car was shooting at you! Are you hurt?" His face and voice seemed so far away to Danie.

"I—I—don't think so." The words echoed in her brain as if she was talking into an empty tin can. For the first time, she felt a pounding headache. "What—what happened?"

"Take it easy, lady. Everything is okay now. Let me help you up."

Her legs felt like gelatin, and she was too weak to stand on her own. For a moment, she couldn't remember where she was or what she was doing there. She was lost inside of what seemed like a garbled dream. After a few minutes, she drifted back into reality as the sights and sounds around her became connected again. From somewhere— she wasn't sure if it was inside her brain or it was real—the wailing of distant sirens got closer and closer.

She was alive.

Chapter 25

Chief Billy Murphy's residence
4:45 p.m., Friday, July 6, 2012

CAL HAD SAT DOWN AT THE kitchen table with a cup of coffee when the doorbell rang. Magic and Billy's coonhounds answered hysterically from the porch while Billy's son went to see who was at the door.

"Uncle Cal!" Dustin said. "Come here!"

Cal heard a deep voice ask if the chief was home. He rushed to the door where a Mt. Pleasant police officer helped Danie inside. She appeared dazed, her eyes were red and puffy, and one side of her face was bruised.

"Oh, my God! What happened?" Cal lifted her chin up so he could see her face.

The officer tried to explain. "Some guy in a car took—"

"I can tell him," Danie said softly. "I'll be okay."

By then, Lindy had come to the door. Danie tried to put on a brave face as she told them about the man who had shot at her twice.

Cal held her to his chest. "Danie. Baby. Oh, Jesus." He walked her over to Billy's armchair in the family room and eased her into it. "Sit here and rest."

He went back to question the officer. "Where is this son of a bitch? I'd like to tear him to pieces."

"I know how you feel, sir," he said. "But the shooter was long gone by the time someone called it in. We don't have anything to go on. No description. No license plate number. Not even the color of the car."

Cal was not in the mood for explanations. "Wish to hell you'd caught that crazy bastard in Summerville. Now he's going after my wife!"

The officer was surprised. "You mean the guy who killed the guard? Lester Beach?"

"Bastard keeps calling my wife. He's still hanging around this area. Obviously."

Cal briefly explained the connection between Danie and Beach to the officer, and then called Billy at the station.

As he listened to Billy vent his anger, Cal had visions of Danie lying in a hospital bed. What if a bullet had hit her and she had died?

"I've got to take Danie home," he said. "That's all there is to it. She can't stay here with a killer after her. No case is worth that risk."

Billy thought about that for a minute. "Is that what she wants?"

"I haven't said anything to her yet about going home."

"Do what's best, but I bet she won't go."

"I know," Cal sighed. "I know."

After the phone call, Cal went back to the family room, where Magic had cuddled up against Danie's legs. Normally the dogs were not permitted in the house, but Lindy had made an exception.

"Sweetheart," Cal said. "I've given this a lot of thought. We need to go back home. This investigation is not worth losing your life."

"A lot of thought? You just heard about it a few minutes ago."

"Well, once I heard what happened, I thought of nothing else but keeping you safe."

There was a long pause before she answered. "I'm not abandoning this case."

He would never consider arguing with Danie in front of others, not even a friend like Lindy, but Danie took the subject off the table, saying she was going upstairs to rest.

"Take Magic with you," Lindy said. "It's okay if he sleeps on the bed."

"Thanks, Lindy. He'll be a good boy."

Cal sat down for a while to clear his head and come up with a plan. Then he went out to his car to make sure his Smith and Wesson .38 was loaded. As he slid it under the driver's seat, Billy's car tore into the driveway. Cal shut the door and leaned against his car as Billy hustled to join him.

"I talked with the officer who brought Danie home," Billy said. "He said only a couple of little kids were around when the guy shot at her, and they couldn't even agree on the color of the car. Thank God he was a lousy shot."

Cal stared into the distance. He was frustrated and angry.

"Come on," Billy said. "I could use a drink. I think you could, too."

They walked into the house in silence. Billy pulled an unopened bottle of eighteen-year-old Macallan single malt from his liquor cabinet.

"Hey, my friend, if ever we needed something to steady our nerves, it's now," Billy said as he poured several fingers of scotch into each glass. "I want you to know how much I appreciate what you and Danie have done to help us, but I agree that she'd be much safer at home."

Cal took a sip and then posed a question to Billy that had dominated his thoughts since he heard about the attack.

"You think Lester did this?"

"Maybe. But if he did, he's a damn fool."

Cal nodded. "Better we should think about why someone would want her out of the picture. Any ideas?"

"Because she's probably touched a nerve. Maybe it is Beach. She's always thought he had it in him to be the killer."

"I know," Cal added. "We just don't have any evidence to tie him to the victims."

"I don't know if you're aware of this, but a couple of the news shows have made her into a bit of a celebrity," Billy said. "Walter's wife pays close attention to what's being said about the case. It looks like reporters researched some of the cases that Danie worked on and got glowing reviews, especially from her former boss at the Bureau. Plus, she's smart and beautiful. Not surprising that the media would focus on her."

"Walter mentioned that to me, too. Danie just laughed when I told her."

"What if she's already come into contact with the strangler?" Billy said.

"I'm not sure," Cal said. "She's interviewed several characters the task force has brought in, but she's never said she thought one of them was the killer."

"I'm betting she's already interviewed him," Billy said. "Maybe he was smart enough to fool her."

"Could be."

They sat in silence and sipped their drinks. The whiskey burned Cal's throat but warmed his belly. His mood began to change.

Billy set his glass down on the end table nearest him. "Danie was interviewing women Etheridge had seduced," he said. "What if he was the one following her? Or it could have been Deveraux. Joe learned he was out of the office all afternoon."

MARILYN J. BARDSLEY AND MARK GADO

Cal said nothing. He was trying to decide what to do next.

"So, has Danie agreed to go back to Savannah?" Billy did his best to keep the skepticism from his voice.

"No," Cal said. "She refused."

Billy cracked a little smile. "I'm not surprised." He paused for a few moments. "Here's something to think about. If Danie insists on staying, you might suggest that you'll agree—if she promises to have either you or one of the detectives with her when she goes out."

Cal was suddenly tired of talking about it and did not bring up the subject during dinner. He sat quietly during the news that Billy and Lindy always watched after dinner, all the while thinking about how to protect Danie. Afterward, Billy talked to him about task force activities for the better part of an hour.

The attempt on Danie's life weighed so heavily on Cal's mind he did not feel like he could contribute anything to the conversation. He said good night and went upstairs to check on her. She was asleep with her puppy curled around her feet. Rather than wake her, he decided he would spend the night sleeping on the back porch with the dogs. He kissed her on the forehead and scratched Magic's ears to wake him.

At first, Magic balked, but finally, he followed Cal downstairs. In the kitchen, Cal took one of the treats Lindy had offered that morning and headed out to the porch. Magic settled in next to him on the couch and waited impatiently for a piece of the frosted pecan roll he knew was coming.

For Cal, the scene brought back the simplicity of their lives in Savannah. Once a month, when Danie went to her hairdresser, Cal would sneak in two large, frosted cinnamon buns. "Fat pills," Danie called them and refused to let the tempting snacks in the house. No incriminating crumbs with Magic around. How he longed for that simplicity again.

Cal decided he liked Billy's face-saving compromise. Deep down, he didn't want to fight with Danie over this issue. If it were only up to him, he would take her back to Savannah immediately. If anything ever happened to her, he would always blame himself.

He lay on the couch while these thoughts and a litany of others raced through his brain like an endless train until he drifted off into a restless and fitful sleep.

Chapter 26

Goose Creek, South Carolina
4:00 p.m. Saturday, July 7, 2012

MIKE PICKED UP THE PHONE ON the first ring. "Detective Cecchi. How can I help you?"

"Hi, my name is Olga Steward. Dr. Clay Etheridge is coming to my house this evening."

That statement left him speechless for a moment. He pushed the recorder button and then asked her where she lived and when she expected him.

She said she lived in the Village of Goose Creek and met Etheridge about a month ago at a fundraiser for a women's shelter. They had talked briefly about the emotional problems of women who came to the shelter. Etheridge told her that as a neurologist, he had some ideas that might help. Unfortunately, he had received an emergency call and had to leave, so they never finished their talk. Steward had given him her card and said she looked forward to hearing from him.

About a week later, she received an email from the shelter's chairman warning her about Etheridge and giving a number to call if he contacted her. She called immediately, she said.

"Ms. Steward, do you mind if I put you on speaker?" he said. "We have other detectives who want to hear what you have to say."

"Yeah, okay."

"Did Etheridge give you his business card?"

"No. I asked him for one, but he said he had left them in his car. He promised to call me when he had a chance. About ten minutes ago, he called and asked if I was busy this evening. I told him I wasn't, and he asked if he could come over to my house. I gave him my home address, and he said he would come by at 8:30." She paused for a moment. "Now, if you don't mind, can I ask why the police want to talk to him? I hope he's not a criminal."

Steward's call injected real excitement into a slow Saturday afternoon. Now was the opportunity to determine whether the mysterious phony doctor was really a suspect or just a liar.

The task force had made finding Etheridge a priority after nine women in the Charleston area had notified the police after the self-styled Dr. Etheridge called them. Most of the women had said they were quite interested in seeing the charming doctor again, but some of them had been cautious and asked him to call back the next day.

Of those women, some had gone online to research Etheridge, trying to find his LinkedIn profile, Facebook page, address and phone number, membership on dating sites, and news articles. They discovered nothing whatsoever about a neurologist named Dr. Clay Etheridge. When several days had passed with no call from him, they had contacted the police to report that a man was trying to meet them using a phony identity.

"Well, he hasn't broken the law," Mike told Steward. "But he's a difficult person to find, and we need to question him about a meeting he had in Charleston. Nothing you should be alarmed about."

"Well, Detective, that's a relief. He seems like such a nice man."

"Can I get your address, Ms. Steward?"

"I live at 800 Hamlet Circle. It's a cream-colored house. Do you want me to give you some directions?"

"That won't be necessary, ma'am. We'll be there well before he arrives. If Etheridge calls again, please don't say anything about us coming to your home."

After contacting the Goose Creek police, Mike, Ira, and the Callahans were on the way to Olga Steward's home, approximately twenty miles from Charleston. They quickly formulated a plan to capture Etheridge when and if he showed up. Cal and Danie sat in the back seat while they tried to imagine every possibility. Mike wanted to arrest Etheridge on sight and bring him in immediately, while Ira wanted to take a wait-and-see approach.

"Once Etheridge drives up to Steward's house, you can get his real name from the license plate and check out his rap sheet," Ira said. "We can run warrants after that."

"That might not work, Ira," Mike said. "The car may not be registered to him. Even if it was, Etheridge might not be his real name. The best thing to do is have him show ID."

Danie jumped in. "Look, I was thinking that maybe I could pose as her and be in the house when he arrives." Cal glared at her, but before he could protest, she continued. "It might be wise to avoid exposing her to this guy if he realizes she called the police on him. If he's our strangler, you don't know what he might do to her."

"Whoa!" Cal said. "And what he might do to you? I'm not letting you talk to him alone, not after what happened in Mt. Pleasant."

"Cal's got a point," Mike said. "How about this? Cal and Ira wait with the Steward woman in the car while I check out Dr. Don Juan with Danie. You can talk to him as long as you want, but I'll be there too, just out of sight, in case things go bad."

Cal's ego was wounded. "Why not me?"

"Cal, trust me," Ira said. "If something goes wrong, you want a cop there to handle it."

Cal relented. "Okay, I guess that makes sense, but I'll be ready to help take him down."

They pulled off the highway into an attractive suburban community. The house on Hamlet Circle was a well-maintained colonial with a wrap-around front porch and a large front yard. They had a good forty-five minutes before they expected Etheridge. A petite redhead in a yellow sundress opened the door before they even made it to the top of the porch steps.

"Hi, I'm Olga," she said with a big smile. "I can't wait to hear more about Dr. Etheridge. Please come in."

They walked into a large foyer with a stairway to the second floor and a hallway to the kitchen. On the right was the living room with a grand piano and expensive-looking French country-style furniture. On the left was a large, formal dining room.

"You have a lovely home," Danie said.

Ira admired the highly polished maple finish on the grand piano.

"Do you play, Ms. Steward?" he said.

"I used to, but my hands are too small to navigate the keys as well as I'd like. Now my daughter, Jackie, she has perfect hands for the piano and plays beautifully. She's amazing."

Mike let the small talk go on for another minute before turning the conversation to the business at hand. He explained to Steward that it would be safer to let Danie wait inside while she stayed with Ira and Cal in the car. He didn't mention that once Etheridge arrived, they would run the plate on his vehicle to ascertain his identity and check for warrants. No sense in letting her think she was bait in a sting operation.

"I'm just thrilled that the police would come all the way from Charleston to make sure I'm safe."

"Your safety is paramount, ma'am," Mike said.

Steward walked with Cal and Ira to the car. Ira then moved the car several houses down from Steward's home.

Meanwhile, Mike had plenty of time to examine the house and decide what to do when Etheridge arrived. He noticed that the laundry room had a small window that was not far from the windows in the alcove off the living room. If they could keep the windows open, he could hear everything that went on in the alcove.

"I think the laundry room is the best place for me to stay, Danie. I can close the door if he comes into the kitchen for some reason. Ira and I are going to text each other on our phones. Let's test this when you get back to the alcove."

Danie walked around the kitchen to familiarize herself with the surroundings. She tried to imagine every possible scenario when Etheridge arrived. She went to the alcove and opened the windows to make sure that Mike was able to hear everything.

At twenty-two minutes after eight, a white Mercury Grand Marquis pulled into the driveway. Danie glanced out the window and then texted Cal and Ira.

Etheridge was tall and slender and dressed in a light gray suit with a gorgeous, shiny, azure-and-silver striped tie. She had been expecting a man in his mid-fifties, but he appeared to be younger. The neatly combed gray hair was a little too perfect to be his natural color, Danie thought, but it made him look older and more distinguished.

As he neared the top stair, Danie opened the door.

"Dr. Etheridge," Danie said. "Please come in."

He had a very engaging smile, and Danie could see why women found him sexy. "My dear Ms. Steward, you've done something different to your hair," he said in a deep, confident voice. "It's very flattering."

Apparently, he had forgotten what Olga Steward looked like. Perhaps after deceiving so many women, he couldn't tell them apart.

"Thank you, Dr. Etheridge. It's so good of you to come. Let's sit in the alcove over here. It's the most comfortable place in the house."

"Please call me Clay," he said. "May I call you Olga?" There was something gentle and sincere in his manner that made Danie feel at ease with him.

"Of course, Clay," she said and offered him one of the cookies Steward had put on the coffee table.

"M-m-m. Thank you. I have no other plans for this evening. I'm all yours."

"Oh, good," Danie said. "I wanted to get to know you better. We had so little time to talk before you had to leave. I was going to call you last month, but I couldn't find you in the local directory. Where do you live?"

"In Florence. I have a townhouse there."

"Any children?"

He laughed. "Not that I know of, and to your next question— no, I'm not married."

"Not married ever or not married now?" Danie said with an impish smile.

"Not married now, but when I find the right woman…" he said with a wink.

It was Danie's turn to tease. "So who would be the right woman?"

He seemed to have his answer right on the tip of his tongue. "Beautiful. Like you. Intelligent. Like you. Concerned about others more than herself. Just like you."

Danie smiled. He was good. His lines were polished and perfect. She guessed they could have played games for a while longer, but there was no point in it. "I understand you've been doing a lot of interviewing," she said.

"Interviewing? I don't know what you mean." He looked genuinely surprised.

"You know, interviews for the right woman. From what I've heard, you've done a lot of research."

Suddenly that handsome face showed signs of panic. "I don't know what you're talking about. I can't imagine where you got that idea."

"Well, Clay Etheridge, if that's your real name, quite a few of the women you seduced made complaints to the police. Were you aware of that?"

"Who are you? You're not the Olga Steward I met last month."

"I could ask the same of you," Danie said. "You certainly aren't a neurologist because that man doesn't exist."

"Why are you interrogating me? What have I done?" There was no anger in his voice, only surprise.

"You were with Victoria Howells before she was murdered."

He seemed incredulous. "Victoria who? I don't know what you're talking about."

"The bar at the Peninsula Hotel in Charleston on June twenty-seventh. You spent the night at the hotel with her."

"Oh, the blonde woman from England? We had a delightful breakfast together the next morning." Suddenly, he stopped talking as he grasped what Danie had said. "She was murdered? How awful."

Danie wasn't letting up on him. "And you were with her again the night she was killed," Danie said as though she had some evidence.

He shook his head vigorously. "No. Definitely not. You're wrong. I only saw her that one time." He paused for a few moments and lowered his voice. "I never see any of them again after we make love. Look, I may have misrepresented myself to women, but we had sex, that's all. They enjoyed it, and so did I. These women that you say complained to the police, did they say that I mistreated them? I'm sure they didn't."

He looked at her curiously. "Just who are you, anyway?"

Danie ignored the question. "You're right. Only one of them said you tried to force yourself on her, but she resisted. They were angry because you used them. You led them on and then dumped them with no explanation."

He looked sheepish. "I suppose I should have let them know I wasn't coming back, but I couldn't bring myself to call and say something that would hurt their feelings."

"You could have sent a note with some kind of apology."

"There were just too many of them. Usually two or sometimes three a week."

Danie was stunned. "Two or three a week? You've got to be exaggerating."

A boyish smile crept over his face. "I really like women."

She couldn't help but smile. "I guess so if that number is really true. By the way, what's your real name?"

He paused for a moment and then said, almost regretfully, "I'm Ford Gaskins."

"Ford?"

"Yeah, Ford is short for Buford, a name I detest. I sell power tools to retailers in the Southeast."

"And I'm Dr. Danielle Callahan, a psychologist and police consultant."

He let that information sink in for a moment. "Police? Am I in trouble?"

"No," Danie said, "but I'm just curious. You said you'd never contact a woman again after you've made love to her. You mean to say you've never had a relationship with any women?"

"Just one." He hesitated and looked down at the floor. "My wife."

"Your wife?" her voice rose with indignation. "You said you weren't married." The wounded look on his face made it clear to Danie that she had hit a nerve. "Does she have any idea how much you cheat on her?"

"I don't know," he said calmly. "She died more than twenty years ago."

Danie did a double take and softened her tone. "Oh, I'm very sorry, Ford. She must have been quite young. What a shame."

He didn't answer, but Danie didn't see much value in continuing the interview. She did not believe he was the strangler and didn't think he could kill anyone. "Ford, I'll be right back. I just need to do something in the kitchen." She went back to the laundry room where Mike sat in a chair with a 9mm automatic in his hand. He stood up and carefully shut the window so they could talk.

"Mike, what did Ira and Cal find out about him?"

"Clean as a whistle, and the car is registered to him. His name really is Buford Henry Gaskins. Ira says he's forty-four years old, lives in Florence, and has no rap sheet. Cal checked social media, and his LinkedIn profile says he's worked for the same company for seventeen years. The photo at the top of his Facebook page is of him and his wife when they were young. In April, several of his friends commented on the anniversary of her death. One said that he had to get over her loss and move on with his life."

"Well, he doesn't seem like a killer," Danie said. "He might be screwed up, but I don't see any indication of violence. Do you want to come out and talk to him?"

"Yeah." Mike put his gun away. "Let me call Ira and have Ms. Steward sit tight for a few more minutes. We'll want to ask him some questions about Victoria."

Danie returned to the living room alcove and told Gaskins that the police wanted to ask him a few questions. She was surprised when he asked her for a business card.

"Who knows," he said. "I might need a psychologist someday."

Danie didn't doubt that and gave him her card.

"Sure, I'll wait," he said. "After all, I haven't seen Olga Steward yet."

When Danie got to the car, she thanked Steward for her help and chatted with her until the detectives finished questioning Gaskins.

"So, is it safe to talk to Dr. Etheridge or not?"

Danie wondered how much she should tell Steward about this man and if the pretty redhead would be his next conquest. Maybe Steward would be the "right woman" who he seemed to be searching for.

"Safe?" she said. "Oh, I think so." She paused for a couple moments. "If I were you, I'd insist on knowing his real name and profession. Ask for his business card. If he won't give you one, I'd advise you to tell him to leave."

Steward seemed puzzled. "So he's not Dr. Clay Etheridge?"

"No, he's not, but that's for him to explain."

"So he's some married guy fooling around?" She looked thoroughly disgusted at the thought.

"No," Danie said. "His wife died a long time ago. You might ask him about her." She made a mental note to contact Steward to find out what Gaskins said and did if Steward followed her suggestion. Such an interesting case and such an interesting man.

After the interview with Gaskins, Mike spoke with Steward, thanked her for her cooperation, and rejoined Danie and Cal. On the way back to Charleston, Mike shared everything they had learned about Gaskins. They all came to the conclusion that he wasn't much of a murder suspect.

"What makes a guy like him tick?" Ira said.

"I know this sounds strange," Danie said, "but Ford Gaskins is still, in many ways, married to his wife. He probably didn't have sex with any woman until years after her death. This compulsion to have one-night stands probably developed gradually. Maybe he found himself becoming too attached to one woman and broke off the relationship.

"In his mind, he can't allow himself to form another long-term relationship. Either out of loyalty to his wife or fear that a new wife might die or leave him. He even asked for my card. Maybe he'll call for an appointment one of these days."

"Over my dead body," Cal said.

Chapter 27

"SHE SAID, 'IF I HAD TWO arms, I would have broken the bastard in half!' That's a direct quote," Joe told Billy during the phone call.

"I wish she would have," Billy said. "Would have saved us a lot of trouble."

The Callahans were sitting with Billy at his kitchen table, discussing Lester Beach. The task force had located the woman Beach claimed he robbed and assaulted. Elisha Goodwin was a fifty-two-year-old, tough-as-nails retired corrections officer who had lost her left arm in a motorcycle accident. She remembered the event well, she said and could describe him perfectly. Goodwin had signed a statement against Beach and said she wanted him prosecuted.

"Lock him up, Detective," she had said.

Billy went over the new information with the Callahans. He had to prepare the mayor for a face-off with Troy Driggers on the evening news. Danie had told him all about the Dr. Etheridge interview. The phony doctor had hotel and restaurant receipts showing he was entertaining a client in Charlotte, North Carolina, at the time of Ackerman's death. If the paperwork was legitimate—and it seemed to be—the task force would eliminate him as a suspect.

That morning, RK had updated Billy on the whereabouts of Dwayne Deveraux around the times of the three murders. Deveraux had been in his office for the entire day Margaret Walsh was murdered. After eliminating Etheridge and Deveraux, Billy concluded that Lester Beach was the only remaining credible suspect.

"Well, we've gone from three suspects to one, Lester Beach, in a single weekend," Billy said. His frustration was evident. "I have to tell you that I'm getting a whole lot of heat on this from every direction. They aren't buying into our theory about these killings. Yeah, there's a lot of similarities to the Boston case, but there are differences, too."

"Who's they?" Danie said.

"The media with all their experts and Troy Driggers, of course," Billy said. "I'm afraid the mayor's having his doubts as well." He paused to pour his fifth cup of coffee. "We've assumed this guy is a lust murderer like the Boston Strangler, who stalks his victims, feels a rush of power as he kills and mutilates, but gets an even bigger kick when every woman in the city is afraid. Right?"

Danie nodded. "That's the assumption because of what he does to his victims, the connections to the Boston case, and his interest in publicizing it."

Billy hesitated for a minute, collecting his thoughts. "Honestly, Danie, I'm having trouble believing that this guy is being driven by violent fantasies. These murders are planned too well in advance to be done by some psycho who can't hold back his urges except on the days that match the Boston case."

Danie didn't answer immediately. "He may feel more powerful pretending to be the Boston Strangler than he gets from the actual murders themselves. If that's true, then he may not be a lust murderer, but he's still a serial killer."

Billy looked confused. "We've been looking for a man driven by violent sex fantasies, but from what you just said, maybe we should be looking for a different personality."

Danie tapped her fingers on the table. She was beginning to feel defensive about the conversation. "Like an egomaniac? I've factored that possibility into every character the task force has submitted as a potential suspect. We don't know his motives. All we can do is infer from the evidence."

Cal had been waiting for the right time to jump into the conversation, and now seemed to be the moment.

"I've done a lot more research on the Boston case lately," he said. "I don't think that killer selected his victims, at least in the first murders of older women. Instead, there's evidence that he took advantage of whichever woman let him in with his phony excuse about being sent by the superintendent to fix something. Considering that the murders here had to be done on specific dates, it would be too risky for our killer to assume that he could talk his way into the homes of our three victims."

"I think that's accurate," Danie said. She looked at Billy to gauge his reaction.

"I can understand that," Billy said. "The Boston Strangler got all lathered up and needed to find a victim, so he knocked on doors until someone was dumb enough to let him in, but Cal's right. This killer couldn't count on Walsh, Ackerman, and Howells falling for something like that."

"Now that we've had some time to think about it," Cal said, "the question in my mind is why is he going to all this trouble with nothing to show for it? He doesn't really rape them and doesn't rob them. He's just copying what his predecessor did. All he gets is notoriety."

"That's all the Zodiac Killer got from his murders," Danie said.

Billy rubbed his temples as if he had a headache. "I need to think about this. Let's talk later."

After Billy had left for the command center, Cal and Danie sat on the back porch, where there was a good breeze coming off the water. Magic and Billy's hounds were stretched out and sleeping on the floor.

"Danie, do you still believe that the killer's motive is satisfying his sexual urges?"

She seemed surprised by Cal's question. "Yes, if you mean that killing and degrading women fulfills his obsessive need for power."

"No other possible motives?" Cal suspected he already knew her answer, but he wondered if she had any doubts, or if she had considered other possibilities and rejected them.

She stood up and placed her hands on her hips. "It's the only one that fits the evidence."

"What if the evidence is manufactured?" It bothered him that Danie was so invested in her serial killer theory.

"You're not making any sense," she said abruptly. "I'm going to the kitchen and look at the recent police reports. Maybe we'll get another suspect out of them."

Cal took off his shoes and put his feet up on a wicker stool. So far, the case had been overly defined by its connection to the Boston Strangler. That link required killing the women on the same day as the Boston victims and with similar crime scene characteristics. Although the selection of rich women had been a deviation from the original case, perhaps it was intentional, to get the killer more publicity.

Cal tried to imagine the three murders from the killer's point of view. Once he had selected the victims, he would have to make sure they were home on the same day as their Boston equivalents.

Ackerman would have been the easiest because she was home most of the time, but Walsh led a busy life, with her charity and her eldest son. Victoria Howells was probably out most nights with some man or another. To fit the timing of the murders to the Boston victims, he would have had to have some sort of relationship with the victims before he killed them. He must have found some reason to contact them, and then made them feel comfortable that he was legitimate and safe to allow in their homes. Probably some kind of service where he could set up an appointment for the day of the killing.

Cal was convinced that the premeditation, planning, and timing that the Boston connection required didn't fit with a person fueled by unpredictable and uncontrollable violent fantasies. The timeline of Margaret Walsh's murder was, at least in his mind, an example of careful planning. The guy knocks at the door in the late afternoon and kills her. Then he hangs around for hours until he deliberately sets off the alarm so that police record the murder on the same day as the first Boston victim.

Then he selected Victoria Howells because he had learned her husband would be out of the country for several days after he killed her. That fit the circumstances of the discovery of the second Boston victim, Helen Blake.

He had probably known that Rachel Ackerman had a maid who worked six days a week and would find her body the day she died. All of these factors pointed to a killer who had done a great deal of intelligence gathering and planning, not some sex-obsessed maniac. What if Danie and Billy had assumed the murderer was a serial killer because the killer had created that scenario for them? He was tired of thinking about it. He lay his head back for a few moments and closed his eyes.

A little after five-thirty, Danie woke him up and suggested they go out for a bite. There was a small neighborhood spot a couple of miles from Billy's where they could get a hamburger and not have to dress up, she said.

It was still early, so even though the bar was busy, they were able to get a table where they could watch the news on the TV over the bar. As usual, the top story was the strangler murders, but this time, Ricky Ramirez focused on how quickly the killings had hurt the tourist business. Already, hotels and restaurants were experiencing lower-than-usual traffic. Two September conventions had been canceled. The Chamber of Commerce had reported that the city was losing tourist revenue rapidly and early in the season. If the case wasn't solved soon, the entire season could be a financial disaster.

Ramirez only had two guests for that segment, Charleston Mayor LC Campbell and Council Member Troy Driggers. Ramirez asked the mayor if it was true that the number of suspects had gone from three to zero. Campbell admitted it.

"You have to understand that we are still very early in this investigation," he explained.

Driggers picked up on the comment. "Mayor Campbell, I understand that you're still putting all your eggs in the basket that the pretty blonde girl sold you. Isn't that so? Why haven't you called the country's best experts to help find this monster?"

"Because I believe that we already have one of the best experts in the country on our team," Campbell said.

Driggers laughed. "Best looking? On that, I agree. Unfortunately, your task force is demoralized with her calling the shots. Let me remind you that some unlucky women are going to die horrible deaths if this guy isn't caught in a few weeks."

Ramirez looked smug. "Were you serious about the mayor and the chief of police resigning if the killer isn't caught soon?"

Driggers repeated his statement that accountability was critical to Charleston's safety and economy. If they couldn't deliver, he said, they should resign.

While Driggers continued to criticize the mayor and the police, Danie was silent. Her cheeseburger and glass of wine remained untouched.

"Let's get out of here," Cal said. "I've lost my appetite." He signaled the waiter to bring the bill and a box for the uneaten food. "Don't pay any attention to this crap. It's all politics."

She didn't answer. Her expression said it all.

As they approached the Rover, Danie noticed a piece of paper a little larger than a postcard on the passenger side windshield wiper. Expecting an advertisement, she picked it up and turned it over. "Oh, God!" was all she said as the paper fluttered to the ground.

Cal snatched it from the gravel, stared at the photo in disbelief, and stuffed it in his pants pocket. "Danie," he said as he held her tight to his chest.

He helped her into the car. "We have to get the hell out of here," he said. "Now, keep down until we get to Billy's." He pulled his handgun from under the driver's seat, placed it on the console, and sped out of the parking lot.

When they reached Billy's house, a subdued Danie said she wanted to rest. Cal brought Magic up to the bedroom to keep her company. Then he went downstairs and showed the photograph to Billy and Lindy. It was the naked corpse of Margaret Walsh. The image of Danie's smiling face from her website had been superimposed on the head of the dead woman.

"Bastard has some nerve," Billy said. "Careful how we handle it. It has to be processed for prints and DNA. By the way, how the hell did he know where you were?"

The answer dawned on him as he asked the question: the killer must have been watching his house.

"Oh shit!" Billy said. He made a quick call to the station, then turned back to Cal. "He ain't gonna be hanging around here no more," he said

"This has been a very tough day for her," Cal said. "It started this afternoon when I questioned her serial killer theory. You know her. She's not used to being challenged because she was right in almost all the cases she worked on."

"Did you guys watch the news this evening?" Billy said.

"Yeah. She didn't say anything, but she was upset by the interview. We left before it was over, and in the next minute, there's this damned photograph."

"She doesn't deserve this," Lindy said. "Not a bit."

Cal needed some time alone to think. He was feeling enormous pressure. He wondered if just being with Danie every time she went out would be enough to keep this bastard from killing her. This case was unlike any other he had ever experienced. Suddenly, it seemed very personal. It was Danie who was at risk now, not some nebulous stranger whose fate would be a few lines in a police report. This was real.

Everything was going to hell.

Chapter 28

I WAS SO SURE, SHE THOUGHT.

After yesterday's ordeal, Danie had barely slept at all. She lay in bed thinking about the recent criticism from every direction. She was disgusted—with herself. It was the same behavior that had blinded her to the seriousness of her brother's condition. Over a month had passed since he had taken his own life, and now she was doing the same damned thing again.

What would her pride cost this time? Another woman's life? She had to undo the singular focus that she had imposed on the investigation. Her original theory was not working. Others knew it, and it was time she admitted it. Just a few days ago, it was inconceivable to her that the killer might be someone other than a lust murderer. Now, after his threats, she believed he might be someone entirely different.

At dawn, she tiptoed downstairs and went outside where the morning sun was just barely showing its edge over the banks of the river. It was a tranquil and soothing scene. Her thoughts were interrupted a few minutes later when Cal walked up behind her and put his arms around her waist.

"Morning, baby." He kissed the back of her neck.

She loved it when he did that. "You're up so early."

He kissed her neck again. "Think I don't feel it when you aren't next to me?"

"I couldn't sleep." She turned around to face him, wrapped her arms around his neck, and pressed her head against his chest.

"Too much to think about," he said.

"It will end soon, right?" Danie wanted his assurance that one day things would be back to normal.

"They'll get him for sure. They've got so many people working on it. I think we'll catch a break soon, and when we do, it's only a matter of time."

He was probably right. It takes time to identify a suspect, but once the police pass that hurdle, things can move quickly. She was emotionally drained from the shooting, the horrible photo the killer had stuck on their windshield, and coming face to face with her own failings.

Though they didn't know who the killer was, they must be on the right path. Otherwise, he never would have taken such chances. His attempt to kill her suggested she may have been too close. The day after the attack, she and Cal had gone over everything they had done and everyone they had spoken to since they arrived in Charleston.

Danie was convinced that sometime during the investigation, she had inadvertently spoken to the killer. They reviewed the daily police reports with the detectives but couldn't narrow their suspicions to any one suspect. By the time they were done, Danie was even more concerned.

"Don't worry, baby." Cal hugged her tighter. "We're getting close to the finish line."

"It can't come soon enough," she said. "Let me make some coffee. Billy will be up soon."

"I'll make you some French toast," he said. "Just like at home."

Billy came down for breakfast. As they ate, Danie told him she agreed with Cal. In addition to their search for a serial killer suspect, they should examine more traditional motives.

"I'm sorry that I caused everyone to be so focused on just one theory," she said. "I'm afraid by doing that, I might have ignored some other leads."

Billy was visibly relieved to hear her say that. "I talked with Walter yesterday about the investigation we normally do during a homicide case. On the Walsh murder, Mike Cecchi and Ira Shapiro were very thorough, but once we all decided that we had a serial killer, we conducted a different kind of investigation. We gotta continue that work, but we also gotta go back to our routine procedures for Ackerman and Howells."

Later that morning, Cal and Danie got together with the four lead detectives at the command center to hear about the Walsh family background. Mike opened the discussion.

"The Walshes had two sons," he said. "Ethan's the oldest. A senior securities analyst at SunTrust for over a decade. Excellent reputation. Makes real good money and owns a condo in one of those big historic district houses. He's not married yet, but he said he's trying to work up to proposing to his girlfriend. Only debt is his mortgage. Not that any of it matters now with his inheritance. Evenings and weekends, he volunteers for an organization to help children with cerebral palsy."

"His mother was very involved in that charity, too," Ira said. "She and her husband donated a small fortune for research."

"And a whole lot of her time," Mike said. "She was a good woman." He shook his head. "It's a goddamn shame what happened to her."

"You should have heard Ethan speak at her funeral," Ira said. "He was devastated—and I really mean devastated—but he wheeled himself up to the podium and gave the greatest tribute a guy can give his mother. There wasn't a dry eye in the place."

"It was at the Episcopal Cathedral, and there were hundreds of people," Mike added. "The place was packed. The mayors of both Charleston and Mt. Pleasant were there. That's how much people cared about her."

"I had no idea she was such a celebrity," Danie said.

"You know, I doubt that most of the people in this area had ever heard of her," Ira said. "I think that, over the years, she made such an impact with her charity activities that many of the families she helped turned out to show their respect."

"At least she had one son who made her proud," Mike said. "But then there was Noah, the one who married Julia."

"I don't have any background on him," Danie said.

"You could look at Noah as a guy who really wants to be an entrepreneur," Mike said.

"He got mediocre grades at a college nobody ever heard of," Ira said. "Followed by a string of minor jobs."

Mike's disgust for Noah was clear. "I insisted he tell me every place he ever worked, the person he worked for, how long he worked there, and why he left."

Ira snickered. "Mike can be so cruel sometimes."

"We went to six of the places he'd worked," Mike said, "and every one of them told us he was fired for lying about his hours, cheating on his expenses, or stealing. The only reason they didn't call the police is that they didn't have enough evidence to prove it."

"With that kind of record, how did he get another job?" Danie said.

"Well, apparently, he realized it was going to be tough," Mike said. "So he changed his game. Instead of trying to get a job, he put the hit on Mom and Dad for money to get into business for himself. I imagine that the lovely Julia suggested it."

"Don't forget to tell them about the trust," Ira said.

"Oh, yeah, the trust. Ira, you know more about the details. You fill them in," Mike said, smirking.

"Okay," Ira said. "Noah's father must have eventually understood that his son was never going to be a successful businessman. Another complication: the German girlfriend was pressuring Noah to marry her. The Walshes were concerned about her, so Noah's father hired a private detective in Germany to check out Julia and her many aliases.

"The report was, to say the least, not good," he said. "Prostitution and shoplifting as a juvenile. Fraud and embezzlement. Enough allegations to make a prospective father-in-law choke. He showed Noah the report and warned him not to marry her.

"Well, Noah married her anyway, so his father did the smart thing. He had his lawyer put together a generation-skipping trust so that Ethan and Noah would never directly get their hands on their parents' money."

"A what?" Cal said, wrinkling his forehead.

"A generation-skipping trust," Ira said. "It's set up so that when both parents passed away, the executor of the trust would invest the money and both sons would receive an income—mostly derived from stock dividends and interest. But they couldn't spend any of the principal unless there was a medical emergency. When both sons died, the trust would be dissolved and their kids, if they had any, would get equal shares of the money. See? It skips a generation."

"What happens to the trust income when one of the sons dies?" Cal said. "Does it get added to the money in the account?"

"If the dead son had no wife or children, the income would go to the other son," Ira said. "Ethan was designated as the executor. In the event of his death, SunTrust would take over that role."

"Did either Noah or Ethan know about this trust?" Danie said.

"Walsh's attorney told us that Noah didn't know about it until recently. On the other hand, Ethan did," Mike said. "When Julia found out that she couldn't get her hands on the money, she screamed at the lawyer, threatened to sue him, and stormed out of the office. The big house will go to Ethan, but the will gives Noah money to buy or to build something comparable. So far the sons are in the clear, but we're still investigating some of Julia's shady friends who have come over from Germany and live in this area."

After the meeting with Mike and Ira, Cal had agreed to go with RK to Camilla Ackerman's home. Joe then asked Danie if she would come along to another interview of Harry Howells.

As they drove toward the marina on Wentworth Street, Joe suddenly made an unexpected turn onto King Street.

"Where are you going now?" Danie said. "The marina is the other way."

Joe nodded his head. "I know. I thought as long as we're in the neighborhood, we could ask Deveraux a couple more questions. It'll only take a few minutes."

Danie was quick to agree. She trusted Joe's instincts and his street experience. She knew that sometimes, hands-on knowledge and intuition was worth as much as, if not more than, academic research.

"Okay with me—as much as I hate seeing that bastard again."

"Something's been bothering me ever since that first interview," Joe said. "Bear with me. I think we may have something."

They parked in front of the Coastal Empire Mortgage offices. The same secretary that greeted them during their first visit was sitting behind her desk. When she looked up, she recognized Joe immediately.

"Afternoon, Detective," she said. "How can I help you today?"

"Is Mr. Deveraux in? Can we see him for a few minutes?"

She picked up the phone and spoke with her boss.

"He said to go right in."

When Joe and Danie entered the office, Deveraux was already walking toward them with his right hand extended.

"Good to see you again, Detective." He smiled. "What can I do for…"

Before he could even finish the sentence, Joe's hands were around his throat as he slammed Deveraux against the wall.

"What the hell…" Deveraux pleaded.

"Shut the fuck up!" Joe shouted just inches from his face.

Danie stood back, shocked but realizing it was better not to interfere.

"Let me tell you something, shithead. If I ever hear that you went near Ruby or Samantha again in your miserable life, you're gonna hear from me, you understand?"

"Yeah, yeah, okay, sure." Deveraux gasped for air but Joe's powerful arms pressed against him like a vise.

"But you know what? I'm not gonna arrest you. I'm not even gonna take you in. One night, when you least expect it, I'm just gonna put a bullet in your fucking head. Do you understand me? Do you?"

Danie could see the fear in Deveraux's eyes. "Yeah, I get it. Okay. I won't see them again. I promise!"

"Make sure, or I'll be back. And next time, you won't like me." Joe threw Deveraux sideways onto the floor where he scrambled behind his desk.

"Have a nice afternoon," Joe said as he straightened his tie. "Let's go," he said to Danie. They walked out of the office and back down to the car.

Danie could feel her heart beating, but deep down, she approved of what she just witnessed. "What if he makes a complaint? He'll say you assaulted him," she said.

"He won't." Joe made a right onto Broad Street and headed toward the marina. He cranked up the air conditioner to the highest setting as Danie simply stared out the window. For a few minutes, they didn't say anything to each other until Joe finally broke the silence.

"Sometimes we have to forget about the law and do what's right."

When Danie and Joe pulled up to Howells's yacht, they saw a sign showing *Victoria's Delight* was for sale. Harry was waiting for them on the aft deck with a bottle of beer. He seemed a bit tipsy and had dark circles under his eyes.

Joe asked him about the yacht. Was he going to buy a different boat?

"No," Harry said. "This was my wedding gift to her. No point in it now." His attempts to sound positive failed miserably.

"I'm so sorry," Danie said. "What are you going to do?"

A big sigh. "Well, doll baby, I'll tell yous what I ain't gonna do. No more running round the world's shitholes. I quit. Next week I'm going back to Naples, get me another condo. My father's down there living with my asshole brother. I need a rest."

The short interview confirmed what Danie had believed all along: the lowborn prince was seriously grieving for his promiscuous highborn princess. From Danie's perspective, he was in the clear. Joe agreed. All the detailed travel documents and receipts from foreign countries Harry had turned over to the police constituted the most unshakeable alibi he'd ever seen.

In the meantime, RK took Cal to Camilla Ackerman's modest home. Cal had already met her when they had taken Rosa to Rachel Ackerman's house in the historic district. His impression of Camilla then was that she was attractive and sophisticated, but that image faded immediately when she opened the door in a tattered shirt and baggy jeans. The graceful upsweep of hair he remembered had fallen into an uncombed tangled mess. Inside, the house smelled strongly of marijuana. She could barely keep her eyes open as they tried to talk to her. Camilla was so clearly intoxicated that RK told her they would come back another time.

"Lots of DWIs," RK said.

"I don't think this is our killer," Cal said as they drove away. "Does she have any boyfriends who might help her get her inheritance?"

"There're a couple of guys she hangs around with," RK said. "They're just as fucked up as she is. I can't imagine either of them staying straight long enough to pull off these murders, but I can set up another interview with them."

Back at the command center, detectives compared the day's interviews. Most were inconclusive, and there were some areas still under investigation. Progress was slow.

As they ate sandwiches and potato chips, washed down with coffee and soft drinks, Walter turned on the evening news as Ricky Ramirez announced the big news in the strangler case: the investigation was doubling down on the victims' families.

"Thanks for the fucking update, Ricky," RK shouted at the television.

Chapter 29

Greg Ackerman's residence
Tuesday, July 10, 2012

"Ever get depressed?" Danie asked him.

Joe seemed surprised.

"Depressed?"

"You know—about the work you do."

He laughed a little. "If you mean homicide, no, I don't get depressed over it." He paused and glanced over at Danie, who seemed skeptical. "Well, okay. Sometimes, it gets me down, but I break out of it right away."

"What about Deveraux?"

"What about him? He deserves worse than what he got."

That was true. Danie never expected Joe to attack Deveraux, but after she had thought about it, she was happy about it. Joe Asher was from the old school of policing—guided by the philosophy that most problems a cop encountered in the street could be solved by a nightstick or a kick in the ass—or both. He believed in "tough love," especially when he dealt with young people.

Joe thought everyone deserved a second chance; it was his strength and, at times, his weakness. He also had no interest in any of the mundane duties of a uniformed officer like traffic enforcement, ordinance regulations, security details, and such. It was all a waste of time to him. What Asher liked to do was be a detective. And sometimes, if that job included slamming someone like Deveraux up against a wall, then so be it.

The workday began with Joe and Danie driving to an interview with Rachel's son, Greg Ackerman, and his wife. Joe just learned some details about Rachel's will from Billy. The family attorney, who happened to be an old high school classmate of Billy's, initially refused to divulge anything because the will had not yet been read. It took an off-the-record phone call from Billy to persuade him to reveal some important details.

Rachel Ackerman had made a ten-million-dollar bequest to a local college and given comparatively modest amounts to her family members. She had told her attorney that she had discussed the distribution of her estate with her family.

When Billy discovered this new information, he asked Danie and Joe to talk to Greg again. As they drove over to Greg's house, Danie had become curious about Joe, who always seemed to have a positive attitude.

"So why do you do this kind of work?" she said.

"It's not what you think it is, Danie. Once you get past the blood and gore, there's a lot of satisfaction in death investigations."

Seeing the expression on her face, he continued. "Oh, we have our ups and downs, don't get me wrong. But when we arrest one of these low lifes who kills an innocent person, that's a great feeling. I'm not talking about drug dealer 'A' who kills drug dealer 'B.' Those guys deserve what happens to them. When we catch a real killer and put him away, that makes our day. We live for it."

Greg and his wife, Betty, were waiting on the front steps when Joe and Danie pulled up to the house. "Betty was in Chicago when her mother-in-law was killed," Joe said.

Greg seemed annoyed as they ascended the stairs, tapping his finger on the railing.

"More questions?" he said.

"We'll try not to take up too much of your time," Joe said.

Greg and Betty spent the better part of an hour and a half answering questions about Rachel and the relationship she had with other family members. With the exception of their son, Leland, Rachel didn't seem to have much affection for anyone, they said.

"What's going to happen to that beautiful house?" Joe said. He wanted to see if Rachel Ackerman had discussed her will with her relatives.

"I can always hope," Betty said, "but then, Camilla probably needs it more than us."

"We don't know yet who'll be the lucky one," Greg said as he filled a glass with bourbon. "I can't imagine she'd give that huge place to Lee. Look, we're kinda tired now. Haven't we told you enough yet?"

"Speaking of Lee," Danie said. "How's he handling his grandmother's death?"

"He's deeply depressed," Betty said. "He told me he spends most of the day sleeping or he goes over to her house for hours at a time. I went there to make sure the refrigerators were cleaned out, and he was just sitting there looking at some old pictures. Very sad."

"Maybe I can offer him some help," Danie said. "Since he was the closest in the family to his grandmother, I wanted to talk to him again anyway."

"I don't believe in psychiatrists," Greg said. "But if you wanna try, go ahead. He's a good kid."

After the interview was over, Danie tried to reach Lee, but he didn't answer his phone. She wondered if Lee's depression stemmed from a feeling of guilt over being unable to protect his grandmother—a feeling she understood all too well.

On the way back to the command center, Cal called.

"Rosa's been hanging around headquarters on and off for the past few days," he told Danie. "She's been making a nuisance of herself by annoying the desk sergeant and asking everyone who walks by if they've seen you."

"She's got nothing to do right now, I guess," Danie said.

"Well, she claims she had a vision. She seems to be in panic mode and says she has to talk to you right away."

Danie sighed.

"There's more," Cal said. "Her husband's quite sick, and she has to catch a bus back to Philadelphia soon. Right now, she's going to St. Mary's of the Annunciation Church on Hasell Street to pray for her husband. She'll wait for you there."

"Okay," Danie said. "I'll ask Joe if he can take me."

"I'll take you," Cal said. "Go to the command center." A few minutes later, he met Danie in the parking lot of the Bay Street office. St. Mary's was only a ten-minute drive from the command post.

Located on a quiet one-way street between King and Meeting, St. Mary's of the Annunciation Church was one of the oldest Roman Catholic churches in the South, with a congregation who had worshiped at the same site since 1789. A fire destroyed the original structure in 1838, but the current building was put up the following year. Its high, arched openings and elegant entranceway were classic Roman design. When Cal and Danie arrived at St. Mary's, they parked on the street and waited for a few minutes.

"I don't see her," Cal said.

"Maybe she's already inside. If she's not there, I'll be right back." She opened the door and stepped out of the car.

Danie walked up the steps to a small landing. Four massive columns supported a large, flat roof that protected a spacious veranda where parishioners gathered after services. The heavy ten-foot oak doors, despite their size, easily swung open, to Danie's surprise. The air was refreshingly cool, a welcome relief from the summer heat. As she stepped inside, the door closed gently behind her with nary a sound, a testament to the workmanship and skill of craftsmen who had lived and died long ago. Inside the church, it was cool and serene, so different from the world outside. Fractured light seeped through the stained-glass windows on each side of the room. At the front of the church, large ornate murals decorated the curved surface behind the marble altar. No one was in the narrow pews, except in the very last row to Danie's right. A lone figure knelt with her head bowed and hands joined together in prayer.

"Rosa?"

She didn't respond.

"Rosa?" Danie repeated. "Are you okay?"

Rosa stared straight ahead. Danie inched closer and sat down next to her.

"It's me, Dr. Callahan."

"I heard him!" Rosa whispered, shaking as she spoke.

"Who?" Danie said. "Who did you hear?"

"He was on his belly. On his belly crawling around on the floor like a snake."

"Where?" Danie said.

"He's a smart one."

"Who?"

"He attacked her. He took something and smashed her in the head!" Tears ran down her face as she sobbed. "He killed her, and he didn't care."

"What happened then?" Danie said.

"I don't know," Rosa cried. For the first time, she turned to look at Danie. "He wants to kill you." Her face twisted in despair. She put her hands on Danie's arms to emphasize her warning. "He has to kill you. You must understand this. I am very worried for you, Dr. Danie. Please, please, you must go home."

"I can't leave now, Rosa. Everyone depends on us. I have work to do. I have to…"

"He's not gonna stop," Rosa said. "He's on a mission."

"What kind of mission? What does he want?"

Rosa wiped away her tears. "I love churches," she said. "I feel at home here. You know, I've had a personal relationship with God ever since I was a child. It has helped me through some difficult times, Dr. Danie. Today I'm asking Him to help my husband with his cancer. I know He will. He always has. I have to pray now."

Danie wasn't sure if she should leave.

"Would you like us to take you to the bus depot?"

"Oh, thank you," Rosa said, "but I have a taxi coming back for me in a few minutes. You must go home, Dr. Danie, please believe me."

"Good luck to you, Rosa." She hugged her. "I hope your husband gets better."

Danie turned to leave, and suddenly Rosa's stern voice stopped her in mid-stride.

"Things are not what they seem," Rosa said. "They never are."

"What are you talking about, Rosa?" Danie said. "What do you mean?"

"I have to pray now." She folded her hands together under her chin like a child in school. "Goodbye, Dr. Danie. You must go home before it's too late."

During the trip back to Bay Street, Danie went over what Rosa said with Cal and tried to make some sense of it. Cal, though doubtful of Rosa's abilities, predictably tried to use the warnings as further proof they should return to Savannah. Danie was adamant about

MARILYN J. BARDSLEY AND MARK GADO

staying until the job was done. After a few moments, she didn't hear Cal's protests anymore. She was preoccupied with Rosa's warning.

As cryptic as Rosa's words were, there was no doubt in Danie's mind that Rosa had a gift. When, at Ackerman's house, Rosa had warned her that the killer knew who she was, she had been right. He had tried to shoot her, and then he put that horrible photo on their windshield. When Rosa said that he had to kill her, Danie believed it; she just didn't know why he thought he had to kill her.

And what about this mission Rosa had mentioned? She tried to imagine what sort of mission would make a man kill three women and display their corpses like grotesque dolls in some horror film. Danie's imagination went wild. A terrible thought jumped into her head: Was she supposed to be the next victim in the series? Was that her role in his mission? Is that why Rosa had begged her to go back to Savannah—so that she wouldn't be killed? Here was a man determined to create a media obsession with his murders. What better publicity stunt than having his next victim be the one who was trying to catch him?

Visit CRIMESCAPE.COM for more action-packed original fiction!   231

Chapter 30

Task Force Command Center
9:17 a.m. Wednesday, July 11, 2012

"LISTEN UP!" DEPUTY CHIEF JOHNSON SHOUTED.

One by one, heads turned to the front of the room. Johnson, Chief Murphy, and the Callahans emerged from their conference and walked into the operations room. All the task force members had heard the rumors that the chief would be forced to bring in the FBI and dreaded the possibility of losing control of the investigation. Walter took the podium. He smiled broadly at the audience before his deep, rich voice reverberated throughout the room. The audience was perfectly silent.

"Some of you already know that in the past couple of days, we've changed our investigative approach. Why? Because we got a killer who's either a sophisticated serial murderer or someone who has devised an elaborate scam to use the Boston Strangler case to deceive us. We don't know which kind he is yet, but we've scrutinized a number of serial killer wannabes and not come up with one good suspect. We'll push on, but our new emphasis will be on murder for financial gain. Dr. Cal, would you elaborate?"

Cal brushed the crumbs of pastry off the front of his shirt and cleared his throat. "Early on, we wondered about the killer's motives.

Why copycat the Boston case so closely, but then have victims that are so different from the originals? The Charleston women were rich, while the Boston women had modest incomes.

"The other factor was his need to publicize his crimes. Most killers don't take risks like that, but this guy wanted everyone to know that he was the new Boston Strangler." He looked around the room and established eye contact with those he thought were the leaders in the audience. "I'm sure you wondered about this as well."

"Our theory is that the killer concocted this massive deception because he stood to benefit financially from one of the victims' deaths. If he had only killed his benefactor, the spotlight would fall on him. If he killed two or more other women, all with the trappings of the Boston case, then the investigation would focus on a serial killer instead of him." Cal looked around the room again and decided that his theory was gaining traction.

"We're talking about large fortunes here. In two of the murders, the heirs didn't know how the money would be distributed. Ackerman's wealth was over twelve million, but only her lawyer knew that most of it would go to a local college.

"Walsh's net worth was closer to eight million, but only one of her heirs knew about a trust that would control how much income would go to the two sons. In the Howells case, Victoria had no real assets of her own, despite lies she told to various male friends about having money from an ex-husband. But there's the possibility that the killer didn't know that."

Cal placed both hands on the sides of the podium and leaned forward. "Because it was critical that the murders happened on the same day as the old Boston case, we're assuming the killer had to contact the victims before the event in order to arrange a meeting. This contact could have been in person or by phone. That's why it's essential we pay close attention to the phone records of all the victims, especially in the month immediately prior to the murders. This theory may be wrong, but I think that's what we need to do. Any questions?"

One of Charleston's senior detectives responded immediately. "I agree with what you're doing, and it shouldn't take long to figure out if you're right, but what do we have in our back pocket if this theory goes wrong? What if this is just some asshole getting his kicks by making us look bad?"

"You mean just to discredit the police?" Cal said.

"Yeah, or the mayor."

Cal got the message. The detective had been watching Ramirez and Driggers making life miserable for the mayor. Cal didn't buy it. "Sure, it's possible there is a political motive, but keep in mind we have two jurisdictions. The first murder was in Mt. Pleasant, which does not have the same political environment as Charleston. If three murders were the catalyst to unseat Mayor Campbell, then they should have all been in Charleston."

Walter took back the floor. "Thanks, Cal. So let's keep up what we're doing. Y'all are doing a good job. Let's review those records and make sure we do everything we can to accomplish our goal. Okay, let's get back to work."

In the crowded operations room, investigators pounded on their keyboards, sorted through the hundreds of tips that had to be processed, and filed a ton of paperwork. A dozen HD screens pulsated with rows and rows of information gathered from police databases across the nation. The computers compared it with other databanks, searching for any sort of a match that would provide detectives with a new lead. It was a massive project that required a great deal of coordination to avoid duplication and repetition.

Joe and RK reviewed the daily reports and tracked the printouts of tips that came in from the public. There was always the chance that an ordinary citizen would supply the single bit of information that would break the case wide open. The infamous Son of Sam case in New York City was solved by a parking summons after a yearlong series of shootings that left thirteen people dead or wounded. The Wichita BTK case was solved by a technician who traced the code on a computer disk that led to the killer. Anything was possible; the task force understood that concept too well. Every lead had to be followed, and every phone call had to be categorized, investigated, and resolved.

A large display board with photos of Walsh, Ackerman, and Howells pinned to it was situated at the front of the room. Statistics of each murder, including dates, times, locations, physical evidence, and a few crime photos were organized directly under each name. Next to the victim's information was a smaller display board that listed the current status of possible suspects.

If a name had been investigated and discarded, a task force member took it from the active board and moved it to still another list, where it joined a dozen other names that had also been rejected. One detective was responsible for each board and was required to keep a log of dates and times when each name had a status change. With one glance, the information was easily available to any task force member.

In a far corner of the room, a CPD detective monitored the results of every subpoena issued during the investigation. He kept track of the specifics of each one: the target, who had issued it, who had served it, and what information or evidence was obtained. Investigators carefully examined the victims' financial records and credit card bills for any questionable transactions. They also followed up on any large cash withdrawals or deposits. Any suspicious bank activity at all had to be investigated and explained.

Victoria's credit card bills were extensive, and it was obvious to investigators that cost was of no concern to her. She made dozens of frivolous purchases each month, including a hundred and ninety dollars for sushi and three hundred dollars for a pair of slippers. Her spending habits were the source of a running commentary in the task force. Any outrageous purchase by Victoria invited derision and a new round of jokes.

Margaret Walsh, on the other hand, was just the opposite. She had made very few purchases, and when she did use her cards, it was nothing out of the ordinary: a lunch, a dinner, or a visit to the salon. Rachel Ackerman had used her cards sparingly, mostly at the same locations: a local wine store, a supermarket, or a nearby gourmet food store.

Detectives faithfully logged in all the data, never knowing which bit of information might lead to the killer. One of the most complex aspects of the investigation and the most tedious was phone record analysis. Detectives were only too happy to share this chore with Cal and Danie.

The phone record section, which was just a small cubicle in the corner of the office, was the depository for all the records and bills gathered during the case since day one. These materials included local usage details and toll calls made by the victims as well as incoming calls made to the victims' phones. It included the listing of each number called, length, time, and to whom the call was made.

It was an enormous undertaking that required special software to sort through the thousands of names and numbers. If there was a call of excessive duration, or if a certain number frequently appeared or during odd hours, that would arouse the interest of investigators. This process could go on for weeks, especially if the target was a habitual caller like Victoria Howells. Some people used their phones sparingly, and their calls were brief. Others used their phones incessantly, making or receiving hundreds of calls each month.

Reviewing Victoria's records, Cal realized one thing right away: Victoria liked to talk on the phone. And she didn't care what time it was, either. Her records showed numerous calls made at four or five in the morning; it was as if she never slept. She would make successive calls to the same number a dozen times, even when no one answered. Then, just as quickly, she would call another number repeatedly. The subscriber usually turned out to be a man she had met or someone she went out with that week. Cal noticed that on one day she called a man she'd met at Salty Mike's restaurant thirty-seven times. When she finally got to speak to him, they talked for less than two minutes.

There was no rhyme or reason to her calls, which made investigators' jobs even more difficult. She would call and talk to someone for an hour, stop, call someone else for ten minutes, and then return to the first call.

"Christ! I wonder when she had the time to charge her damn phone," Cal said.

"It's going to take weeks to get a handle on her calls," Joe said with a sigh.

"At least," RK said. "By the way, we finally have all the records for Rachel Ackerman. The phone company was very slow, especially with the incoming call listings. We got the May and June records last. I went through some of them already, so I can tell you the analysis isn't gonna be as tough as Victoria's."

Though Ackerman had a cell phone, she did not use it nearly as often as Victoria. She used her cell primarily for the grocer, hair appointments, and such. If it was a call for personal business or family, she used a landline. Her phone bill was average, unlike Victoria, whose bill was usually a few hundred dollars each month.

Joe was accustomed to reviewing phone records; he had done this type of tedious work many times during his career. Although he did not really enjoy it, he was well suited for it because he had one of the fundamental qualities necessary for investigative work: insatiable curiosity.

He went over each phone record carefully, making notations of interesting calls or patterns. After the data was entered into the database, he would file the record in the hard-copy file, make a list of things to do on the current record, and move on to the next. Then he and RK would go over the notes and formulate a plan. Sometimes, more subpoenas were needed to find out who Ackerman had called. Other times, there was no need to go any further.

After Joe had explained his process to Cal and Danie so that they could help by noting special calls or patterns, the three of them looked at a sample—the list of phone calls for the week prior to Ackerman's death. One entry on the list jumped out at Cal immediately.

29 Jun 12 2025 843-234-5678 2056 Duration: 31 minutes

"Does this line mean someone talked to her for over half an hour several hours before she was killed? I'm assuming that '2025' is the time of the call," Cal said.

"It is," Joe said. "The call was at 8:25 p.m. That's a pretty long call for her. Who was the caller?" He looked at the month's detail and saw the same number again. One additional call was made from that number on June 7, five days earlier, for nine minutes.

"RK, could you run this number through the database?"

The task force's identification database contained every phone number from every victim's phone records for the previous twelve months. When a call was identified, it was entered into the program, which included subscriber information: names, dates, and addresses. If anyone made or received a call from that number in the previous year, it would show up. RK entered the data, requesting all calls made by the Ackerman caller, and the results immediately flashed on the screen.

17 May 12 1017 Walsh, Margaret 1027 duration: 10 minutes

07 June 12 1405 Ackerman, Rachel 1414 duration: 9 minutes

13 June 12 1700 Walsh, Margaret 1704 duration: 4 minutes

25 June 12 1642 Howells, Victoria 1659 duration: 17 minutes

28 June 12 1845 Howells, Victoria 1856 duration: 11 minutes

29 June 12 2025 Ackerman, Rachel 2056 duration: 31 minutes

Joe was amazed. "What the hell is this?"

"This is what I was hoping we would find," Cal said. "The first call to each victim might have been to set up the appointment for whatever he told the women he was going to do for them. A home repair or a service of some type. The second call was probably to confirm the appointment."

"Look at that!" RK said.

"That's our killer right there," Danie whispered. "It has to be. What's the odds that some innocent person knew all three victims and called all three shortly before they were murdered?"

"Astronomical," RK said.

They ran the caller number for the subscriber name and address, which returned as an unknown listing.

"I'm not surprised, RK, I'm betting it's a burner phone," Joe said.

For the next hour, Joe and RK made a dozen calls to trace the origin of the suspect number. They discovered that the phone was, in fact, a "burner" manufactured for the T-Mobile network within the past six months. T-Mobile was unable to ascertain who was using the phone or who purchased it.

However, it was a new model and had only been available for retail sale since April. This particular phone had been one of a gross shipped to a Target store in Summerville. Joe contacted the store manager and made an appointment to investigate further.

"I know where that store is," RK said as the two detectives and the Callahans hurried to their unmarked car.

"Lights, no siren, RK," Joe said as he called the chief to let him know what was going on.

They raced up I-26, exchanging various theories. They soon agreed it was unlikely the buyer would have used a credit card, but they had to do everything they could to find the transaction. They drove the twenty-five miles to Summerville in eighteen minutes flat.

Chris Garrett, the store manager, was a young, energetic man who was eager to cooperate. Joe explained what they were after, noting that the information was an important part of a homicide investigation. First, Garrett had to notify the legal department before he could do anything.

"Mr. Garrett, we really don't have a lot of time," Joe pointed out. "The information we want is just some purchasing records. We can get a subpoena, no problem. But we're here now. How about you get security to help us, and I give you my word we won't take anything against your wishes, or until you get the okay from the lawyers? Would that work?"

The young man thought for a few seconds. "Okay, it's a deal." He pressed his intercom on his lapel. "Justin, I'm sending some detectives over to your office. Give them what they want, but no paperwork until you hear back from me."

"Okay, got it, Chris."

Garrett directed them to the security office where Justin, a balding ex-cop and chief of security for the Target store, greeted them.

"How are you doing, detectives? Justin Fowler retired from Columbia PD after twenty-five years of service. Nice to meet you guys."

"Thanks, Justin, appreciate it," Joe said and introduced his three companions." Joe provided the phone information and asked what could be done to find the purchaser.

"Not much as far as who is using the phone," Justin told them. "The store doesn't keep track of the actual calling numbers of the phone. Just the phone itself. We have no idea who is using which phone."

"Crap," RK said. "I figured that."

"Let me ask you this, Justin," Joe said. "Can you tell us how many of these particular phones were sold—since May 1, for example?"

"Sure, that's easy. The computer tracking system can tell you when each phone was sold, what time, and how many. That's no problem."

Joe sat down in the chair in front of the computer terminal. He read off the model number and brand of the phone. Justin punched in some numbers and letters. Within a minute, a row of data appeared on the screen.

"We sold ninety-six of those phones," Justin said. "Here they are."

"Now what I would like to do, if possible, is to get a printout of those purchases, including the times. Can you do that?" Joe said.

"Yep. Here we go." A nearby printer spit out a single sheet of paper.

"Do you retain video on the premises?" Cal said.

Justin nodded. "Sure do. Our cameras are on the registers every single minute of the day, one hour before and one hour after closing or until Chris presses in the code that shuts it down."

"I'd like to pull every video of each sale working backward from June 7. Can you do that?"

"Stand by, Joe." Justin worked the computer for a few minutes until the first video appeared on a separate screen. "Okay, let's move over to this terminal. This is our master system, which controls all the surveillance video in the store. By typing in the code, I can zero in on any register for any time in the past ninety days."

"Where's the code?" RK said.

"It's on that printout sheet. See that seven-digit number at the front of each line? That tells me which register recorded the sale of that item listed on the line. Just read me the first code from June 7."

RK supplied the code, and Justin punched it in. The screen went blank for a moment and then the image of an employee making a transaction with a customer at a register appeared. The video's clarity was excellent.

"This is great video," Danie said. "I can see the phone on the counter."

"It sure is," Justin said. "State of the art. HD at its finest. Wish we had this when I was on the job."

For the next hour, RK read off the transaction codes, and Justin pulled up the videos. They looked at each purchase of every phone, day by day, going farther back into the month of June and eventually into May. For the sake of expediency, if he saw a female purchaser, he skipped over it. He could always go back for another review if they decided to later.

Justin's intercom sounded.

"Okay, I spoke to the legal department," Chris said. "They want subpoenas before we release anything. So no paperwork to leave the building until we get a subpoena. I'm going to lunch. See you in an hour."

Justin looked over at RK. "That's his way of helping you guys. If he's not around, he doesn't know what you did. I know my boss. He's a good guy, Joe."

"Glad to hear that. Let's go to the next code."

"May fifth," RK said. "It looks like 3:46 in the afternoon."

The image of another register appeared. They saw an employee and a customer. The buyer was holding the phone until he reached for his wallet and pulled out some cash. His face was plainly visible on the screen.

"Freeze it!" Joe yelled. He rose from his chair and put his nose inches from the screen. "Can you zoom in on that, Justin?"

"Sure." The image grew larger until the face of the customer filled the screen in blazing, crystal-clear color.

"Holy shit!" Joe whispered. "Look at that! Danie and Cal, come here."

"What? What?" RK said.

Joe's voice was barely audible. "That man buying the phone."

He felt the hair on the back of his neck bristle. It was as if he could not believe what he was seeing. He had read somewhere that the human brain can sometimes function faster than any computer ever invented. This was one of those moments. During the time it took him to process the image on the screen, the truth screamed inside his head like the blast of a firehouse siren.

When Danie saw the video of the man buying the phone, she thought of Rosa's warning: "Things are not what they seem." How right she was.

"Who is it?" Cal said.

Danie's left hand covered her mouth as if she could barely say the name. "It's Greg Ackerman!"

Chapter 31

Task Force Command Center
2:20 p.m. Wednesday, July 11, 2012

WHEN JOE, RK, AND THE CALLAHANS arrived at the command post, Billy was waiting at the front door.

"Joe, let's pick him up." He glanced at his watch. "Where does he work?"

Joe explained that Greg Ackerman worked as a contractor for the state DOT. His company, Transport Engineering Services, had an office on Broad Street. When Joe called the office, a temp said everyone was out, and she had no idea where Greg was. Joe called Greg's home on the off chance he was there, but there was no answer. Billy ordered a car to wait outside Greg's house in case he returned.

"Guys," Danie said, "I promised Greg's son, Lee, I'd talk with him today. We hate to leave, but I'd like to get there early and ask him some questions before you grab his father."

"You go ahead, Danie," Billy said. "We'll keep you posted."

Right after Danie and Cal left, the temp called back to say that Greg was probably on the Ravenel Bridge waiting for an inspection. She said he was on the eastbound side, around a half-mile out from where the SCDOT was doing repairs in the right lane. Billy and RK wanted to go directly to the bridge and arrest Greg. Joe disagreed.

"We don't have enough," he said. "The phone calls aren't enough. What are we gonna charge him with?"

Silence.

"Do you see what I mean?" Joe said. "We know the calls are incriminating, but it doesn't show he actually killed anybody. There could be more than one person involved, and maybe Greg was never at any of the murder scenes. Or maybe he never made those calls himself. There are a lot of possibilities. I'm just playing devil's advocate, Chief. And you know already what the solicitor is gonna say: It's not enough."

"Yeah," RK said. "The solicitor's office wants a signed confession handed to them on a silver platter."

"Exactly. I think we should talk to Greg first and see what happens. Let's make him think we know everything, and let him believe that we're gonna arrest him. We've done it a hundred times before, and it usually works."

Billy still wanted to arrest Greg, but the more he weighed the possible outcomes of an impetuous move, he began to understand Joe's caution. It was better to wait until they had a chance to talk with Greg. He could make an incriminating statement, and if he did, then they had their man.

"Joe's right," Billy said. "Let's talk to him like he said, and we'll go from there."

Billy, Joe, and RK headed out to the expressway, where traffic was moving briskly, but not yet tangled in the daily rush that appeared each day around four o'clock.

Nearly two and a half miles long and over a hundred and eighty feet high, the architectural design of the Ravenel Bridge was unique. The two separate bridges that it replaced in 2005 were obsolete, and the eight-lane architectural masterpiece became the pride of

Charleston. The architects, mindful of the damage caused by Hurricane Hugo in 1989, the worst storm in the history of Charleston, created a super bridge that could withstand wind gusts of three hundred miles an hour and earthquakes exceeding seven on the Richter scale.

As the police car approached the center of the span, orange cones gradually cut off the right lane, forcing traffic to the left, and provided room for work crews to function without danger from passing cars. A multitude of trucks and other work apparatus gathered on the right side of the span a few hundred feet in front of them. They inched forward until they reached an available space between the traffic cones. Joe switched on the red grille lights, put the portable light on the roof, and weaved into the closed right lane. They slowed to a crawl as a worker with a white hard hat waved his arms frantically for the police car to stop. Joe parked the unit close to the rear bumper of a work truck.

"Okay, let's see if we can find our guy," Joe said.

The worker came closer and directed them to a group of a dozen men about a hundred feet away. A powerful and steady wind swept directly across the bridge from north to south. It was an effort to walk straight ahead without grabbing onto something. The entire structure, the equivalent of a twenty-story building two hundred feet above the river, was moving from the force of the wind. They could feel the gentle sway of the deck beneath their feet, a sensation much like standing in a rowboat. As they approached the work crew, Joe saw Greg and pointed him out. Greg suddenly turned around, looked for a moment, and then turned back without saying a word.

"Hey, Greg!" Joe shouted. "We wanna talk to you for a minute."

Anger was written all over Greg's face. "Why're you bothering me while I'm at work? I don't have time for this bullshit. We're waiting for an inspection."

Joe would not be intimidated. "We just wanna ask some questions. What's the big deal?"

"I've already answered all your questions," Greg said. "This is fucking harassment."

"Okay," Joe said. "So I'll let your bosses know you refused to cooperate and see what it gets you. Maybe we could get you transferred to the city dump or some other shithole."

Greg pulled away from the rest of the men so that his co-workers couldn't hear the conversation. His face was red with anger. "You cops don't get your way and right away you wanna fuck with people."

A gust of wind slapped the side of RK's face like a wet towel. He had to hold on to the side of a truck to keep from being tossed around.

"We don't wanna talk to you here," Joe said. "We're taking you to the station."

Greg turned around and clenched his fist by his side as if ready to do battle. "The hell you are!" he said.

RK made a slight move back and placed his hand closer to his holstered gun. He could feel his palms sweating, and his heart raced as fast as the traffic speeding by. A struggle with a potential murderer on top of this bridge was the last thing he wanted.

Joe put his hand up and pointed his finger at Greg.

"Listen up, my friend," he said. "Either you talk here and now, or you're coming with us. The choice is yours."

Greg froze in position and stared at Joe, contemplating his next move. They stayed like that for a few seconds, eye to eye, neither one budging an inch. Joe was smart enough to be the one to talk first.

"You wanna have your buddies see you in cuffs and dragged over to that cruiser?"

Greg seemed to understand that this cop was not going to back down. "Make it fast."

MARILYN J. BARDSLEY AND MARK GADO

"We have a video of you buying a phone at the Target store in Summerville last month. What did you use that phone for?"

A smug smile spread across Greg's fleshy face. "None of your goddamn business."

Asher took the cuffs out of his pocket. He hoped it wouldn't come to this. "Let's go!"

"Wait a minute! Wait a minute!" Greg said and stepped back. "What's this bullshit about? I don't have to tell you why I buy something."

Up until this point, Billy had been silent. When it was clear to him that the conversation was going nowhere, he decided to step in. "We're taking you in. You had your chance, now you're coming with us."

"Okay. Okay. I bought the fucking phone," Greg said. "So what?"

"Where's the phone now?" Asher asked him. "You have it?" He saw a phone clipped to Greg's belt. Asher took a step forward and snatched it off his waist.

"Hey!" Greg yelled. "What the fuck do you think you're—"

"Shut up!" Joe said as he examined the phone. To his surprise, it was the wrong brand.

"It's not the phone," Greg said to RK.

"Where is it, then?"

"Why?"

"We want that goddamned phone!" Joe said, his anger growing by the second. He grabbed Greg's arm and began dragging him over to the police unit.

"I don't have it!" Greg pleaded. "I swear to God!"

RK pulled out his cuffs and slapped them on Greg who pushed back and then tried to hold onto the bridge railing. Billy jumped in to pry Greg away while RK grabbed him around his neck. The

249

four men grappled with each other for a full minute as they moved precariously near the edge of the roadway. RK could see the river two hundred feet below.

"Where's that fucking phone?" Joe yelled.

"I don't have it!" Greg screamed. "I gave it to Lee!"

Everyone froze in place.

"Lee?" Joe said. "Your son?"

"Yeah," Greg said as he fell to the pavement. "He wanted one, so I bought it for his birthday. I think he still has it. What's the big fucking deal?"

"When did you give it to him?" Billy asked.

"A day or two after I bought the phone at Target," Greg said.

"All right," Asher said. "Lee's not in any trouble. We just need to talk to him, that's all. Stand by a minute." He slipped Greg's phone into his pocket. Billy took a few steps back so they could talk without Greg hearing the conversation. If they left Greg alone, he would immediately call his son to ask about the phone—and if that happened, Lee would dispose of it.

Billy requested a patrol unit to respond to the bridge and told Greg that he would have to come to the PD for a written statement.

"It's just routine, Greg," Billy said. "A uniform will be here in a minute, and when you're ready, he'll take you over to the PD and then take you back. It won't take long, believe me. It's just a formality. Detective Karlovec will wait with you."

Greg cursed and carried on but eventually agreed after it finally dawned on him the cops weren't going to give up. RK removed the cuffs, and Greg seemed to calm down. A patrol unit rolled up.

"Okay, let's saddle up," Billy said. "Head back to the command post." They drove to the other end of the bridge to turn around because concrete barriers prevented a U-turn. After they had headed westbound toward Charleston, Billy had a terrible thought.

"Joe, I just remembered something," he said. "Danie is on her way to meet with Leland."

"Jesus! That's right," Joe said. "Let me try to get her on the phone."

"Yeah!" Billy said as he turned on the siren. "We've got to stop her before she gets there. No telling what he might do. He's already tried to kill her once!"

Asher frantically dialed her phone, but it went straight to voicemail. "By the way, did she say where she's meeting him? At his rooming house, his grandmother's place, or his father's house?"

"Hell, I didn't ask her," Billy said in a panic. He slammed down on the accelerator. "We already have a car outside Greg's house, so you can contact them about what to do if Danie shows up there. If you can't get Danie on the phone, try Cal. Call Bert and Walter Johnson, too. Have the sector people keep the streets open. Where's Shapiro and Cecchi? Call them too! Call everybody, God damn it!"

Chapter 32

Rachel Ackerman's residence
3:45 p.m. Wednesday, July 11, 2012

"I'T'S BEEN A WHILE SINCE MAGIC's been off Billy's back porch," Cal said as Danie got into the Range Rover. They had enough time to liberate him and then take Danie to meet with Lee Ackerman. Magic showed his appreciation by licking Danie's face and nuzzling up against her shoulder.

"My good boy," she said. "Looks like we'll be going home soon. You'd like that, won't you? Won't you?" He lay on her lap all the way to the Ackerman mansion. As they drove down Meeting Street, Danie called Lee and told him she would be a bit early. He invited her to come to the side door on the veranda.

"I'll wait in the car with Magic," Cal said as Danie closed the passenger door behind her. Charleston's summer heat precluded having Magic alone in the car, even with the windows lowered. "Maybe I'll take him for a walk, too."

"Okay, I won't be long."

Danie opened the wrought iron gate and walked through the garden, where two large shade trees offered protection from the afternoon sun. The sound of the wind chimes on the veranda was so pleasant; it reminded her of their home in Savannah. She knocked gently on one of the leaded-glass double doors.

"Dr. Callahan?" a man's voice said on the intercom. "Just a minute, please."

Lee Ackerman appeared and opened the door. His tan shirt was unbuttoned at the collar, and his khaki pants were perfectly creased—he was the epitome of a southern college student.

"Hi, Dr. Callahan," he said with a broad smile. "Good to see you again. Come in, and call me Lee, please."

"Thank you, Lee." She walked into the breakfast room next to the kitchen where she and Cal had talked less than two weeks ago.

"I'm glad you called and even happier you could visit," he said. He seemed buoyant and not the least bit depressed. "Let's go into the family room here to the left. We'll be more comfortable there."

Danie followed him into the family room. After she'd entered, he said, "You know, Doctor, when I spoke with you on the phone earlier, I was kinda surprised you would call me at all. I mean we only met that one time. If I didn't know better, I'd think my father had something to do with that call."

"He's very proud of you, Lee, and really worried about how hard you were taking your grandmother's death," Danie said.

Lee sat in a large wingback chair and motioned for Danie to sit in one of the two sofas whose ends faced the entrance to the room. A handsome stone fireplace capped by a thick wooden mantel stood behind the sofas, and between them, an oval coffee table was the resting place for all sorts of magazines and books, as well as a large glass of red wine. Next to it was an almost empty bottle of Bordeaux.

"The couches are the most comfortable furniture in the entire house." He lifted the wine glass. "Would you like some? It's a 1986 Haut-Brion." He pointed to the bottle on the coffee table. "I think there's some left."

"Thanks, Lee, but I'll pass. That's a French wine, isn't it?"

He took a sip from his glass, clearly enjoying the flavor. "One of my favorite Bordeaux. Let me know if you change your mind. I was planning to open another bottle anyway."

She was surprised at Lee's knowledge of wines. She thought immediately of the bottle of expensive Silver Oak cabernet sauvignon left in the kitchen after Rachel Ackerman's murder.

"I thought all college students drank beer," Danie said, covering her concerns with a friendly smile. "That's all I could afford when I was in school."

He laughed. "I can't afford it, either. Not yet, anyway. It won't be the first time I drank some of Grandpa's stash." He emptied his glass but kept it in his hand.

As she watched him drink the wine, Danie mulled over what "not yet" meant. "You know, we always wondered about the origin of the bottle of Silver Oak found in your grandmother's kitchen that morning."

"Yeah," he said, "me, too."

Danie wanted to keep the conversation on Rachel. "Maybe your grandmother said in her will that you should get all your grandfather's wine collection," she said. "She was very close to you, from what I heard, and probably knew what you would want from her estate."

"Oh yes. Very close. Right up until the end." He paused for a moment. "She needed me, and I needed her. I can't think of anybody who liked her more. She was so difficult and demanding. But she wasn't as hard on me as everyone else."

"Why do you suppose she was nice to you and not your father or your Aunt Camilla?"

"She trusted me to do the right thing." Lee sat back in the chair and crossed his legs. "You see, she knew they hated her, and she hated them. Both my aunt and my dad never made anything of themselves. They dropped out of college, had bad marriages, and never had a job she could brag about. Camilla's an addict, and my dad's a drunk. All Grandma did was rag on them. That's why they avoided her."

Danie found his candor jarring. "Perhaps she treated you differently because she wanted to encourage you to finish your education."

Lee stood up, wine glass in hand. "I almost laughed when you said she was nice to me. She was always nagging me, too," he said. "The difference was that I put up with it and never complained. I was always good to her, no matter how bitchy she was. That's why she gave me so many things. My car, my tuition and rent, this expensive wristwatch, a hefty allowance. It was a game. She bought me what I wanted as long as I called and came to see her. If I stopped giving her attention, she would've stopped buying me things."

Cold-blooded. No love there. "Your dad said that you were experiencing bouts of depression after she died."

"Oh, I'm fine now." He poured some wine into his glass. "Depression is fleeting sometimes."

Something seemed very warped about Lee's character. The fancy wines, his deception about being depressed, and the exploitation of his grandmother—psychopathic tendencies. Her instincts kicked in, and she felt a strong impulse to get out of the house as fast as possible.

He put his wine glass down on the end table. Instead of sitting in his chair, he approached the sofa where she was sitting.

"I'm glad you're feeling better," Danie said with a nervous smile as she quickly stood up and started toward the door. "If you start feeling depressed again, please give me a call."

"Where do you think you're going, Doc?" he said with a frightening grin, blocking her escape path between the two sofas.

"I have to get back to work." She prayed her fear didn't show in her voice. "I'll give you a call tomorrow—"

"Shut up!"

Danie froze.

"Just shut up, you fucking bitch!"

"Look, I'm leaving now," she said.

"No, you're not!" He almost spit the words out. "You know, people like you make me sick. You think you know everything, don't you?"

"No." She reviewed her options. If he put a hand on her, she would kick him in the groin and run for the door. She should be able to get to Cal before Lee could recover. "I don't think that at all."

His menacing smile turned into laughter. "Tell me, did you ever think that dropping a goddamn pen could save your life?"

At first, Danie wasn't sure she heard him right. "What did you say?" The image appeared in her brain like a bolt of lightning. She remembered dropping the pen as a bullet streaked by her face. No one knew exactly what happened that day in Mt. Pleasant except her—and the one who tried to kill her.

"Yeah, I saw you drop it on the porch." He smiled. "One second later and you wouldn't have anything to worry about ever again. No husband to take care of and no strangler to chase. So, for the sake of a dropped pen, you lived. But not so today, Doc."

Lee reached down to the coffee table and picked up a large hunting knife that lay hidden under a newspaper. He held it straight up with one hand on the handle and the other hand on the blade.

Danie backed up a step, looking for something to help her. She couldn't kick him because the table was in the way. The door was too far away, and Cal would never hear her if she screamed.

"This is going to be very enjoyable for me," he said. "Maybe not so much for you."

"Stay away from me! My husband is outside. He has a gun!"

He moved closer. "You're a lying slut!"

Danie backed up toward the fireplace until she felt the heavy handle of a metal poker behind her. She grabbed it and swung at him with all her strength, but he ducked, and she missed entirely. At the same moment, Lee took a step forward and punched her squarely in the face. It hit her like a hammer, and she fell to the floor, losing the poker, and scrambling to find anything to save herself.

"Bitch!" he screamed.

Still groggy from the punch, she crawled away from him, toward the door, which seemed so far away.

Lee picked up the poker and raised it high over his head with his right hand. "Time to die, Doc!" he shouted.

Danie looked around for something, anything that would shield her. She screamed in utter desperation.

A door from the side veranda slammed open with a bang, and she heard footsteps. A deafening explosion went off at the entrance of the family room. The noise paralyzed her. Lee was thrown back violently. The poker flew out of his right hand, and the knife tumbled to the floor. He staggered backward and put both hands on his chest.

Danie saw a blur of movement out of the corner of her eye and something jumping directly over her, pouncing on Lee like a wolf. Magic knocked Lee to the floor. Straddling his chest, Magic bared his teeth and snarled just inches away from Lee's face. Cal stood next to them, his smoking gun still pointing directly at Lee.

"You all right, Danie?" he said.

Danie tried to stand up, but she was too dizzy. Her jaw ached from the blow.

"Take it easy, baby," Cal said. "The troops are on the way. It's all over."

"Cal? I...I...what happened? He was going to kill me. It was him. He killed them all, Cal. He was the one who shot at me in Mt. Pleasant."

"I know."

Keeping the Smith and Wesson .38 pointed at Lee, Cal helped her to her feet and then eased her into the wingback chair. Magic pressed hard on Lee's chest, growling and snapping.

"Billy said it was Lee and not his father who used the phone to call the victims. He'll be here in a flash."

Already there were men's voices coming from the veranda. "Cal! Danie!" someone yelled. It was Billy.

"In the family room!" Cal shouted. Billy, Joe, and RK rushed in with guns drawn, quickly surrounding Lee, who was groaning in pain. Magic was still on his chest, barking wildly at the rescue team.

"Here, Magic," Cal ordered, pointing to the wingback chair. "Come here, boy."

But Magic wasn't through with the man who hurt Danie. He snarled again, and his teeth moved very close to Lee's face.

"Down, Magic! It's okay," Cal urged. "Come here, boy! Come on! Good boy."

This time, it worked. Magic jumped off Lee's chest, trotted over to Danie, and put his paws on her lap.

"Magic! Magic!" She grabbed him around the neck, hugged, and kissed him, so happy to feel his warmth next to her.

Billy went right to Danie's chair. "You all right?"

She didn't tell him that her jaw was killing her and that she wasn't touching her nose for fear it might be broken. "Yeah, I'm a little banged up, but I'll be okay."

Billy bent down and patted Magic on the head. Danie's "spoiled canine prince" had redeemed himself in his eyes. "Good boy, Magic. Good boy," he said.

Joe keyed up his police radio and ordered an ambulance while RK examined Lee.

"Looks like one shot to the upper chest, Chief!" RK said.

As all this was going on, Lee swore at everyone and whined like a baby. "He fucking shot me! I need a doctor. Am I gonna die?"

"Okay, people," Billy said. "Let's get the crime scene gang over here. RK, cuff him up. Joe, notify the solicitor's office, and you might as well call Walter to get a search warrant going for this entire house, his car, and the room he rents. Let's move Danie and Magic into that library next to the staircase. She needs to relax for a while. It's gonna get crowded in here soon." He looked over at Danie. "How's that sound?"

"Sounds good," Danie said. "Thanks, Billy."

Cal helped Danie up and took her to the large Chesterfield leather sofa in the library. Magic followed automatically and planted himself next to her. She was getting her senses back. Gently, she put her finger up to the bridge of her nose and wiggled it slightly. Thankfully, it didn't seem broken, but her hands were trembling.

Cal knelt next to her. "Feeling better?"

"Yes, I…I think so."

"It's over," Cal said. "It's all over."

She looked into his eyes but was unable to say a word. Her thoughts could only focus on the man she loved, her partner, best friend and now, her everlasting hero.

Chapter 33

Charleston Police Department
Thursday, July 12, 2012

"YOU THINK LEE WILL GET THE death penalty?" Danie said.

"I think he'll plead out," Joe said, "but we have to act as if the case will go to trial. Better to do the prep now rather than in two years, when our memories aren't as good and we're involved in something else. Now the real work begins."

The day was a blur of events that kept everyone on the move from the early morning hours. Billy and Bert Allman held a press conference along with the rest of the investigative team at ten a.m. Danie and Cal were celebrated as "valuable members of the extraordinary police coalition that broke the strangler case and put an end to an evil man's killing spree." Nancy Grace sent over a representative to sign up the Callahans for an exclusive appearance on her show while Greta Van Susteren's producers burned up the telephone lines seeking an appearance for Danie.

"You should go," Joe said. "There might not be another chance, and let's be honest: It would be good for your careers."

"You're probably right," Cal said. "We'll go on, I'm sure, but not right now. We want to go home first. We need to recharge."

The office phones rang without pause throughout the day. Most were media outlets looking for comments on the case or requesting appearances on news broadcasts. After the fourth cup of coffee, which carried her to almost noon, Danie heard some commotion outside the door of the squad room. Billy walked in and quietly announced that Mayor Campbell was on his way up.

"Everybody behave, please," he said with a mischievous grin, but he meant it.

A few seconds later, the mayor, accompanied by a half-dozen of his entourage breezed in with a cameraman not far behind. An expert at feel-good speeches, Mayor Campbell expressed his sincere gratitude to the team for solving the shocking murders in less than a month.

"Great work, Danie!" Billy grabbed her shoulders from behind. "The mayor is happy, and that makes me and my department happy."

"I wish we could have identified Lee much earlier," she said.

"Stop it!" he said. "You and Cal did a fine job and were a part of the team. All of us feel the same way."

"It's been a great experience," Danie said. "I really mean it. We've learned a lot."

"Listen," he whispered. "We're having an unofficial meeting at the Tiger at eight o'clock. Be there!"

By evening, everyone in the office was exhausted from the turmoil of the last twenty-four hours. Some detectives had worked through the night and went home by late afternoon. Cal and Danie spent the last few hours reviewing and adding to their notes from the time they arrived in Charleston. They wanted to document their thoughts and conclusions so they could understand what they did right and, more importantly, what they did wrong.

Later, when Cal and Danie arrived at the Blind Tiger, Joe, Cecchi, RK, and Ira were already situated at their favorite spot at the end of the bar.

"Welcome aboard," Joe said with a hefty glass of beer in his hand. "Oscar, drinks for the Callahan team."

"So, where's Mr. Ackerman?" Cal said. "Still in the ICU, I assume?"

"The bullet was embedded in his upper left chest, but no damage was done to his heart if he has one," Ira said. "They moved him out of the ICU. He's gonna live."

"That's too bad," Joe said.

"What did he say about the murders in his confession?"

"He did it for the money. We know that for sure. Rachel Ackerman told him he was in her will for millions. He just didn't want to wait years for her to kick off, so he thought he could speed up the process a little."

"What a bastard!" Danie said.

"So what's next?" Cal asked.

"Well, Lee will be indicted for the murders, and then it's up to the court," Cecchi said. "Whether it goes to trial depends on his attorney. Oh, I don't know if anyone told you this, Danie, but Lee faces additional charges of attempted murder for shooting at you in Mt. Pleasant. You'll be expected to testify before the grand jury sometime in the next few weeks. By the way, he told us where he tossed the gun off the Ravenel Bridge. We're diving the Cooper River tomorrow morning. With a little luck, we'll find it, I hope."

Billy pulled Cal out of earshot. "How are you doing, partner? I know it's not easy to shoot someone, even if he is a killer."

"I just acted on reflex," Cal said. "Over and done. I have no issues with it at all."

"Glad to hear it," Billy said. "The solicitor's office needs you for the court, so expect a call from him soon."

When they rejoined the group, Billy put his arm around Danie. "You did a tremendous job," he said. "You had a close call, very close call."

"I'm okay," she said. "I admit I was scared, but I'm better now. Why did he try to kill me, anyway?"

"He said he was worried that you were getting too close to him," RK said. "Apparently, the task force didn't bother him, but having a forensic psychologist after him really spooked him."

"Yeah," Ira said, "he was afraid you were gonna bill him."

For hours, they went over every detail of the case, every suspect, and crime scene. There was a great deal of discussion on what they did wrong, but their successes far outnumbered their missteps. There were a lot of laughs and genuine relief the pressure was finally off.

"Now I can get back to normal," Billy said.

They carried on until almost two in the morning when the meeting began to dissolve. Mike and Ira said their goodbyes. Then RK finally left for home and Bert a few minutes later.

"Oscar, the tab, please," Billy called out. Oscar came over with empty hands.

"No tab, Chief," he said. "Already taken care of."

Billy was annoyed and yet, flattered. "That Bert! He's not getting away with it. This was my night."

Oscar wiped the bar. "No, Chief," he said. "Bert didn't pay. It was Danie's friend."

Danie was surprised. "A friend of mine?"

"Yeah. Yesterday a guy came in and asked if I knew you. I said sure. He said he was an old friend of yours, and the next time you came in with friends, the tab was on him. He gave me a card, I ran it through, and it was approved. He said money was no object."

Danie was shocked. "Who was he?"

"I don't know." Oscar folded the towel into quarters and placed in on the bar in front of them. "He was a weird dude, though. Didn't stay long."

"Did he give a name?" Danie asked.

"No," Oscar said. "But the name on the card was Higgins."

"What!" she said.

"Yeah, Stanley Higgins. You know him, don't you?"

"It's fucking Beach!" Cal said.

"Okay." Billy pulled his phone from his pocket. "I'm putting every resource we have to find this son of a bitch. Don't worry, Danie."

But Danie was strangely calm. "I don't know for sure," she said, "but I have a feeling this was his way of saying goodbye."

"I'm putting a police detail on you twenty-four hours a day, Danie. Starting now." Billy reached for his phone again to call the PD.

"No." Danie put her hand on his. "Not necessary. I don't want it, Billy, but thanks anyway. If Beach wanted to kill me, he would have already done it."

"Danie, we will do—"

"We're heading back home tomorrow," she said. "It's time we got some sanity back in our lives."

"She's right, Billy." Cal put his arm around her. "Beach will be caught sooner or later, wherever he is. It's time to call it a night. See you back at your place, buddy."

They left the bar and walked out into the deserted street. To their surprise, a fog had moved in during the evening and blocked much of the light from the crescent moon. They could barely see the tops of the palm trees that lined the sidewalks or the traffic light at the corner. The streets were oddly peaceful, but the pavement glistened with the remnants of a passing shower. The familiar sound of a boat's horn from somewhere on the river covered the dim echo of a ship's bell, bouncing with the gentle rhythm of the waves. As they walked down the avenue, Danie leaned against Cal for support.

"It's chilly," she said.

While he held her close, Cal tried once again to make some sense of the past few weeks. He thought of the evil that seems so prevalent in life these days: the greed, insanity, and murder that had been so much a part of his profession. Does it ever end?

Lee Ackerman was intelligent, born into enormous advantages, had a solid future, and yet, he killed three innocent women so he could have more money. How can anyone prevent that kind of evil? How can it ever be defeated? And what do we do about it when we find it? Ignore it? Turn our heads? Pretend it doesn't exist? No, none of that will work, he decided. It's what we do when we're confronted with evil that counts. The battle has to be fought and won, over and over again.

"It's the only way," he whispered.

Danie clutched his arm tighter. "What did you say?" She glanced at him for a moment. "You okay?"

He emerged from his thoughts as if from a dream.

"I'm fine," Cal said. He took in a deep breath of the cool night air. "Let's go home."

Afterword

THE BOSTON STRANGLER MURDERS STRUCK TERROR in the minds of the people of Boston and all the surrounding communities. The public believed that one man killed the eleven women, but investigators believed there were at least one serial killer and several likely copycats. The first five "official" Strangler murders which occurred between June 14, 1962, and August 20, 1962, provided the strongest evidence of a serial killer.

> June 14, 1962, Anna Slesers, fifty-five
>
> June 30, 1962, Nina Nichols, sixty-eight
>
> June 30, 1962, Helen Blake, sixty-five
>
> August 19, 1962, Ida Irga, seventy-five
>
> August 20, 1962, Jane Sullivan, sixty-seven

These five victims were white single women of modest income and respectable lifestyle. All five women lived alone. Their ages ranged from fifty-five to sixty-seven. Two possible additional victims were eighty-five and sixty-nine years of age. The killer did not force his way into their apartments.

Police believed the victims had voluntarily let their assailant into the apartment for repair or maintenance. The killer strangled each victim with her clothing, sexually assaulted her with an instrument or object, and posed her in a sexually degrading way. The man who strangled these five women used a square knot with a double half hitch for the ligatures.

The killer searched each woman's apartment thoroughly, and in several cases, ransacked them. Drawers were left open and their contents disturbed. The murderer even emptied waste baskets and rummaged through the trash. The police determined that robbery was not the motive because with one exception valuable items and cash were not missing. The chaos of disorder and ransacking was seemingly for nothing.

The Boston area was in a panic and the newspapers shamefully exploited it by publishing detailed accounts of each murder, victim, and the crime scene. Perhaps the unintended consequence of such reckless reporting was enabling copycats to stage murders to appear like the Boston Strangler homicides.

The remaining six "official" victims died between December 5, 1962, and January 4, 1964. If one killer was responsible for all the Boston Strangler murders, his pace slowed considerably after the first five victims in the summer of 1962. In 1962, he killed two women on the same day.

> December 5, 1962, Sophie Clark, twenty
> December 31, 1962, Patricia Bissette, twenty-five
> May 6, 1963, Beverly Samans, twenty-three
> September 8, 1963, Evelyn Corbin, fifty-eight
> November 23, 1963, Joann Graff, twenty-three
> January 4, 1964, Mary Sullivan, nineteen

Boston had a three-month breather that ended December 5, 1962, with the murder of Sophie Clark, a popular and attractive

African-American student at the Carnegie Institute of Medical Technology. Forensic experts believed that from this point in time, the differences between the first five murders and the ones that followed suggested the work of possibly another serial killer and copycats. Sophie was black, young, and she did not live alone. For the first time, there was evidence of semen at the scene of the crime.

Three weeks later Patricia Bissette's boss and the apartment custodian found her in bed with the covers drawn up to her chin. Underneath the covers, she lay there with several stockings knotted around her neck. She had recent sexual intercourse and was in an early stage of pregnancy.

In March, Mary Brown, sixty-eight or sixty-nine years old, was beaten to death, strangled, and raped in her Lawrence apartment. She is not on the official list of Boston Strangler victims. Her killer ransacked the apartment. Like the first five Strangler victims, she was white, elderly, and lived alone. The police report indicated, "What appeared to be a knife or a fork was stuck in her left breast up to the handle."

In May, a friend of Beverly Samans, a graduate student, opened the door to her apartment and found her on the bed with her legs spread apart. Her hands had been tied behind her with a scarf while a stocking and two handkerchiefs were tied together into a ligature around her neck. He had stuffed a cloth into her mouth and placed another cloth over it. Despite the appearance of strangulation, four stab wounds to her throat were the cause of death. Her left breast had eighteen stab wounds in a bull's eye design. There was no sign of rape.

In September, youthful-looking, fifty-eight-year-old, Evelyn Corbin lay on her bed nude. The killer had strangled her with two nylon stockings and had stuffed her underpants in her mouth.

Police found lipstick-marked tissues that had traces of semen on the floor around. The autopsy surgeon identified spermatozoa in her mouth, but not in her vagina.

The following month, Joann Graff, a twenty-three-year-old industrial designer, was murdered in Lawrence. Around her neck were two nylon stockings tied in an elaborate bow and there were teeth marks on her breast. The outside of her vagina was bloody and lacerated. Her assailant had ransacked the apartment.

In January 1964, two young women came home after work to their apartment at 44A Charles Street. They were stunned to find their new roommate, nineteen-year-old Mary Sullivan, strangled in a shocking fashion: first with a dark stocking; over the first stocking a pink silk scarf tied with a huge bow under her chin; and over that, another pink and white flowered scarf. A bright "Happy New Year's" card lay against her feet.

She was in a sitting position on the bed, with her back against the headboard. A thick liquid that looked like semen was dripping from her mouth onto her exposed breasts. A broomstick handle had been rammed three and a half inches into her vagina.

People were angry at the police, but serial killers are very hard to find. Despite unrelenting media coverage and frequent warnings to women about the dangers of allowing strangers into their homes, women were continuing to let a killer or killers into their apartments.

A couple of weeks after the murder of Mary Sullivan, Massachusetts Attorney General Edward Brooke took over this case that spanned five police jurisdictions. His people coordinated the various police departments and assigned permanent investigative staff.

The forensic medical experts saw important differences between the murders of the older women and the younger women. For that reason, they thought it was unlikely that one person was responsible for all the killings. In other words, there were copycats.

The medical team developed a profile of an individual who would be capable of such murders: he was at least thirty years old, and probably a good deal older. He was neat, orderly, and punctual. He either worked with his hands or had a hobby involving handiwork. He most probably was single, separated, or divorced. He would not impress the average observer as crazy. He had no close friends of either sex.

A couple of years before the Strangler murders began, a series of strange sex offenses began in the Cambridge area. A man in his late twenties would knock at an apartment door, and if a young woman answered, he would tell her that he worked for a modeling agency. Someone had provided her name to the agency. His job was to get her measurements and other information if she was interested. Apparently, some women cooperated.

He seemed like a nice enough person with a charming, boyish smile. He told them that Mrs. Lewis from the agency would be contacting them if the measurements were suitable. Eventually, some of the women realized it was a hoax and told the police.

On March 17, 1961, Cambridge police caught a man trying to break into a house. He confessed to being the "Measuring Man" as well as the breaking-and-entering charge.

Albert DeSalvo mugshot

His name was Albert DeSalvo, a twenty-nine-year-old man with numerous arrests for breaking into apartments and stealing. He lived in Malden with his German wife and two small children. Biltrite employed him as a press operator in their rubber factory. The judge sentenced him to eighteen months, but he was released after two months in April 1962, two months before the murder of first Strangler victim, Anna Slesers.

Albert DeSalvo was born in Chelsea, Massachusetts, on September 3, 1931. His parents, Frank and Charlotte had five other children. His father was a violently abusive man who regularly beat his wife and children. Throughout his adolescence, DeSalvo went through periods of very good behavior and then lapses into petty criminality. He and his mother had a good relationship. DeSalvo met his wife, Irmgard, while he was in the Army from 1948 through 1956 when he received an honorable discharge.

In 1955, the mother of a young girl who DeSalvo allegedly fondled refused to testify. That year, his first child was born with congenital pelvic disease. Irmgard avoided sex out of fear of having another handicapped child. DeSalvo was oversexed, needing intercourse several times a day. Between 1956 and 1960, police arrested him multiple times for breaking-and-entering, but he received suspended sentences. In 1960, his son, Michael, was born without any physical problems.

Despite his arrests, DeSalvo stayed employed. Most people who knew him liked him. His boss characterized him as a good, decent, family man and a good worker. He was a very devoted family man and treated his wife with love and tenderness.

Aside from being a thief and liar, he had another serious character weakness: he was a confirmed braggart. He always had to top the other guy, no matter what the situation was. Police Commissioner Edmund McNamara summarized the problem: "DeSalvo's a blowhard."

In November 1964, police arrested DeSalvo again.

On October 27, a newly married woman lay in bed dozing just after her husband left for work. Suddenly, DeSalvo was in her room and put a knife to her throat. "Not a sound or I'll kill you," he told her.

He stuffed her underwear in her mouth and tied her in a spread-eagle position to the bedposts with her clothes. He kissed her and fondled her, and then he asked her how to get out of the apartment. "You be quiet for ten minutes." Finally, he apologized and fled. The description the woman gave to the police reminded them of DeSalvo. While released on bail, his photo went out over the police teletype network. Soon there were calls connecting him to a sex offender called "The Green Man" who wore green work pants.

He admitted to breaking into four hundred apartments, assaulting 300 women, and a couple of rapes in a four-state area. Considering DeSalvo's tendency to aggrandize, it was difficult to tell if the number was that high. Many of the instances had gone unreported, and in those that were, the women were reticent to describe what he'd done to them.

DeSalvo went to Bridgewater State Hospital for observation. While police did not believe he could be the Strangler, they wanted the psychiatrist there to examine him. Shortly after, George Nassar, a dangerous man with a near-genius IQ, also became an inmate. Nassar's ability to manipulate people was highly developed. He was put in the same ward with DeSalvo and became his confidant.

Months earlier, DeSalvo suggested to another of his lawyers that he was the Boston Strangler. "What would you do if someone gave you the biggest story of the century? They discussed the reward money for information leading to the conviction of the Strangler. Nassar and DeSalvo mistakenly assumed that $10,000 would be paid for each victim of the Strangler or a total of $110,000 for the eleven official victims. If Nassar turned him in and DeSalvo confessed, they could work out a deal to split the money. He thought the story might bring some money for his family. The lawyer believed DeSalvo was insane and began a quiet inquiry.

Bailey heard about DeSalvo from Nassar and went to visit DeSalvo with a Dictaphone on March 6. Not only did Albert confess to the murders of the eleven "official" victims, but he admitted to killing two other women, Mary Brown in Lawrence and another elderly woman, Mary Mullins, who died of a heart attack before he could strangle her.

Before Bailey could let DeSalvo confess to authorities, he had to protect him from execution. After a lot of legal arguments, DeSalvo confessed to all the murders in chilling detail. Still, there were doubts about the confession

Nobody who knew DeSalvo believed he was the Strangler: his wife and family, his former employers, his lawyer, an eminent prison psychiatrist, and even the police who had become very familiar with him from his frequent arrests for breaking-and-entering. Everyone who knew him thought of him as a very gentle, decent family man, who just happened to be an incorrigible small-time thief.

Susan Kelly in *The Boston Stranglers: The Public Conviction of Albert DeSalvo and the True Story of Eleven Shocking Murders* made a persuasive argument for DeSalvo being innocent of the Strangler murders.

- At that time, there was no physical evidence that connected him to any of the murders.
- No eyewitness could place him at or near any of the crime scenes.
- Various eyewitnesses to the probable killer did not recognize him as the person they saw near the crime venues. However, two victims who saw George Nassar and Albert DeSalvo together, leaned toward Nassar as most resembling the individual they saw.
- The detailed and voluminous media coverage of the crimes enabled false confessions.
- There were numerous errors in DeSalvo's confession.
- Crime experts dismissed the possibility that the murders were committed by one individual because of the significant differences between some of them.

- Serial killers tend to select similar types of victims, whereas the Strangler victims differed widely in age, race, and physical attributes.

DeSalvo never went to trial for the Strangler murders, but in 1967 he was convicted on the Green Man charges. As expected, the judge sentenced him to life in prison, where he died from stab wounds in 1973. Officials believe the murder was related to a prison drug operation.

In October 2001, Court TV reported there would be DNA tests performed on evidence taken from the remains of Mary Sullivan, the last victim in the Boston Strangler case. James E. Starrs, a professor of forensic sciences at George Washington University, led the team of scientists who performed the autopsy. In December, Court TV reported that DNA evidence taken from Mary Sullivan's remains did not provide a match to Albert DeSalvo.

The case against DeSalvo closed? Not so fast. In 2013, new DNA technology was used to test the seminal fluid from the Sullivan crime scene against DNA taken from a water bottle discarded by DeSalvo's nephew. Consequently, Albert DeSalvo's body was exhumed for testing, resulting in an unprecedented level of certainty that Albert DeSalvo raped and murdered Mary Sullivan.

Does this prove that Albert DeSalvo killed all eleven official victims attributed to the Boston Strangler? No, but it does solve the murder of Mary Sullivan and explains the death of Mary Mullens, who died of heart failure in June 1962. In the Green Man trial, Virginia Thorner testified that DeSalvo told her that he had killed an elderly woman, but police didn't know about it.

Sources

Gerold Frank's book *The Boston Strangler* (Open Road Media, 2013). A thorough account of the Boston Strangler case.

Susan Kelly's *The Boston Stranglers* (Pinnacle, 2013) makes a persuasive argument that Albert DeSalvo was not the Strangler.

A&E Biography Video: *The Boston Strangler*

F. Lee Bailey in his book *The Defense Never Rests* (Signet, 1972) devotes several chapters to the Strangler case. He takes the position that DeSalvo was the Strangler.

Boston newspapers are an excellent source of contemporary information on the murders as they happened and their impact upon the people of the city. The *Boston Globe, Boston Herald,* and *Record American* had the most extensive coverage.

A major feature film *The Boston Strangler* premiered in 1968, starring Tony Curtis and Henry Fonda.